This edition first published 2018 by Fahrenheit Press.

ISBN: 978-1-912526-32-1

10 9 8 7 6 5 4 3 2 1

www.Fahrenheit-Press.com

F 4 E

Stoned Love

By

Ian Patrick

Fahrenheit Press

For my daughters.

Life will throw you curveballs. Just keep batting them out of the park.

Love, Dad.

xx

"Now I wanna tell you of a great love
Oh, it will light up
It will surely light up
The world
If you'll just believe."

The Supremes

1

I observe the rat. It's twitching, convulsing, foaming at the mouth. Its eyes pulsate at odds with its erratic heartbeat. I haven't touched it. I'm just watching it die. I don't wish to intervene in a sentient being's death. It's chosen this path and taking any drug has its consequences. You see, this dirty rat has just consumed a corner of my kilo of cocaine and is now having a seizure as a result. This rat has cost me money but has shown me a valuable lesson in the dark side of my business. It's time to get shot of the last five kilos I have sat in a salt bin, in the wood by the cottage I've inhabited for the last month. I'm here because the police have put me here. They have a duty of care to all serving police officers, of which I am one.

I enter the adjoining garage and find a coalscuttle scoop with a broken wooden handle. I need to get rid of the rat. I clear dead leaves and bracken from the strip of corrugated iron that covers the hole where my cash is buried in an old ammunition box. I'm mindful not to disturb any creature that has bedded down in the vicinity. Why should they suffer as a result of a drug-addled rodent?

I started off with one hundred and sixty kilos of pure white powder and now have five kilos, less the rat's share, to shift. I have a buyer lined up for four but I know he'll take the five. I pick the rat up by the tail. It's dead. I decided against the scoop in case I was careless and pierced the already open package further. Every trickle of white dust is money. I look up and see a red kite hovering over the fields looking for prey. I throw the rat towards the open area of grass.

As I do, the sound of an engine enters my senses. It's a car, not an agricultural vehicle. I move further into the wood and crouch down. The dyke wall hides the driver's window but I can see the red roof. It's a post office van. I hear the engine stop outside my cottage, the metal cattle gate open and close. The sound repeats, the engine fires up then fades as the car drives off down the hill towards the farm. The silence returns. I wonder what's been sent. I only get mail from my employer. It's never good news.

I raise a corrugated iron strip that lies abandoned on rotting vegetation within the wood. I dig down using an old spade propped in a lean-to wood store. The spade hits metal. I clear the remaining soil by hand. The earth's crumb disappears through my fingers. The lid opens. The money stares back at me. It's all neatly bound and secured in waterproof bags. I break a seal and stroke the cash, grab a fistful of twenty-pound notes and close the lid. I replace everything as I'd found it.

As I leave, I look back and check its appearance. It looks like a derelict area of wood where a tenant dumps his shit. The cocaine can wait. I observe the road before I leave. It's quiet save for the Limosin bull observing me from the field opposite. Rain is beginning to fall as the sky turns black. I grab some logs from the wood shed before entering my temporary dwelling. The only mail is a plain envelope and some flyers the postal service have to deliver. I have no need of continence pads so dispose of the paper as firelighters. The flame envelopes the logs and I sit back and rip open the letter.

I'd rather read a Dear John. It's from the promotion board. I've passed the Inspectors' exam. I throw the letter on the fire. The paper's a poor grade and the fire starts spitting. I have five years to complete the rest of the process. The police have halted promotion but they have to continue letting Sergeants take the exam. Inspector will be my last hoorah, if I want it. I've no intention of going beyond DCI. The next rank is Superintendent and mine is a complete arsehole. I'm earning a good wage and keep under the radar. There isn't any overtime but I don't need it now I have other income streams. The phone jolts me from my thoughts. The call screening kicks in.

"It's Mike, pick up!"

It's the arsehole I was referring to. He's also the authorising officer for my work.

I press one. The line connects.

"What do you want?"

"A good morning sir would be nice."

"Get your mistress to tell you that; I'm busy."

"Fuck off, Batford. You've been sat on your arse for a month. Something's come up and your name's been thrown in the pot to take it on. A courier is on way with a train ticket. Meeting at The Yard at oh nine hundred hours tomorrow. Wear a suit. I know you have one – it cost us a fortune."

He hangs up. I have no choice. You don't when you're a Detective Sergeant working as an undercover officer for the Metropolitan Police. I hear a knock at the door. I check the camera monitor. He doesn't wait for a signature and an envelope drops through the letterbox. That will be my tickets then. This is no ordinary cottage. It's a safe house in a remote part of Scotland. I'm here because I fucked someone off doing my job and he wants to know where his missing cocaine is. That man is Vincenzo Guardino, aka Big H. He's already started his hunt for the robbers and he's killed two. One of them I was close to, in a professional way.

I miss Stoner. She was a bad girl with a heart of gold. She should have been dripping in cash, not blood. News reports suggested two people had been shot dead in retribution for a drugs deal gone wrong. The murder team are no further in the investigation. You wouldn't be when you have limited resources investigating murder in the capital. This is 2020 and the consequences of cuts are kicking in. Times have changed since the public sector austerity measures were first imposed. The then-Home Secretary became Prime Minister and still persisted with the draconian measures despite public backlash. Not even Thatcher touched the police and most thought she was brutal.

I put the kettle on the Aga and gaze out over the fields. I have a day to kill before my train from Edinburgh to London. I've enjoyed the break and the solitude. City life has ground me down. My problem is the pace and vibe of the city is in my blood. It's part of my DNA. I love its tension coursing through my veins. I adore the adrenalin rush when a job comes off. I also enjoy the rich pickings from the criminals I infiltrate. I have no intention of completing thirty years' service. I need to top up my pension pot before I leave, though. I subconsciously check my leg and experience reassurance at the feel of titanium. I intend to upgrade and add to my prosthetic leg collection once this next job is over. Whatever my bosses have planned for me, I always turn it to my advantage.

I watch the bull. He's in the field for a purpose. His job is to fuck at every opportunity. He has no competition. He's Mr Big surrounded by his bitches. He strolls over to a cow. She's wary but carries on eating. As he approaches, she flicks her tail. He takes the hint and mounts. A ton of muscle thrusts twice. Job done. Every bull has his day, though. Old age will render him useless. All lives have a price. The whistle indicates the water's ready.

The thing I love about the police is they will always look after you. That's unless you need to be further away than London for a cool-off period. There are no mod cons or city flats to escape to here. The cottage has seen better days and let's just say the police estate doesn't run to cover the costs of refurbishment or maintenance beyond a working fire alarm.

Damp permeates the walls and paper hangs from the ceiling. The heating is oil and at least they've kept up the contract to enable that still to work. The furniture would look good in a seventies sitcom. The solitude has given me time to think. In many ways it's been a good thing but today it hasn't. A month alone has taken its toll. Memories have haunted me and sleep has been fitful. My left leg's phantom pain has revisited me and haunts my mind like a feral ghost taunts a medium. The pressure of feeling hunted and getting rid of that amount of cocaine hasn't been easy. I'm only here because of the death threat. The police can tick the box over duty of care. If it weren't for this, I'd have rolled straight on to another job.

I've had help. How else could I accomplish such a task without appearing overloaded with class A and attracting the wrong attention? Cocaine stores well if packaged correctly but the use-by date is brief. The longer it's stored, the greater the risk of contamination from the wrong kind of filth. A rodent is the least of my problems. A rat of the informant kind is my greatest enemy.

I've been lucky here. The cottage is remote and the nearest farm believes it's a retreat for overworked city types to come and get away from it all. If only he knew the hell that could follow any one of us if it became public knowledge that this is where the police hideout after they've fucked off a crime lord and had his importation away.

The money's been good. I've turned a profit on my half. I'm not a greedy man. Greed leads to complacency and that leads to capture. I'm not flash with the cash. I have a good accountant who takes care of my earnings. I give a percentage to charity too. I bring him the money and he takes care of my investments. These investments have good growth and are currently earning ten percent each year. I can live off my salary very comfortably. If it all comes on top the police will have a job linking any of my extra-curricular earnings to me. A life mixing with the criminal elite has its benefits. Politicians are top of the criminal pile but I've no intention of having a beer with any of them.

The coffee tastes good. I move into the living room and

contemplate packing. I've always hated this part of any trip. Not knowing what clothing you'll require for the job ahead, and Mike hasn't given me the best heads up as far as that's concerned. I decide to take what I came with, which is easy, as I haven't unpacked any of it. The two-seated sofa has made a great wardrobe. I no longer have a watch as that got used on the last job and the police have decided not to return it to me. I don't blame them. That watch had a ten-thousand-pound price tag and the commissioner needs to save money.

I haven't been back to London since my inception here. I have a sense of trepidation that doesn't amount to nerves before a new operation in the field of crime. These nerves are ones of uncertainty, isolation, despite the vast swathes of people who move through the capital like they own it. I think of Zara Stone. Poor Stoner wiped out in a game of hunt the snout. She'd done well to survive as long as she had in her world of men and violence.

Who I'm to infiltrate next? I have no idea. I will do what I have to survive despite the legality of my position as a servant of the Queen. She's not my Queen. The only person I serve is myself and that in turn serves the society in which I choose to belong.

I look out the open kitchen window. I hear a banging coming from the corrugated roof of the garage. At first I think it's tree branches lightly tapping on the roof. But this sounds different. A definite bang every now and then, and the wind is light enough not to sway the trees. I move out of the kitchen into the tiny hall and grab the baseball bat by the back door.

The bat of choice is a Rawlings wood composite. Fits well in either hand, feels light enough to swing repeatedly but heavy enough do serious damage to someone's head when it connects. I still recall my long baton training and the instructor's emphasis on all the energy exiting from the tip, causing the most damage to an assailant.

I'm right handed and in no mood for entertaining guests.

The cottage door opens easily and without sound the side door to the garage remains shut. The bang happens again. I move along the garage wall towards the door. I haven't locked the side door since I arrived.

An unwelcome gust of wind blows up dust. I temporarily can't see. I'm conscious of getting my body weight shifted on my left so my balance is good. I'm not as useful if I go to ground but have some techniques I can employ. I've made my decision to rush any intruder. This isn't based on any theoretical training but on the necessity for me to catch my train.

I place my left hand on the door and push the handle down. I hear the lock disengage. The banging starts up. I shoulder the door and move in at the same time. The bat's over my shoulder, ready to swing. The first hit is swift, straight to my face. The next one skims the top of my head at speed. I drop the bat out of confusion, duck, then let out breath. My arms go up around my face in an instinctive defensive pose. If the intruder lives, then pathology will see defence marks in the forms of gashes along my forearms. I can already feel my forearms bleeding from striation marks.

I'm up from my crouched position, sight fully restored. I fleetingly see the enormous crow that has chosen the garage as a roost. A strange domain as they normally choose a higher location. I guess it got trapped coming through any number of gaps in the wall. I wait. The mass of feathers exits the doorway cawing. Its impressive wingspan inspires awe at such close proximity. Fucking wildlife gets everywhere. As I regain my composure, all I'm left with is a sense of relief, laughter and an angry paper wasp queen who's busy building her lair in the garage roof eaves. I approach it. She hovers near the entrance but appears happy to continue her intricate work with me observing.

I can see the coombes forming from within the small entrance hole. She weaves her structure with care and attention. An ecological way of using recycled paper she has scavenged. A worthy home for her brood of soldiers keen to carry on the next generation of workers. Still a fucking pest, though. One sweep of the bat scatters the nest raining wasps down into the garage like an unwanted piñata at a Mexican street party.

I underestimated the fury of a wasp scorned and am thankful the side door is open. My exit is swift and the door closes on the angry swarm. Fuck the country life; the city beckons. I grab my belongings and after leaving the wood with my packages, sling the bag and contents on the back seat of my chariot and head towards Edinburgh and my train connection to The Smoke.

2

I arrive in Edinburgh earlier than expected. I take refuge in an internet cafe in a side street away from the bustle of tourists. I'm aware I could be classed as one but I regard this visit as a stopover and have no intention of sightseeing. Thankfully Edinburgh has long-term parking and for once I feel a sense of safety at being able to leave and return to find my car where it should be.

The venue isn't much of a cafe at all. It's basic, does repairs and printing if you need it. All I need is to check up on emails and contact an associate. There are a few students inside. All of who feel the need to be old school despite having free Wi-Fi on campus or in a national coffee house. One of them stops the conversation and indicates they take the money up front for the hour session I will require. I pay him cash and he points to the booth I can use.

"Make sure you back up anything you need. We forensically wipe all data once each session is over. Coffee's from the vending machine and we have chocolate in the fridge, enjoy." He walks back to his group, and they all huddle around a laptop and continue watching shit on Netflix. I put my bag between my feet and make sure my right foot is in contact with it.

I haven't got my phone turned on. I won't until I'm on the train. I need my solitude. The computer is quick. This is reassuring despite the shop's squalid facade; the technology is where the money is invested. I've a good view of the outside world and the booths are designed that no one can see over your shoulder when you're online.

I don't use any mainstream search engines for my line of business. I find the anonymity of the darknet more amenable to my needs. The Onion Router (TOR) is the best way for me to make contact with the people I need to engage with. One of these happens to be my accountant. He isn't the kind of guy you just contact by phone. He doesn't own one. With a click on a link, I'm in and secure in my underground world. I don't have much time for the good old U. S. of A., but I am thankful for them setting up this wonderful system and not having the benefits of a seer where it could all go wrong.

For the uninitiated, this was set up by the US government to share classified military information. It's now been taken over by the anonymous amongst society to conduct our own lines of business and research. To shut it down would mean the internet would no longer exist. It's called TOR because, like an onion, the information being sent or searched for travels through so many layers it's near impossible to establish its source.

The downside is it has become a marketplace for criminality with no way of policing it. That's why I love it. I find my contacts' message board and request a meeting. I have a substantial cash deposit to make and his opening hours are not advertised. I scan the outside whilst I wait to see that it's sent. Water races down the window. The tourists make a break for cover. I get an automated response back. Before I close down, I wipe my browsing history from the main server and get rid of cache data too. They can't see where I've been and I have no reason to doubt they will wipe the computer history after each session. Old habits die hard. I zip up to my neck on my waterproof coat and pull up the hood. The baseball cap will catch the rain. I don't have far to go.

I saw my marker from the cafe window. He's parked in a vehicle opposite reading a paper but glancing over at regular intervals. I know he's looking for me. I saw the car from the street. The index plates showing a London car hire firm. He's not police. He looks in his rearview mirror as a traffic warden approaches the line of cars he's parked in. His engine is running. He glances at me then back at the warden. My gut instinct kicks in. It's time to disappear. I get up and head over to the counter where the group still congregate. I address the guy I paid.

"Hey. There's a guy across the street checking this place out. Where are your cameras? This could be a robbery." The self-appointed lead looks at me, then over at the window. I intercede. "Don't look at him. If you spook him he may have others and none of us want a kicking."

The youth looks back at me "How do you know he's going to rob us? We've got no cash." I'm done buying time. I need an exit. "He's a lookout. Is there a back way? I don't want to be caught up in any violence." The cafe owners are spooked now.

"Look, you're off your head, mate, and you need to leave. There's no back way out. I'm calling the police." I have outstayed my welcome.

The car door's opening. The warden has left. I have two options. Front him out or leave. It's a brief thought. He's across the street looking left, right and heading towards the cafe. He has a three-quarter length coat on, dark shades and a shaved head. He's twenty feet away. I take a right. His pace quickens. There are enough people about that he will need to get in close if he wants to take me out. He won't want witnesses. I see a newsagent up ahead. I approach the window and wait, looking in. My tail is on the opposite footway now, searching for a vantage point to hold. I've left him nothing. I see the shop owner move towards the rear and another worker come out front. I enter the shop.

The shopkeeper reacts. "Hey, where are you going? You can't go back there it's private!" The shopkeeper's words blur as I move past him and into a rear storeroom. There's a fire door at the back. I take a fire extinguisher from the floor and smash the lock mechanism. It opens on a courtyard. I hear other shouting now, then a scream. My pursuer is strapped. The screams of 'gun' confirm that.

I pull myself up and swing over the courtyard wall. An alley runs along the rear of the shops. I see a large blue industrial wastebin three shops down and make for that. I manage to get in just as the sound of feet hit concrete. I remain still. Flies buzz. It's like being entombed in a scene from a sudden death where the body has lain undiscovered for months. I hear footsteps outside. They're getting closer. Other waste lids are being opened and closed. I try and slow my breathing and prepare to strike should my only barrier from certain death open. I can't move. I'm pinned down amongst fish heads and rotting veg.

The sounds of lids opening and closing are getting closer now. I need to know who he is and why he's after me. No one knows I'm here other than my unit. Sirens pierce the air. Not just one set. Multiple sets. The cavalry has been called. He's outside my bin. I hear his feet shuffling and the rock of the bin as his hands grip the lid and it starts to open. I hold my breath. What pressure I can exert on the inner lip I do. I know that it's futile but doing something is an option I always take. The sirens are louder. They're close by. The lid is left untried. All I hear is my heart; my assailant's hands leave the lid and the deafening sound of sirens coming from the street.

I remain still. I hear voices now in the alleyway and police radio chatter. Then I hear what I was hoping for: "Nothing at the back. Mark it up as area searched no trace, over." Once they've left, I emerge. Grab clean clothes from my bag and change behind the bin. I dump the clothes farther down the alley, spray myself with deodorant and head for the train station and my link to London.

It was thoughtful of my Detective Superintendent to ensure the reserved seat had good legroom. Not that it matters as I have my lower left leg sat next to me. I've taken the shoe off, of course. It wouldn't be appropriate to have a shoe on the seat. No one asks for me to move it to sit down.

That would be impolite. I turn my phone on. There's one message: *Pico's @20:00.* That will be me on a tube to Vauxhall, then. I'm on edge. I'm being hunted. I have an idea who's behind it. Whoever it is, is professional. They're also being fed information from inside and that's what bothers me most. I settle back for the journey and listen to a meditation podcast. It takes me back a month.

I was living in a Buddhist centre biding my time before the job against Big H that ended up with my haul of cocaine and Stoner's death. I know the closer I get to London the more on edge I will become. I felt safe in Scotland. That illusion is now shattered.

The carriage is filled with the usual suspects making their weary way to the capital city. Most wear suits but the women carry them better. DCI Klara Winter is one such woman who rocks a suit. Hers clings in all the right places emphasising femininity and an appearance of comfort in her own skin. Mess with her though and that comfort suit becomes a flaming cloak of rage. She's a smart cookie and a tenacious investigator. I'd never tell her that. I've no desire to meet her again. We didn't hit it off. She doesn't have time for my kind of resource. I need to blend in where I shouldn't belong. The best undercover officers have no air of ego or the appearance of a police mannequin. After all, one sniff of pig and your ass is bacon. I've no intention of being served up at any criminal's barbecue.

The journey's been uneventful and I'm glad of that. I watch through the grime-framed window as the train pulls into St Pancras. It's time to switch on and tune in to the sights and sounds of London. I won't be sightseeing in the usual way. My messenger will know I'm on the move. I'm in no doubt he'll know where I was heading. I will need to be alert for a follow by foot or car. My jackpot win was their sour bet. The only issue now is they want to check the numbers on the winning ticket, as they doubt its authenticity. I'm not about to give Big H or his crew the satisfaction of interrogating me and ascertaining whether I have their missing coke. I check the station clock. I have an hour to get across the water. My luggage is lighter now. I grab a cab and head towards my next destination and my initial meeting before the main event tomorrow.

As the cab drops me by Thames House I stare up at the array of satellite dishes and aerials. I feel at home. I've returned to the environment I live, breathe and love. I cross the bridge Vauxhall side, and enter the courtyard area underneath the apartment block that overlooks the Thames. The pub is busy. I avoid this, as I know it's a favourite haunt of off duty police. A good place to relax, away from the public eye. I enter the lift area and press the button for the sixth floor. I exit right and there's flat sixty-four. It's twenty hundred hours. I'm bang on time. The door is answered by my meet.

"Hi, Mike. Long time no see." My Detective Superintendent checks the corridor then lets me in, shuts and double locks the door.

The flat's spartan in furnishings. It could be described as minimalist. Some of the seating hasn't had its protective covering taken off. The furniture is from the Conran shop and fits the hip city dwellers' setting perfectly. A balcony has two Eames chairs with matching footstools and overlooks the Thames. Both doors are open letting in a warm September breeze. Chatter can be heard from below. Mike shuts the patio doors and the voices cease. Mike's edgy and so he should be. I have five kilos of cocaine in my bag and he has a buyer lined up tonight.

"Nice place." Mike deserves that credit.

"Thanks. Cost me enough but should be a sound investment. Drink?"

"Whisky, straight, no ice." I watch Mike as he moves towards the drink.

Mike goes to a bar area, grabs a bottle of Laphroaig and two glasses. He's lost weight since we last met. Not a good sign. He was a good UCO in his day, but he went for promotion and now he regrets the move. The pension may be good, but he misses being hands on. By hands on, I mean getting his hands well and truly filthy.

"Nice watch." I compliment him on the ten-thousand-pound Brietling he's wearing. I recognise it, as it was the same he'd given me for the last job. The same one I'd activated the emergency button on that told him where his share of the seizure was. Another indicator he conducted the collection himself.

"You didn't think I'd hand it back in, did you?" He's the one taking an overt risk, not me. I can resist the temptation for flash, but Mike has an addiction that needs satiating.

He pours out the drinks. We each occupy our single, overly expensive, leather, low-backed chairs with walnut legs and arms. I take a sip and look out of the main window. The sky is starting to burn red as the atmosphere changes both outside and in the flat.

"So, you brought the parcel?" He wipes his brow with a serviette.

I push the bag over the walnut, engineered, wood floor to where Mike is sitting.

"It's all there." Mike opens the bag, checks inside and zips it back up.

"Great job. You weren't comprised in any way? In Scotland?"

"Why would you ask that? I wouldn't be here if I was. It's all gone well. Any news from the Commander? She still happy?"

"She's good. Very good. We've copped another job. We'll talk about it tomorrow. You'll need to be a good actor and suck it up. I'm on the move. Surveillance commissioners came and did an unannounced inspection. We were slaughtered. Bad practice, poor record keeping, you know the thing. Commander went spare and gave me my ticket back to division or retire. I'm seeing this job through then I'm taking my pension. She's sailed close to the wind with us in terms of turning a blind eye to get the job done. She hasn't a Scooby what we've had off over the years. Of that

I'm certain. She feels let down and I can't blame her. She kept me on a loose lead but now she's applied a choke chain and I've no time for being yanked about."

He takes a sip of his drink. His hands are shaking as he leans forward and cups the crystal glass. I say nothing. Let him take some time before he speaks. We are in this together, but he's not holding up the way I expected him to. We both made the choice to line our pockets and top up our retirement funds. It was all meant to be small, under-the-radar stuff but then he got greedy. I was under the cosh and had little choice. I've managed my money off grid where Mike appears to be doing the opposite. The flat we're in is worth millions.

"What will you do with this place? I'm not in the market for this kind of property but need to know for my own security of mind."

Mike hesitates. "Keep it. It's not in my name and will be a good bolthole when I'm in London. My Florida retreat will become our main home and we can stay here when we're back visiting her family."

'Her' just happens to be Mike's marriage wrecker. A lithe brunette, mid thirties, pert arse and tits to match. He met her in a Pilates class. He wasn't doing Pilates; he was waiting to pick up his teenage daughter from swimming and was caught ogling through the studio window. She liked what she saw and the rest is history, as was Mike's twenty-five year marriage. His ex-wife got his house in Chigwell and will get half his pension and a lump sum on retirement.

She's unaware of his other business acumen and he intends to keep it that way. He's lucky as he's also renting a one bedroom flat in Ilford. He stays there when his daughter visits, giving the appearance of poverty and a man on his arse through divorce. I've seen this so many times before and that's why I relish my single life. That and childhood trauma just about sealed my fate.

"So, what's next?"

"This is our last hurrah." Mike sounds certain. I'm not

assured.

"It's all done, Sam. We agreed we'd call it quits if the status quo changed. I can't take any more risks. I'm out after this one, if you're up for it?"

I take a sip of whisky and sit back. I don't need any more money, but I know the cash will run out. It always does and I need a secure future. I feel Mike's opinion of his role is overinflated.

"Risk? Sat on your fat arse nursing a Laphroaig and a guilt complex? Give me a break. You don't know what fuckin' risk is. You're making me nervous. You're shaking and I'm not convinced you're telling me everything." I await his response.

Mike looks up from his hunkered position, his brow furrowed like a ploughed field. His eyes tell me he's on edge. The eyes are the windows to the soul. Tell a person all they need to know about how he or she is going to react next. I know Mike is angry. As sure as bears shit in the wood, he displays this by firing his glass at me.

It passes my right ear with speed. I hear crystal and the contents explode against the wall behind me. I don't move and take another sip. "Feel better now, sir?"

"Don't patronise me, Batford. I'm under pressure! Massive pressure. It was bound to come out at some point. I can trust you to keep my display of it under wraps."

"Of course. Now let me tell you something. I don't appreciate having a crystal tumbler thrown at me and despite our business arrangement, and your rank, if you ever do that again, I'll fucking put your head through that window and leave you for the gulls. Are we clear on that count, sir?"

Mike stands, makes his way to the bar and grabs himself a fresh glass. He returns and fills both our glasses and smiles in my direction. My message has been received.

"How long have we got until you off load those parcels?"

"An hour. A trusted of mine will pick them up and bring back the cash once the deals done."

"He comes here?"

"Don't be a prick, Sam. I meet him well away from here. Look, I'll see you tomorrow, oh nine hundred hours, New Scotland Yard. We'll have a briefing. Be on time. I need some head space before tonight."

I knock the drink back and bid my farewell. I'm not interested in talking shop, the state he's in or explaining what happened in Scotland. "I need to change. I know I stink." I get up.

"Your gear's in the spare room. You're right; you fucking reek like Billingsgate market." I shower and change, then grab the lift back down. I'm relieved the bag feels lighter, as does my mind.

I have no room booking; I'm tired and hungry. What I do have though is cash and plenty of it. I hail a cab and head for The Connaught, Mayfair. I've phoned ahead they have a suite. I sit back as the cab fails to indicate and joins the stream of traffic heading over Vauxhall Bridge. The city lights dance on the Thames and the movement of the water causes them to ripple and fade in and out like a lava lamp.

It feels good to be back and as hungry as I am for food, I'm hungry for work too. I felt stale after a month of administrative seclusion and psychological rest. The job insisted on it after my last role. They know there are few of us left willing to take on the workload and disruption to life. There's also a lack of appetite and tighter control on what work the police are willing to commit to.

The cab stops in the middle of the road outside the hotel. I alight and pay his fare. I don't believe in excessive tipping, especially cab drivers that earn enough as it is. The doorman leads the way and another staff member makes an effort to take my bag. I indicate I'm happy carrying it. He shows me to the suite and after an introduction to the room, leaves and quietly closes the door. I grab the room service menu, dial and order. I'm back and ready to roll.

3

I'm stood outside the latest home for the elite and powerful of the Metropolitan Police. Traffic noise rumbles by at a slow pace, police motorcycles exit the drive. It's become a home for the top brass and little else. The original building in Victoria is long gone. The latest Yard now looks more like a top London hotel than the pinnacle of policing power. I'm waiting in the canteen for Mike's arrival.

I can sit here with little recognition from colleagues. There was a time when I knew so many but now so few of us remain thanks to cuts, resignation and early retirement. I see Mike as he scans the floor in search of me. He finally sees me, nods and makes his way over.

"Morning, sir. I trust you had a pleasant evening?"

"Very pleasant, thank you, Sergeant. My delivery arrived so I'm most pleased."

"Good to hear. Get the coffees in then."

He leans forward, smiling this time.

"Get the coffees in, sir." He's laughing, as am I. A few heads turn to see where the laughter is coming from. It's a rare sound these days, especially so early in the morning.

"Meeting still on, sir?"

"Yes it is. The Operational Team's Senior Investigating Officer is here talking to the Commander about the paperwork. Commander Barnes has changed her tune, Sam. She's a fucking stickler for everything being in order since the inspection."

Mike leans in closer and looks out of the window as he speaks. I do the same but listen.

"The job's good, but you'll need to keep your mouth shut and get on with the work. I think you're ideal for the role. You fit the profile of the network in terms of age and credibility. This won't be like the last one. Times have changed in the short time you've been away. The wheel has turned back. No more solitary pursuits. You'll need to keep thinking outside the box on this if we're to benefit."

"I look forward to the challenge." We leave together. I take the lift. He takes the stairs up to the next floor. He's been told by his bit of skirt he needs to shed some timber. I wait at the doorway to the stairs and hear his wheezing and coughing as he finally arrives. Coffee from the disposable cup hasn't had a good trip and some has attached to his shirt. His efforts to clean it have failed. He does his suit jacket up in an attempt to disguise his carelessness.

He swipes his warrant card through the door to the main floor and punches in his code. I follow. Mike turns to me. "Remember to keep your mouth shut unless you're required to express an opinion." He opens the door to the Commander's Personal Assistant. The PA's changed. He is now a she. A fast-track Detective Inspector with a mission to conquer. She invites us to sit and wait. The Commander is talking behind her closed office door to an unknown. I hate this part of the job. The pomp and bureaucracy to tackle criminals is easier than the shit required to get a job authorised, approved and off the ground.

DI golden hair picks up her phone and announces our arrival. She puts down the receiver, her pinched face not cracking a smile. "The Commander will see you in a minute. Can I get you a tea or coffee?" I decline as does Mike. The door opens to the Commander's office. Mike enters first. I follow. The room's an adequate size for someone of this status. A large table dominates, capable of seating ten people comfortably. She has a desk to match the domineering decor and commendations adorn the wall. A desk nameplate with

Helen Barnes, Commander sits proudly. If you didn't know whose office it was by the time you entered, you should be sacked. What I didn't expected is the other occupant she's speaking to.

"Hello, DS Batford. Long time no see?" She hasn't changed.

"Detective Chief Inspector Winter, how wonderful to see you again after, what, a month?"

"Yes. How time flies when you're waiting for the next opportunity to work together."

She sits down. I greet the Commander who proffers me to be seated. Winter smooths the sleeves of her dark blue suit jacket. I notice her shirt now has longer collars but still befits her rank. She has her gaze locked on. I cannot resist the need to join her in the stare off. She acquiesces first as she has to open the formalities as Operational Team Head. I take a coffee, as the Commander has poured. No paper cups here. The PA comes in and sits down with a note pad and pen. The Commander dispenses with introductions and kicks off the dialogue.

"Well, we all meet again. I do hope this meeting can be completed without incident." She glances at both DCI Winter and myself. "Right, Klara, I understand you've come to the Covert Intelligence Command with a view to us assisting in an operation you have running, called Kestrel. So we're on to names of birds for our operational names now, how lovely. Do continue, Klara."

The Commander sits back and Winter takes the floor. There's no computer presentation or death by PowerPoint. This is always a verbal briefing and a need to justify my use. It's one of the few times I get to feel wanted. The Commander already knows she will authorise my deployment and to what end my authority will extend. I bide my time and relax with the show.

Winter begins. "As you are aware, this operation has been running for a short time and has amounted to intelligence gathering and some lifestyle surveillance of our target. The

Met's Special Projects Team were initially given the job but they've had a long-term operation go to an arrest phase and have handed it to me at the National Crime Agency."

Alarm bells are already ringing in my head. That team would never give up a job if it had legs.

"Talk of a job involving a team of armed robbers has come up in conversation on another operation. There won't be any cross over as far as targets are concerned, but it cannot be left. The team consists of three men: Johnny McKivor, aka Razor; Gavin Deal, aka Trigger; and Martin Nolan, aka Snowy. All have previous for firearms offences and armed robbery. Razor is the main man and imports firearms via Ireland to the mainland. The talk was of a major hit. We don't know where, but intelligence suggests they're waiting on the guns for the job."

"So why an undercover officer and for what purpose? Can this operation be completed with the current telephone facility in place and conventional methods?" The Commander asks.

Winter responds, "In short, no. The team drop numbers regularly. We've no way of keeping track of them. We know that they're looking for a motorcyclist; we don't know any more than that. That's where we thought an undercover officer could come in. The group regularly meet at the Ace Cafe in Wembley. It could be a good location to get to know them and hopefully get taken on by the group to learn more about where, when, and how they plan to carry out the robbery. We know they're actively seeking another recruit. The only reason we don't know is why they want to bring in an outsider."

I can see as much thought has been put into this as Brexit. The police are all about getting quick results on the cheap. Cash has run dry since the referendum on 23 June, 2016, and years later it is no better. Cuts have kicked in. The service is on its last legs. Recruitment is at an all-time low. No one wants the hassle for a poor wage. Retention is a joke. Brexit has bitten the country's arse and has no intention of letting go. The National Crime Agency is busy and requests for Metropolitan Police help are increasing. Mike knows I'm not amused and so he should be. A great job for us, he said. He must know more than he's letting on.

"Since when has an operational team dictated undercover tactics?" I have to ask, as the 'sitting here quietly' isn't working for me.

"Nothing has been decided. It's a suggestion based on the lifestyle of the group and phone chatter of where they are looking to recruit from." Winter is on the boil. I intend to up the gas. She needs to get the upper hand of the Commander on this job as she was pissed off with me on the last one. I thought the seizure of ten kilos was adequate. She was expecting another one hundred and ninety. I found that first though, and the rest is history.

"I'm sorry you don't approve, Batford, but if that's the case, there must be someone else who can step in?" Winter looks at the Commander, then at Mike. Pretty poor to bite at the first challenge and a weak one at that. The Commander is the first to respond.

"I decide on who I authorise. I've read enough of the background. I'm satisfied that the deployment is proportionate and necessary to combat the serious nature of the crimes the group are looking to commit. Thank you, Detective Chief Inspector, that will be all. I need five minutes with Detective Superintendent Hall and Detective Sergeant Batford. They will meet with you afterwards and discuss a way forward. Good day."

Well, that was quick. Winter looks flustered but happy she has the support. She makes her way out of the room and Mike indicates he'll call her by pointing at his phone and back at her. The door shuts. The Commander sits back in her chair. We wait. Once she's satisfied Winter is clear, she opens her desk drawer and removes a brown file marked *Secret.* This is going to be good and I feel the anticipation of work rising from my gut.

"Right, I've spoken with the Special Projects Team.

They've hit on a cell that was of interest to us in the early nineties. Razor has other business interests so the thought of an armed robbery seems odd. As a team they've been on and off our watch. In truth we don't know what they have planned but something is on the cusp of being active. We need success out of this as the department's taken a hammering from the inspection and we must recover."

She opens the file and hands it to Mike. He puts down his cup and takes it from her. The Commander continues her diatribe. "Winter and her team were selected for the job to mask our interest. This lot know their stuff and know our methodology for surveillance, so it makes sense to have her on it. On the plus side, if she screws up, egg will be on her face and not ours. You'll have authority to deploy in two hours, as I need lunch. Any questions? Winter will sign off your terms and conditions, Batford. You'll have a new pseudonym for this operation."

"Why a new one, ma'am? I know the back story for the one I have and all the paperwork with it to back it up." The Commander shoves a piece of paper in Mike's direction. I grab it first.

"*Batford!* I will not accept insolence in my office." She's angry, as she wanted to soften the blow that Mike has to deliver.

"I know an R v Osman death threat letter, ma'am. With respect, I'd like sight of who wishes to kill me first, and why, before my Detective Superintendent." She leans forward. Her gaze locks on to mine. There will be no competition here. She always wins a stare down. Only a fool would take her on and my jester's coat is in the lobby.

"Contrary to what you believe, I have your best interests at heart, Batford. It will come as no surprise that Vincenzo Guardino, aka Big H, wishes to catch up with you over his missing cocaine. He's spoken with Zara Stone and Terence Sullivan and as you are aware the conversation ended when they were executed in a car on the Barnsbury Estate in Islington." She pauses to get my reaction. I continue concentrating on my breath to keep my emotions in check. My mind feels numb.

From the corner of the office, I see Stoner leaning against the wall, smoking. "Fuck me, lover. You're right in the shit with no way out. You've got it coming just like me."

"Earth to Batford." The Commander's voice infiltrates my mind.

I snap out of my surrealist dream.

"Sorry. Miles away."

"The information is considered accurate. We still have the phone facility on. They've now returned their focus to you, hence the new identity. Sign it and our job is done. You know the limits the job will go to and I know you see this as an occupational hazard."

I look at the paperwork and do nothing. The Commander continues. "With any luck it will come to nothing. I've arranged your accommodation and Mike has the details. Times have changed. Our resources are scarce. I can't give you the support you deserve in the field as we used to. Due to sickness and cuts, I have no DI to assign as cover officer. I am working on that though. In the interim, report back to Mike until, or if, one can be arranged. DCI Winter will cover your outside deployments with her team."

She looks at her watch, then at us both as she rises from her throne and we rise too. Respect is everything. I respect the Commander despite my actions seeming otherwise. She does have a heart, but no one has risked smashing the glass case to access it in case of emergency.

"One last thing." Her voice is determined.

I stop leaving and turn back as does Mike. "Screw this up or fuck Winter about again, and you will both be back in a main CID office within a day. Good luck, gentlemen."

With that we leave and exit towards Spring Gardens and lunch at Pico's.

4

Pico's is on the light side for diners this lunchtime. We take a table at the back where it's calm and away from the small bar area. I sit and observe the window. Mike has his back to it. I need time to see what the job will entail and where I come in. I'm not interested in the how and why. I'm interested where the benefit is to me in terms of the financial growth of my future investments.

"So what did you make of that?" Mike looks up from his menu.

"I make that the Commander is unhappy with us and expects a better return for effort than the last job."

A waiter comes over and we order. "So how did it go last night, Mike?"

"It went well. The gear's all gone. The money's away in the safe until I can move it on. This job won't be as good but there may be room for us to move on it."

Mike looks around the room before he continues. There is more staff than diners so I'm happy for him to speak. "I put Razor away for a robbery in the nineties. I produced him from prison to clear some jobs up to reduce his sentence. He agreed to talk. He's been talking to me ever since. We've done some work off the books. He's not a bad man, just misunderstood."

He takes a drink of beer and I indicate to the waiter we need another as he's almost downed the glass.

"So who's running him now? Who's his handler? This

could become a risk to me if he sniffs a rat knowing some of our tactics."

Mike shifts in his seat. "I never handed him over to any Covert Human Intelligence Source Unit. He'll speak to me and that's the way it's been my whole career. Some of the pricks they have now can't handle their own cocks let alone an informant. I wasn't taking the risk with him. I pass on some information but some I leave and he sorts me out a cut. That's how it was back in the day before the Regulatory Investigatory Powers Act. This job is big though. It will be good for us but we need to be amongst it to make sure it gets done properly."

"So, if I've heard correctly, you're running an unauthorised informant and you've ensured, through your contacts on the Special Projects Team, that we get the job so you can send me in and do what exactly?"

"That part's unclear right now." Mike smiles. He's the only one.

"Why in the fuck would you put me amongst the wolves not knowing how we'll benefit from it? We've made loads off the last hit. Have you lost the plot?"

His smile's disappeared. "This firm aren't a bunch of kids on mopeds trying their luck armed with pickaxes and sledgehammers. We're as good as undetected *if* we're on the inside and controlling Winter and her mob. Just like the last time. This will be my swan song, then I'm off."

Mike starts eating. I say nothing. Fact is I underestimated how much I was enjoying the down time. I'm now drawn into a plan I have no control over, but the wheels have already been set in motion whilst I've been in Scotland.

Mike knows I can't refuse. Why? I can't refuse because he knows too much. I'm not saying he'd grass me up, but I do know he's feathering his own nest and the cuckoos are at the door. He also knows I will say nothing about his business ventures outside of the police. Astonishing how the corrupt can climb so high and operate within an environment of secrecy and collusion. The irony isn't lost on me.

"So what do you see me facilitating in this 'job'? How do you see me gaining access to a tight cell of people who've done work together, served time together, and have probably done each others' wives?"

Mike shifts in his seat. "What I do know is that Razor needs a courier and you've got the skill set. He owns a club in Euston. He's got a pad in Mill Hill. He's got a good supply chain going across London clubs. He's been looking for a courier and you're going to apply for the job. The job's clean. I've told him nothing, other than I might be interested in the action. Razor's playing me like a well-used fiddle. I think the job's big but not the one Winter thinks it will be. He can't keep his mouth shut as he loves to gloat when we meet up, so I'm hoping the truth will out."

I'm as circumspect as I can be in my response "So you want me to act as postman whilst he's off tearing it up around London? You've lost the fucking plot. Winter will think it strange that an undercover officer is out delivering god knows what whilst her target is off elsewhere. I'm done, Mike. Find some other mug for this job." I get up to leave and he grabs my forearm. His grip is meaningful and not in a sentimental way. I don't make a scene, not here. I sit back down and he leans in.

"Calm down, for fuck's sake. You'll be on his job. Use your skills to become indispensable to him. You're good at that, I should know or we wouldn't be sat here would we? Why are you so touchy all of a sudden? A month of celibacy got to you?"

He grabs the calamari and pours it on his plate. Privilege of rank. "You crack on, I didn't want any!" Mike holds the empty plate up in the direction of the waiter along with a ring of the calamari. The waiter nods and phones through to the kitchen. Mike gorges on the fish in his hair-encased mouth.

"Go and see Winter, then get your arse down to Lambeth. They've got a bike for you. Before you ask, it's been adapted so you operate the gears by switch and not foot. See, I do think about your needs. Now, I've got to go. Here's your new package: driving licence, passport and address of your new digs. Keys are in there, too. I hope you like rural living. Get the bill, son. I'll sign it off on expenses."

With that, Mike gets up and passes me an A5 padded envelope, then he's gone. Sauntering his way out past the waiters who see me and bring the bill. I leave cash and don't take the receipt. My treat. I'll make sure Mike pays one way or another once the job is underway. I go to the toilet, enter trap one. I rip open the top and take a look at its contents.

My new identity stares back at me from the driving licence photo. The photo's me; at least they've got that right. I look deeper – ther 's a booklet that will contain my back story and a smaller envelope that contains a set of keys. On it is an address in Watford. Hardly rural but he sees it as such.

Having to work there will be tight but I can cope with that. I know that's the way now as there aren't many of us left to operate in different areas of the capital. When a job comes up, we take what we're given and accept the risk of compromise or worse, death. I shove it all in my man bag, check my leg, flush and leave for Spring Gardens and a meeting with the lovely DCI Klara Winter.

The sky is clear. I don Ray-Bans and the street becomes a filter of shade. My inner ear vibrates. The sounds of Carter USM's "Sheriff Fatman" causes me to smile as an image of Mike swaggering away comes to the fore. All is well in my world. I'm in good form and enjoying not being able to breathe too well now I'm back in the smoke. Scots air is pure where this air is acrid with diesel and tobacco. I've noticed there's an increase in vapours. Not the type that inhabit the air but the people smoking e-cigarettes, or plastic smokers as I call them.

They may as well stick a pen in their gob. If you're going to smoke, then for fuck's sake smoke and enjoy the ride. Our final drive will always be in a hearse so why fret. I don't smoke, well not often, filthy fucking habit. I will when I'm in role. That's a given. Only tobacco. Nothing stronger, unless for medicinal purposes. Even then, I bring my own horticultural medicine to the party. My drug of choice? Tramadol. Not often, as it fucks with my mind. I must be alert. I'm not a pill head but when it's available, why suffer for your art? My art is espionage and I never repeat the same canvas.

Originality has kept me alive and I intend to keep it that way. I was trained to act within the law and I do when needs dictate but in my world, the lines often get blurred. I arrive at the reception to The National Crime Agency and try my swipe card I was issued a month previously. It's been deactivated. I go through the security gate and into reception where the same desk guardian is on duty. This time he just nods. I wonder how Winter will be on this jaunt. I soon find out as she enters the room, bag in hand, motioning to the door I've come in by. No tea and biscuits then. I exit first and she follows.

"Office being refurbished?" She stops and turns, looking directly at me. Her hazel eyes wide with contempt.

"My lot wouldn't piss on you if you were on fire and I'm not about to test the notion. The merry dance you led them a month ago hasn't been, and won't be, forgotten. You crossed a line, Sam. You forgot who you're working for and what your job is." She pauses and we continue walking away from the building and towards her car. I know it's hers, as she never changes it. "Get in." I do as I'm told on this occasion.

I'm not looking for any confrontation, at this stage. I know how she operates from the last jolly. She pulls out a manila folder and hands it to me. "This is your briefing package. Read it and ask me anything you like. You've got twenty minutes, I'm late for a meeting." She pushes a button and the driver's side window disappears into the doorframe. She removes a packet of Rothmans and lights up.

"I never knew you smoked." I was aware she did by the smell from the car. She doesn't react so I push some more. "Surprised at your blatant disregard for the no-smoking policy in company vehicles, though. Definitely not your style at all." This serves my childish purpose.

"Read and shut up. I'm in no mood for you. Yet again I get saddled with you as you're in the age range of the subjects of this operation. Note to self – target the youth in the future. Sign this; it's your terms and conditions of use." I ignore her rant, sign where I need to and glance at the research paperwork. The firm is top drawer, as Mike had intimated. All have previous convictions that would make fine epitaphs. From the surveillance footage, they like to party and party hard. Razor runs a club called Harvey Browns. They like their music, fast bikes and women. I'm already salivating at the opportunity presented to me. Winter will have her result but so will I. If this lot are as good as they appear, then the haul will be mighty.

I pull out a surveillance photo of a woman, white, blonde hair, with long bangs in a pixie cut. She has a slim, defined face, chiselled cheekbones, natural eyelashes that women pay good money for, plump bottom lip with a thin top to make a perfect set. She looks like she's in her thirties. If only she was smoking, the transition would be complete. Out of the factory and into the fire. She's sat on the back of Razor's bike. She's looking into the camera but would have been unaware she was being photographed. I shift in my seat as I react to the image. Winter has noticed.

"Thought she'd get your attention. Razor's security. She's been identified as Kat Mills, thirty-five years of age, born in London. No previous convictions but has been documented travelling to Ireland on a frequent basis so she may be a courier too. Always uses the ferry as a foot passenger and likes her ink. You should get along well."

I put the image away and hand her back the envelope. I have three minutes of her twenty left. She's absorbed in her own thoughts and nicotine.

"For the record, I've had an Osman letter served. Big H is looking to kill me. I did my job very well, I'd say. You got what I had and that was the ten kilos of coke and MAC-10 on my lorry." I start to open the door, as she looks my way without any notion of empathy. I have the final say.

"I've seen what I need for now. I need to get a phone and I'll text you a number you can get me on. Be ready to have your team out tonight. There's a Brit bike night at the Ace Cafe. They'll be there and so will I. Keep your team loose on me. No one inside the premises. I'll be there at twenty hundred hours." I nod and exit her car before she has the chance to speak. Fuck her. This is my job now and she'll follow like a probationer on his first day out on the street. I just hope the bike Mike has sorted for me is British. I head for Lambeth to collect. I check my jacket's inner pocket for the release paperwork that was in the package Mike gave me. It's all there.

The Thames is choppier than a cheap haircut. The tide is in, testing the masonry of the barrier wall. A police launch patrol's looking for any floaters to collect. Suicide is on the up since the country has plunged further into recession. Increased patrols on the main bridges have done little to prevent the need for some to take a dive. I've contemplated it on occasion when the thoughts of the past and the physical pain of walking on an artificial limb take their toll. Thoughts have never transcended into action, but I'm aware I'm not immune.

I follow the footpath at Lambeth Bridge. I move alongside the vehicle barrier that now protects pedestrians from terrorist attacks by car. The coffee hut where Mike and I meet is busy with people getting their fix. Above me, an open window from the block of flats lets me in on a row between two over-privileged city dwellers. I stop and take in the conversation.

It would appear she's upset over him entertaining his legal firm's understudy. He's making a feeble attempt at playing it down but failing. You can tell who has the greater skills in presenting the case at court. She is winning hands down. On this show of verbal épée, I'd have her represent me. I leave as he withdraws. Hands in the air in surrender. The window closes.

I carry on round the corner and the entrance that contains the garage area becomes apparent. A vehicle barrier splits the entrance in half and a keeper inhabits the gatekeeper's dingy hut. He comes out of his cubical. I show the release letter. Car horns blare from the depths of the garage basement. Sounds of warning as they arise from the depths of the garages. I pass him and wind my way down the ramp into the garages. There is a quiet calm down here. A rest area for weary vehicles. Some are being worked on, others just sat awaiting collection.

The echoing hum of the various size vehicles' engines being turned over is a mechanic's wet dream. Oil and diesel fumes add to the ambience. I find hut B and see the feet of Little Chris appearing from under the engine compartment of a Volvo XC90. He hears my approach and slides his six foot seven frame from out under the vehicle. I reach forward and he accepts my offer of a hand up. He has a slight frame but muscular build, so little effort is required on my part other than balance.

"Haven't seen you in a while. You're the reason everyone's getting heaps of shit to drive these days." He wipes his hands on a rag and hands me a tin of old engine oil. "Thought you could use this for that leg of yours." A mutual smile shows him I'm okay with the piss taking. You never fuck the guy off who has the keys to the undercover fleet. You never know when you need to call a favour in.

I've seen blokes come back with cars that I would never be seen dead in for a job. It can make or break that first introduction if appearances aren't maintained. Why have the Ferrari when you can have the Ford? He takes the tin back from me, goes to his hut and returns with a set of keys. We walk over to the bike bay and see Mike's done well for once. A two-year-old Triumph T120 in matte black, peashooter twin exhausts to facilitate the 1200cc engine. Chris throws me the keys; I sign the release form and he takes the paperwork.

Little Chris gives an introduction. "The leathers and helmet are on the floor. It was a seizure by traffic, all been re-plated. Sometimes they do a good job and remember us. Fill it up before you leave; there's fuck all fuel in it but I've looked it over and it's fit for purpose. I don't expect it back now it's with you, but if you could return it when it's no longer needed that would be good." Chris gives me a wave as he saunters back to his domain and another customer. It's been a while since I've ridden but the training I had in the Army and this mob will still be there.

Physically I've changed but I know how to apply the laws of physics and pull on the leathers and helmet. The leathers are a good fit and complement the darkness of the bike. Other than the bike's lights, there's nothing reflective about me. I like this. The police are full of health and safety shit but when it comes to my job, they show a degree of relaxation. I lean the bike in towards me, get good form on my right leg and swing my left over. I choose my good side, as I'd hate to over balance on the first try out. I start the ignition. Contact, lights illuminate the wall; I move the bike back and go.

The engine sounds incredible as it echoes through the basement. The front light illuminates the tall concrete walls of the basement tomb and cast shadows as I turn. I weave my way to the fuel stop at the top where daylight fills my retinas, making me squint. A uniform Territorial Support Group officer is at the first pump refuelling the meat wagon. The crew sit about. Banter's going on as the sounds of laughter from the bus is heard.

I swipe the fuel card, type in my registration and refuel whilst sat on the bike. I breathe in the petrol fumes and mentally plan my route to Watford and my new pad for the duration I'm south. Tonight will be crucial. I need to be prepared for anything. I replace the fuel line and secure the fuel tank cap. The rear exit barrier rises. I'm out, free and back on the front line.

5

Decision log initial entry, 7th September, 2020
DCI Winter – Senior Investigating Officer – NCA

Here I go again. Same old shit, different day. It's becoming like a play. Same script, same cast, different audience. I'm getting hacked off at the belittling of the Met. Having to beg for covert resources is becoming a joke. I have my own, but terrorism is taking priority at the National Crime Agency.

However, I've waited for this job since the last debacle and now I have my chance.

I will be expressing my thoughts and feelings throughout this log, which is marked as sensitive. It will not be disclosed to defence in the event of prosecution. Nothing I say here should undermine the prosecution or assist the defence's case. I will have a revelation meeting with prosecution council where any issues will be ironed out.

I have developed vetting and a strong history in detective policing at a pro-active level. In short, I am fit for purpose. My purpose is to infiltrate a criminal network and bring the offenders to justice.

This includes any corrupt officers involved in the planning or commission of offences.

Operation Kestrel originated following contact from the Metropolitan Police's Professional Standards unit. Their specialist enquiry team hit on none other than Mike Hall, aka Detective Superintendent Hall of the Metropolitan Police, after he was seen talking to Johnny McKivor, aka Razor, in Mill Hill Broadway. The two were enjoying a nice coffee in Costa when the team were out behind Razor following a tip he had a person in the police supplying him drugs.

No drugs were seen. It's still unknown why the two men were together. There is no need for a man of Mike's rank to be with Razor. The Met looked at recent investigations Mike had a hand in. The last one was Vincenzo Guardino, aka Big H, where a limited amount of class A drugs were recovered instead of the two hundred kilos expected. Now a threat to life has been made against DS Sam Batford, the undercover officer on the enquiry, whose cover officer was, and still is, Mike Hall.

Big H wouldn't go to this trouble over ten kilos. The investigative team believe Mike Hall intercepted the other 190 kilos of cocaine.

At present, this is pure supposition. I have always believed both Mike Hall and Sam Batford are as corrupt as they come. I have now been given the chance to prove this and I intend to do so.

I have had a meeting with Commander Barnes. She has handed me the enquiry to gain distance from her own force. Any back story as to the origins of the enquiry are false. The Special Projects Team heads within the Met Police have colluded with the enquiry and reinforced the deception by bringing a job forward to arrest phase. Superintendent Hall has taken the bait.

I have agreed with her to undertake this investigation and I am as satisfied as I can be that Commander Barnes is clean.

The Commander and I will give the appearance of being antagonistic towards each other in the presence of Mike Hall and Sam Batford. This will fit with the investigation and draw suspicion of collusion away.

The investigation will be recorded on paper only and locked in the incident room safe in my office. A/DI Hudson and myself will be the only two people with access.

Cometh the hour, cometh the woman.

I intend to mop this firm up once and for all.

Klara Winter DCI
National Crime Agency
Senior Investigating Officer
Op Kestrel

6

Hotel, Central London
Persons present:
Helen Barnes: Commander
Klara Winter: NCA
Alex Kennedy: covert human intelligence source (CHIS)

These minutes are transcribed from a recorded interview prior to the commencement of Operation Kestrel. These minutes are for operational purposes only and not to be disclosed if this case is brought to trial. It has been decided to use a covert human intelligence source (CHIS) in this investigation in addition to current resources. The CHIS is already amongst the group and is providing actionable intelligence.

CHIS Alex Kennedy is on time and of reasonable appearance. They do not smell of alcohol or appear under the influence of drugs. They agree to a random drug test and this proves negative for class A drugs. Test conducted by myself (DCI Winter). Results are recorded separately.

Commander: Welcome and thank you for being prompt today. I have reviewed your CHIS record and history and I am satisfied your use will be proportionate and necessary in the interests of detecting and preventing serious organised crime. It goes without saying the risks are high and the tactics we will employ will be bold and direct.

Before we continue with the details of the investigation, you must agree to and sign these terms and conditions of your use. Please read these conditions fully before you agree to anything.

Alex Kennedy is handed the paperwork and reads through all documents. I am satisfied they have the capacity to read and understand what is being requested of them.

Alex Kennedy: They're good. I've read and signed them.

Commander: Thank you. This operation is now effective. DCI Winter will run through what is required of you. I must leave as I have other pressing engagements. I would like to personally thank you for your commitment to us; it's greatly appreciated. Any issues, contact DCI Winter.

Commander Barnes leaves and Acting Detective Inspector Hudson enters room. Introductions done. Hudson will act as Acting Detective Inspector for this operation. All contact with Alex Kennedy will come through me and A/DI Hudson, who will run the outside team. Direct reporting to me due to confidential nature of enquiry.

Winter: You will be known as Alex Kennedy for the purposes of this operation and for phone contact. You will not disclose your role to anyone including family members or close friends. I'm to understand you know the people in these pictures I'm showing you?

Alex Kennedy: Yes. Johnny McKivor, Gavin Deal and Martin Nolan. Johnny's called Razor. Rumour has it he cut a bloke up who nearly knocked him off his bike at traffic lights. Gavin Deal is called Trigger, as he's good with guns. Martin Nolan is Snowy, as he loves the white. They work as a unit. They move cocaine and heroin. They're always tooled up. I've known them a few months now and they're slippery. Razor's got a villa abroad. He likes to spend the winter months away from here. He goes first, then his wife follows.

DCI Winter: Have you ever seen either of these men with them? (Slides two photos across desk to Alex Kennedy)

Alex Kennedy: Not him (points to surveillance image), but I have seen him, the older guy in the suit (points to separate surveillance image). He was over the other night at a hotel Razor uses. He delivered about four keys of cocaine and went away with one hundred and twenty thousand pounds. I know this because I counted it out. The cocaine's long gone though. The guy looked pissed off as he took a big knock on the price. It was like he just wanted shot of it.

DCI Winter: Were you wearing gloves when you counted the money?

Alex Kennedy: Yeah. It would look strange if I didn't. Razor is cute around forensics.

DCI Winter: There's a British bike gathering at the Ace Cafe tonight. We expect them all to be there. Here's a hundred pounds. If you see either of the two men in the images you've just seen, get in contact.

Alex Kennedy: Don't I get to find out who they are?

DCI Winter: No, not at this stage. We believe both are associated with the three you already know. You've confirmed one of them; we just need the other now. Any names you hear, let us know along with anywhere they may be going. You know the drill and what we need. We have your number. Here's ours; you can get hold of us twenty-four hours a day. A/DI Hudson will be overseeing the investigation too. Any questions? No? Call in as soon as you're down at the Ace Cafe.

Alex Kennedy: Of course.

Alex Kennedy leaves the room and is escorted by A/DI Hudson. No follow from the building and no compromise reported on leaving.

I now have confirmation that Detective Superintendent Hall has met with Razor and is purported to have supplied four kilos of cocaine. CHIS was shown a picture of Detective Superintendent Hall. DS Batford has not been identified at this stage. I will have an early meeting with the Crown Prosecution Service and discuss this revelation.

Tape ends.

7

It's nineteen thirty hours. I'm in a McDonalds off the A406 contemplating another cheeseburger or just skipping to the apple tart. I have a promotional sticker and I've won a Big Mac meal. Choice is made. My view is clear from my window seat. My bike is already attracting attention from those getting back into their cars. This pleases me. Getting noticed is stage one in the operation. I take a sip of the weak coffee and take stock of how much time I have to get in role.

The bike has helped. I rehearse the back story in my head, should I need it, and breathe slowly. I feel the heat on my top lip and the chatter in my skull calms down to a monotone whisper. My mind races again. I feel a shudder through my body. This isn't good. I've been away too long. My body temperature is increasing in the full leather suit despite the cool air conditioning. Stoner appears again; this time she's opposite me.

"Some other mug waiting to be fucked over by you? You're an arsehole. A complete fucking arsehole. You will die on this one, babes. You're way out of your depth. Always trying to scratch that itch. This itch is the mother of all rashes, darlin', and you are far from a chemist." I put my head in my hands but can't shake her away.

The entry door swings open and a biker comes in still wearing their crash helmet. They don't remove it and head towards the counter and order. They're scanning the room. If this was a bank, I'd be nervous. I don't facilitate eye contact but survey the car park. Their bike is next to mine. I'd missed it. The bike's a Triumph Bonneville Thruxton R, top of the range 1200cc powerhouse in Diablo Red.

This subject has cash, of that there is no doubt. The bike costs over ten thousand pounds and the leathers are a cool grand's worth. The biker stands with their legs shoulder width apart and stock rigid. I know they're not surveillance; the bike is way out of budget for them. The rider's five foot nine, athletic build, self-assured. The rider orders a coffee to go. The gloves come off to pay and I note from the hands the biker is female. I relax. If it was Big H's goon, I'd be dead.

She takes the coffee and makes her way outside to her bike. I remain and observe. The helmet's still on as she places her drink on the floor. Never placing anything on the seat is a good sign. She either wants a hot drink or doesn't want a wet arse. Now it's time for the reveal. From her presentation, I'm assuming she's heading to the Ace Cafe. Her left hand is clean of jewellery. The only addition is a leather wrist cuff. She's either not married or just doesn't wear that shit. She takes the underside of her helmet in both thumb creases and slips it back over her head.

I stop drinking as the form of the photo Winter showed me earlier comes to life. Kat Mills. I feel a tingle at the nape of my neck as my neurons fire in recognition. This is good, very good. She's drinking and sat over her bike on its centre stand. She's looking at my bike and taking it in. She reaches out and touches the tank, tactile, feeling the tank's smooth contours. Her fingers gently stroke the paintwork, then she retrieves her hand quickly as though she's been shocked.

I can't make out much of her face other than her right side. Her beauty is infectious. She's everything the picture displayed and more. I tell myself she's not my target. Razor is, but I'm a heterosexual male and it's in my evolutionary DNA to look and be aware of the attraction she has stirred. I've been on many deployments surrounded by some of the most beautiful women, but none have caught my attention in the way she has. Not even poor old Zara Stone could compete with Kat Mills for looks. I take the decision not to go out. I'd rather wait to see if the others arrive. I inform Winter, though. I press the speed dial and she answers on the third ring.

"Winter."

"It's like summer here. A beautiful vision of serenity." Winter's moving paper and swearing.

"I've got a pen. I take it your cock stirrer is at the cafe?"

"Close but no cigar. I'm at the Macky D's on the 406. How's things with you?" I keep the conversation light in case an undesirable is overhearing me.

"All good this end. You've got cover, but at a distance, as you requested. No one from my side is at the cafe."

I check the window and she's still outside drinking. "Good. I forgot to ask how your old man is? Still got the fish?" An old reference to her husband's penchant for caring more about his fish than her. Cruel, I know, but in a warped way it shows I care.

"He's living elsewhere, with his fish, thanks for asking. Not that you give a shit and I've no idea why I told you." She pauses and I look down at my coffee. She clearly wants to talk. At least that's the thought in my Neanderthal mind. There's never a good time when you spend your life out chasing scum.

"Sorry to hear that. Maybe we could do lunch sometime and you can tell me more?"

"If you were the last man alive I'd rather starve. You have a charm that should be extinct. Stick with the job and remain focused."

The line goes dead. I smile. I'm back in the game. I watch as she removes a phone from her jacket pocket. She places it to her ear and listens as she looks around. She blows a kiss down it, leans down and takes her helmet off the floor. I down the remaining coffee and grab my lid. As I go to get up, the car park comes alive with the abuse of three motorcycle engines. There's no subtlety here as the bikes come into the bays near the entrance adjacent to Kat.

They stop. Kat gets off her steed and walks over to the lead bike. The rider nods at her as she punches his arm by way of greeting. The rider removes his helmet. It's Razor. The crew is complete and all with identical rides. The other two flank him. All have their engines running. The rear two are restless, eyes about. Razor talks to Kat over the din. They separate and Razor waits for her to get on her bike. She joins them, and they disappear in a symphony of noise.

When I'm happy it's clear, I leave via a side entrance and go towards the bike. I check the bike over. Nothing has changed or been added in the form of a tracker. The addition would be quick and it had been out of sight for a moment whilst I took a natural break. I mount the bike, drop the stand, and head towards Wembley and my first encounter with the firm.

The roads are busy. I enjoy weaving my way through the exhaust fumes. I'm on my mirrors looking for follows but none appear. It's early in the job and not even Winter would be that foolish to go against my judgment at this stage in the game. The throttle is light and a joy to twist. The engine responds with a low, powerful howl as the machine cruises past buses and travellers stuck in their metal-encased hell. The sun is low; my tinted visor comes into its own. The tint's enough to elude the rays and confuse an outsider looking in.

As I approach the cafe, it's getting busy. I can see my targets have arrived. They're off the bikes talking. All admiring one another's machines. I ride past first. I turn around under the bridge and pass briefly before heading back. The cafe's on my right. I've seen the spot I'll choose to park up. It's neutral so as not to piss off any of the regulars. I have plenty of time for that. I can't see any of my mob and that's a good sign. I use the time to phone Winter. She answers promptly.

"Winter. You'll have to speak up. I can barely hear you under that bridge."

I'm reassured. "That's all I needed to know. There will be no further contact until I'm away." I don't give Winter the opportunity to respond.

I hang up, pocket the phone and walk towards the gathering crowd happy that I'm covered.

The cafe is full, the long tables occupied. The evening is pleasant enough to be outside despite the falling temperature. We're in leathers. A slight breeze is a welcome pleasure. I open my jacket to let out heat and not create moisture. I see Kat again. She catches my glance. She's with a crowd that includes Razor and his cronies. Now is not the time to make any move towards them. I don't know them and they don't know me. It would be like crashing a party with no coke. A poor show. This mob loves the limelight despite their preference for sharing shadows. They clearly adore the attention they and the bikes are getting. That is until someone approaches them with a phone and points it in their direction.

Razor turns his back. Only the bike is captured in front of him. Snowy's mountainous back moves across and the cameraman moves away. Message received. Snowy's muscles form in his leathers and there's no mistaking how he spends his time. It must be a shock to him to be outside a gym. His six foot six frame supports his bulk well. Trigger is the opposite. Muscular looking, taught face with a wiry physique. He's less than six feet in height. He too looks after himself but spends less time on his hair than Snowy, as his head is buzz cut.

Snowy runs his fingers through his blonde locks and returns to his bike. Razor is more relaxed now. The routine is a well rehearsed one between the two of them. Kat has disappeared. I walk in between the bikes nodding casually in recognition of the owners. I see her in a queue. I take this opportunity to go inside. Proximity is everything. I can see how the possibility of getting close as an outsider is going to be tougher than I thought.

She's relaxed and more at ease here than in McDonalds.

She has one person in front of me, then that person gives up and leaves. I maintain an appropriate distance whilst the queue moves forward. I can't see the others. I'm conscious of my hands beginning to sweat. I've put the gloves in my lid I'm carrying. It's not the temperature in the room but my internal temperature setting off again as I get closer to contact.

She smells of leather and pine. Reminds me of a posh car air freshener but one you'd want to replace. In that moment of thought, she turns and smiles. I smile back and nod in recognition, nothing more. It isn't an acknowledgement of attraction but more one of 'Hey, we're at the same place, into the same thing, waiting in a fuck awful line to be served'.

"Hello again." She focuses her eyes to mine. Pupils small and unmoved. I respond out of politeness, more than a need for conversation, but seize the moment.

"Hi. Sorry, have we met before?" She moves backwards as the line shifts.

"Not exactly. You were in McDonalds. A girl notices these things, you know. I saw you arrive on the same bike too. Nice."

"Ah. It was you! Always interested in a fellow biker. I hope I wasn't that obvious. I did see you touch my bike though. Not that I have a problem with that."

"Bikes are a tactile thing for me. That's why I like it here. Haven't seen you before, though. New hobby?" She's acting cool, just pleasant conversation, which is good for me.

"A return after some time out." I don't add anything more. Let her explore if she wants to. She doesn't. Just nods. We're at the bar now and both ordering at the same time. She's got more drinks than she can carry.

"Can I help with those? I'm Billy-no-mates so only getting the one." She looks back at the crowd she has to work through.

"Sure. Why not? Take that tray if you can." I put my drink on it, pushing my arm through the crash helmet visor. Now is my opportunity. I intend for it to pay off.

I balance it as best I can and dance my way through to the exit. She moves with confidence and people part as she disrupts the crowd. She is well ahead of me by the time I reach the external door.

8

Observation Point

The nondescript OP van remains stationary as the rear occupant picks up the radio and sets down the camera on the ply-lined floor.

OP: "DI Hudson, from observation point. Are you receiving, over?"

DI HUDSON: "Go ahead," Hudson responds.

OP: "Batford is out of venue and carrying drinks towards main targets. He has made contact with subject Mills, over."

DI Hudson: "Contact with Mills received."

Radio silence for a brief period. DI Hudson leans back in the front seat. His lounging is brief.

OP: "Batford is now approaching main targets, thirty feet away. Subject Mills is with main group and they're looking in Batford's direction, over."

DI Hudson: "Received. Keep commentary going."

OP: "Subject Snowy is moving towards Batford along with subject Trigger. View of Batford obscured by subject Snowy.

View is lost! View is lost! No eyeball of targets, over."

Hudson sits up.

DI HUDSON: "Let me know when you have renewed contact, over."

Short pause ensues. Hudson sips coffee from a Styrofoam cup.

OP: "Active message from OP."

DI Hudson: "Go ahead, go ahead!"

OP: "Subject Snowy has Batford by the neck. He's lifting him off his feet. State action."

DI Hudson: "What do you think the situation is?"

OP: "Looks like he may throw him. Crowd has gathered. We can't get outside team in though."

DI Hudson: "Stay where you are. I'll get uniform to drive by."

OP: "Received. Standing by as directed."

9

As a rule, I'm not used to being lifted off my feet. When you fake a stumble and send a tray of drinks crashing into your targets, you can't expect a civil response. I'm apathetic at this point. I'm dry and Snowy has lifted me out of the debris of glass and spent alcohol. He's prevented from throwing me by Razor.

"For fuck's sake, put him down. You're making a fucking scene." Razor is right. Snowy should do as directed or I'm about to show him why. He doesn't see his boss's reasoning. His grip isn't relaxing.

"He's just slopped a tray of drinks down me and he thinks it's funny." Snowy's brow is taut and he's squinting. He blows a stray hair out of his eyes as his hands are locked around my throat.

I'm not thinking anything's funny right now. I am thinking I could have thought my strategy through some more as my eyes invade his. I don't give a fuck what the state of play is with the operation – no man takes me by the throat and doesn't receive a lesson. Petty, I know. All cops are supposed to be trained to take all kinds of shit. I'm one of those cops. All cops have their limits. A crowd of bikers have gathered to see what the commotion is.

I have no comprehension how many know this group and who would wade in should I kick it all off. Some are aware I tripped and sent the drinks surfing into Snowy. What they don't realise is that I faked it. Leaving the drinks and being told thanks, now piss off, would lead to nothing. Without information and knowledge, the operation is dead.

Snowy hasn't taken heed of his boss's message. Time to deliver mine. I continue my gaze. I raise both arms to the sky then windmill my arms down and up through his with my hands together in prayer then open again as my forearms drive through his arms and release his grip. I drop and remain on my feet. He responds with a right hook. I duck back and use his motion to two-hand push him into the bikes behind him. It's worked; he's over balanced and topples onto the saddle and due to his size, goes down with the bike. As I expected, the crowd circle increases in circumference as they step back. The next move I didn't anticipate. Kat steps in as Razor makes his move. She forms a protective barricade between us.

"Leave it. He fuckin' tripped and that stupid arsehole deserved what he got. He's not on the door now and didn't listen to you. He should have let go when you told him. We don't need any more attention." She has her hands out against Razor's chest, and Razor's breathing like a rhino on speed. Eventually he sees her point and his facial skin tissue eases from the contortion of rage. The crowd have seen enough and go back to their smaller groups. I hear a siren approaching. I know I don't have long. Razor has shot Snowy the same look as me. He keeps himself busy picking the bike up. I take my chance at addressing the main man

"Hey, it was a mistake. I'm sorry for the damage and the scene. Whose bike is it? I'll see them right on repairs." He steps forward and Kat moves aside. Razor's invaded my personal space. We're nose to nose.

"That bike's mine, you jumped-up little prick and I'm telling you the repairs will be way out of your league. You've crossed the wrong man, my son."

"Look, I hear sirens. Let's just say we're not aware of either of us. I'm more than able to cover your costs, so take this as a goodwill gesture. Give me your number and I'll settle the rest."

I reach into my leathers and hand him a wad of cash. All twenties and folded like a dealer. He's looking at the cash and I know he's clocked the way the cash is presented. He pockets the money, all five hundred notes' worth. The siren grows louder and stops. The Old Bill has arrived. I hear the opening and closing of two doors only. We both say nothing as two uniforms approach.

The older of the two arrives first. He's in his mid twenties, seems like a sensible guy. I step in. "Evening, officer. No idea why you've been called, as we're all good here. Completely my fault. Spilt some drinks and fell into the bike, knocking it over. Just about to get this gent's number so I can sort out the bill for the repair." The copper's having none of it.

"Well that's not the report we had. A fight in progress and you two fit the description."

"Fight? There's no fight here. Look, can you see any blood, any bruises? I think someone's wasted your time."

He takes a look at the two of us and the crowd that have now gathered. Snowy is up and away into the throng so as not to be picked out. A struggle for him due to his size but so far so good.

"Well, it all seems in order apart from the bike there. I'll see you swap numbers, then I'll be off."

Razor looks at me then gets his phone out. It's a pay-as-you-go ten-pound job. He's giving me his dirty line. It will be untraceable and he knows it. I get in first.

"What's your number?"

Razor reluctantly gives it up whilst the copper looks on.

I type it into my phone and I can see he's noted I have a similar shit product. I call the number he's given. It doesn't ring. The copper looks at Razor.

"I must have put the wrong number in. Can you repeat it back?" Razor does and the 995 become a 998. I punch it in and call again. His phone comes to life with 'Back in Black'.

I accept blame. "Must have been me. You've got my number now. I'll be in touch and arrange payment for the damages. Anything else, officer?"

"Not from me. Nice to see two people sorting things out in a civilised way. Enjoy the rest of your evening." With that the two coppers leave and get back in their patrol car. Snowy is back now and as the cops leave, I consider my exit. Razor has other ideas and he begins to look over his bike. The side stand is fucked, the throttle handle damaged, along with the exhaust. The fuel tank is scratched and dented. It's rideable but he's not seeing that right now.

He's crouched down, surveying the carnage. His right shovel hand wipes the top of his bald head. His broken nose didn't come out on the surveillance photo but is prominent when you're centimetres away from it. Trigger is in the background not intervening and appears to be lookout. Some fucking lookout. He didn't even tell us of the Old Bill. Once Razor's done, he heaves his lump of a frame up and delivers his speech.

"I came for a good night out with my pals and you have royally fucked that up. I don't take kindly to people I don't know asking for my number and especially someone who rings it to make sure it's kosher. To do that in front of the Old Bill leaves a sour taste. My instincts are telling me you're used to a bit of confrontation and getting your own way. Now I don't mind that in a fella unless it affects me. Tonight it has. You owe me a clear two grand on top of the money you've given me. I only have your number so I reckon this will be resolved by me taking your bike until you bring me the cash. Call when you've got it and I'll tell you where to come get your ride."

With that he hands Kat fifty quid and sends her to get more drinks. I'm in a tight spot and he isn't going to budge. I don't have access to the money now. I only have the bike as a means of collateral. It's a gamble. If I give it up, he may never call and ditch the phone just to teach me a lesson for embarrassing him in public, getting police down and chinning his henchman. On the other hand, he may think it's an easy bit of pocket money and I'll turn up loaded and ready to settle my account. I prefer the second option and decide to take it.

"I'll leave you my bike. Show you I'm a man of my word. I know how much a bike means to a man and I trust you to look after mine for a night. I'll have the money for you tomorrow. I just need to know where to bring it and who I'm talking to." He shifts his feet and rubs his broad chin as he nods.

"Good choice. Call me tomorrow. I own a bar and club in Euston called Harvey Browns. Come down at happy hour from nine pm. If you bring the cash, I'll have the bike delivered to a place of your choice. If you don't show up, then that's your funeral pal. This must be one of those times you wished you hadn't been such a fucking gentleman helping a lady. Now, until tomorrow, give me your keys. I saw you come in so I know your bike. As for who I am? That's none of your concern."

He's finished his speech. I've no intention on filling him in around the adaptations. I don't expect to see the bike back in one piece. At least I'll have proved Little Chris right, albeit sooner than he expected. I throw Razor the keys and he throws them to Trigger.

"Till tomorrow then." I turn to leave. Kat is coming out with another full tray.

"I'll leave that to you this time."

"Good choice." She's concentrating on me but not enough to engage me in further conversation. I'm on my way out. I need to contact Winter, get scooped up by her lot and brief her on how she needs to come up with two grand and a further grand for me to go out on the piss tomorrow night. All in all a good night's work. Contact made, number obtained, along with a further meeting. All is well in my world.

10

I take the back roads away from the Ace Cafe. Although I look strange carrying my lid, dressed in full leathers, without a bike, I'm glad to be clear of the target area. I see my lift. Winter is en route, which is interesting. She's decided I need closer supervision. Probably both. I walk past the car and see A/DI Hudson and another I don't know. I walk farther down the road and turn right. They follow and I get in the back.

It's seconds before Hudson's sounding off.

"What the fuck happened back there and where's your bike?" Hudson's tone isn't conducive to my mood.

"Why are you asking that question? You should have seen all that was happening. Where were you when I was about to get the shit kicked out of me? That's the question I want to know, pal."

"It's 'sir' or 'guv' to you. Now answer the question. Where is the bike?"

Hudson isn't driving. He's delegated that to a DC who has taken the sensible approach – do her job and drive. She looks like a deer in the headlights. If her gut is telling her what mine is, she'll put her foot down and head to the meet point for the debrief, on the hurry up.

I lean forward to the back of the headrest that supports Hudson's neatly combed head. "If I were you, *sir*, I'd look straight ahead and say nothing until we meet your boss. You're a wannabe who's been sat on their arse whilst I've been at the coalface supporting your fucking job. Now, if you want this to be your first success at playing DI, then give me some space, sit back and shut the fuck up, *guv*." He takes the message. First sign of weakness. I would have told the DC to pull over and taken the conversation outside. Horses for courses.

The ride is continued in silence apart from Hudson telling the DC which way to turn. I've been a twat to him, but I haven't come down yet. I'm still in role. I need the space to look out the window and move through the evening's events in my mind, before I see Winter and give her the good news that she's about to meet my Superintendent to tell him the bike's gone and that I need three grand cash by tomorrow night.

I'm unsure whether they'll look at this as an opportunity or discipline me for loss of police property. By discipline me, I mean put me in front of a central disciplinary board to get rid of me from the job. It's all about reducing numbers. I need to get my game plan on for a night on the tiles with a bunch of villains who consider wringing your neck as an acceptable form of handshake.

I see a twenty-four-hour Starbucks up ahead. We've been on the M1 North for twenty minutes and Chiswell Green is the meeting venue for Winter. Works for me. The DC can drop me back in Watford. The DC pulls in. The car park is full but it's only ten pm, so that's expected.

"Put the car there." I point to a spot; she hesitates and looks at Hudson. Hudson says nothing and she parks up. The venue is full of people using free Wi-Fi and sipping mochas. The spot I've chosen isn't conducive to patrons but is beneficial to us should we need to make a hasty exit.

"Latte for me," I order Hudson as I walk towards Winter. He hesitates. He was about to meet Winter, who's occupied a rear table where no others are sat, making conversation easier. She's already got herself a drink. Winter has chosen the dominant seat leaving three spares. I pick the one next to her. It gives the appearance I'm her go-to man. In a way, I am, but she won't see it as such this evening.

"Evening. I see you sorted yourself out with a drink whilst the troops were out doing your work." I'm smiling. She looks up and takes a smug sip. She has froth on her top lip and I don't mention it. I wait for the cheap thrill of her licking it off. "Pass me a serviette, will you?" I reach behind me, grab a fist full and hand them over. She takes one and wipes her mouth.

"So you managed to hit things off pretty well, I hear? A fight, uniform called in, and I see you're without the bike. Great job, well done." She begins a slow clap.

The others have returned now. Hudson has slopped his drink though, which makes me happy. Winter kicks things off.

"Right, what went on out there? I will hear from you first." She nods in Hudson's direction.

Unusual to hear from the guy sat on his arse with no idea what was talked about. I sit back, wait for the response. I know it will be good. He takes a sip of his coffee and spills more down his chin. The drip runs off onto his Berghaus coat.

"We arrived as agreed. DS Batford entered the target area. He milled around looking at bikes then went into the cafe. We lost him briefly as the instruction was to remain static with no foot follow. He came out carrying a tray of drinks followed by Mills. They appeared to be in conversation. Visual got lost due to a passing lorry. We then saw Batford being held by the neck by Snowy. Batford broke free and sent Snowy into the bike behind him. Mills intervened and that's when the uniform I had called turned up in case we needed Batford out." Hudson finishes his appraisal and all eyes turn to me.

"My turn then? Well, the acting Inspector's script reads well. I won't go over that again. I had to make recompense for damages to Razor's bike. Razor and I agreed he could keep my bike as surety. I gave him my five hundred notes as a goodwill gesture. He wants a further two grand for repairs tomorrow night. Oh, I got his mobile number. So all is good. I just need the money for him and flash money for me." I pick up my latte and raise it, smiling in the direction of the wide-mouthed frogs in front of me.

Winter is the first to fire her salvo. "That bike was Met Police property. Not my agency's but your service's. That is your problem, not mine. Any 'flash' money is coming from your pot. That includes unauthorised payment offered or otherwise to the lead subject in a criminal investigation." She's had her say.

Now it's back to me. "I've done what you asked. I have the main man's dirty phone number and a meeting with him tomorrow night where I plan to party and earn his trust. If I don't turn up with the money, then your job is dead and buried. I don't give a flying fuck whose budget covers what. Let me know by oh nine hundred hours tomorrow whether I need to collect it or not and from where. I need a lift home. I'm tired and on overtime so it's in your interests, ma'am." I leave her with that and start to get up.

"You're not going anywhere, Batford. Until we've sorted this issue out, you'll sit your arse down. Let me remind you, this is my job. I'm in control of what happens on it. You had too long a leash last time. This time you're on a retractable one. I will enquire about the money first thing tomorrow when the Commander calls me for an update. If she's in agreement, then cash will be drawn and you can sign for it, no problem. If she says no, then we have to look at the options. So get to bed and rest up. Tomorrow will be a long day. I will call you once I know anything. Now if you've nothing else productive to say, I will leave and Hudson will get you home. Hudson, a quick word outside before you go."

They both depart. The DC who's left says nothing. I'm glad. I have no desire for conversation, just scotch and a bed to crash in. Winter and Hudson are talking animatedly outside. I can't hear what they're saying. Hudson is now on his phone and walking farther from the car. His lips aren't moving. The phone stays stuck to his ear. The other person has answered as his lips have started to move. He's too far away for me to read them. The conversation is brief. He strides back towards Winter. Both nod at each other, then she leaves. Hudson returns to the car and gets in. I look at the DC. "Guess that's our cue to leave." She raises her eyes and pours her coffee into a takeaway cup she's retrieved from the counter.

"Right, where to?" He's looking in the rearview mirror. I've moved behind the driver for more legroom and commandeer the whole back seat. It feels good to stretch out. "Watford train station. I'll get a cab to where I need to be." He nods to the driver and we set off. He's on his phone typing away. I can only imagine it's a long, weary text to his partner saying how he's sorry that he'll be late again, but he'll make it up somehow when he has more time. I shut my eyes and let my body be taken by the motion of the car.

I am bitter. I have neither the temperament nor skill to maintain a relationship, friendship or otherwise. I scraped through on selection for covert duty, the psychologist questioning my ability to stay calm under duress. She was right, but the course leaders decided to take the risk. The country's in desperate times. I've been performing the role for a number of years and the psychs have been told to use discretion widely. My attitude isn't conducive to twenty-first century policing. I know that but see it as a strength. Criminals don't give a shit about political correctness or public feeling. The best just look at more devious and underhand ways to get the job done undetected. I consider my failings to be a skill set. I always get the job done to everyone's advantage. I'm here to protect and serve society, after all. I haven't forgotten that I am a member, too.

The young DC who's been driving will have a strong career. She knows when to stay silent and out of confrontation. She uses a local map and has a good memory. She doesn't rely on a sat nav. That's why she's the one in control. In a surveillance situation, there's always a need to stay ahead of a moving target and predict where they will be going based on observation. A team is only as good as the driver getting them there. I feel relaxed now and safer than I was earlier. I've shaken off my alternate persona. I'm now back as myself and rest my head against the blacked-out window, shut my eyes and succumb to the motion of the car.

11

"Where are we going? This isn't the way back."

"You don't give the instructions. I do. Now shut the fuck up." It isn't Hudson.

The car lurches forward and accelerates, weaving between cars. I'm woozy but can see from the back seat. My head feels disconnected from my body. My vision is as hazy as a fogged camera lens. I'm on a three-lane carriageway, the motion makes me want to retch but I'm aware my situation wouldn't be conducive to this action. The car doesn't remain in one lane for long and the front seat occupant's constantly search their surroundings as we progress on an unknown route. Every now and then the driver glances into the rearview mirror, his visage but a blur.

I hear the indicator click as I slip between conscious and unconscious states. The car exits left, slows and turns left again. I see the tops of tall trees through my limited windscreen view and nothing else. We're on the edge of a wood. The car now rocks and bounces in trance with the rutted road. Treetops increase in density as the car slows to a stop. The engine stutters to silence. A door opens and closes. I hear feet on dried leaves, then feel hands on my feet, pulling.

My legs exit first. The back of my skull follows and greets the car doorframe with a nod before it hits earth and my legs are dropped. I can't open my eyes – they're sore and sting. I taste blood and my neck feels damp from my skull's impact.

Whether it's blood or cerebral fluid, I don't know. The smells of earth and pine enter my nostrils and bring some relief from the last memory of my nose being covered. If I'm to die now, I can think of worse places to be. I lie still. My options limited.

There is a familiarity of scent from the car that I can't place. It's not the smell of the upholstery, as that stinks of smoke; it's a soap smell mingled with a deodorant or aftershave. The man towering above me is distorted but I make out swirls of smoke, and I hear him cough. My vision becomes steeples of light. I make out signs of the sun breaking through the tree canopy and bathing the area in a quasi-religious scene.

I feel sacrificial. I squint and in my frailty, decipher a face. A male. His hands different shades of dark and toned streaks. He's undoing his trousers and starts straddling me. I'm on my back. I realise my hands are bound. Light screams through the trees and dazzles me as my vision adjusts. My breathing has become laboured. I shout but my voice is feeble. It's useless. I feel a warm jet of fluid across my face. No matter how hard I close my mouth, it finds its way in. He's waterboarding me with his own piss. Behind him appears another image, smaller with a demure sway about the walk. The form gets closer and stands beside Mr Pissmeister. The stream of urine stops, but he shakes every last drip onto me, laughing. I force open my eyes. The images appear clear.

Both have exposed rib cages from where they'd been blasted by Big H's men with twelve-gauge shotguns. What was a heart is a mangled bloody mess of sinew and muscle tissue. Blood seeps from the open chest wounds. The female form is Zara Stone; the other is Terry Sullivan, aka Barclay. I push into the ground to get away from the shattered human form in front of me. Stone has blood-streaked hair and an exposed jawline where the shotgun pellets have eaten half her face. The left eyeball hangs loose yet still moves as she turns in my direction. Barclay moves away as Stone takes her stance. The blood from her face has formed a river as it runs down the valley of her torn clothing. Her jaw opens and she speaks as she bends closer to my face.

"Alright, lover? Thought we'd say hello after you fucked off and left us for dead. Guess what? You were right; I never should have met Barclay again, like you said. But I was lonely, scared, and he was the only one there for me. We were a good team, me and you, and it's time to team up again and go to work." Her tongue is out and licking the top of what would have been her upper lip but is now shattered bone. From behind her back, she produces a sawn-off, pushes both barrels into my forehead and leans in. I feel the two circles of metal encasing my skin as she puts pressure on the butt.

"I want to see you suffer as you cross over to the dark side with me. I can watch, because I'm already dead. I wanna feel your blood cover my face and enter my head like you're a part of me again. This time I'll make sure we can't be separated. Thing is, lover, we were meant for each other, but you just couldn't see it. Now it's time for me to do the educatin.' You just shut up and take notes. See you soon, babes."

Stoner winks once with her good eye, then pulls the triggers.

"NO! STOP!" I sit up and smash my head on the roof of the car.

"What the hell are you on? If you need more room fucking ask and stop kicking me in the back." Hudson looks away and then turns back to me.

"We're here, time to get out."

I say nothing. I exit the car as quick as I can. Sweat's forming on my brow and stinging my eyes. I bail out and they drive off. A cab waits in the rank and I jump in the back and give him my address. I struggle placing the key in the communal door to the converted house, but eventually open it and step inside. Mine is the first-floor flat. I climb the stairs and insert the other key and get inside, double bolting the door. I know it was only a dream, but the realities of the situation they were in before they died have never left me. I had to leave her. I told her what she shouldn't have done. She went against that advice.

I was always taught to remind a suspect that their lawyer's advice is just that. They need to make their own mind up whether they take it or not. Stoner didn't. She paid the ultimate price. She should have been a means to an end for me. A snout. Nothing more. But it felt good having her around. She deserved better. I feel vulnerable. A feeling I've struggled with historically. I'm hoping I didn't say any names out loud or talk in my sleep. My bag's here. Mike must have sorted that out.

I throw the keys down on the side table next to a two-seated sofa. The brown leather looks as though it's been savaged by a cat but is still usable. Shabby chic. The living room overlooks a quiet residential street. I leave the living room and move along a short landing. A bedroom is situated opposite the stairs. The bathroom is at the back off the kitchen and off that is a door that leads to a covered wooden glasshouse. From there steps lead down to the garden below. I need to be aware of how to get out of the place in a hurry. Especially after Edinburgh.

There's basic equipment here. Enough for me to manage and space to chill out after deployment. Mike has left a bottle of scotch. I open the top and poor a large measure into a mug bearing an image of Homer Simpson. I throw my coat over the bannister rail and sit on the edge of the bed. There's no bedding, only a sleeping bag. I detach my leg and place it against the wall. The stump looks red. The knee is still great and that's the main thing.

The thin curtains are drawn. The moon invades the darkness through the cheap fabric and creates a strange shadow of my prosthetic foot and shin in the air. I raise my stump and observe its form. I'm used to seeing this now. I wonder what my life would be like if I hadn't lost my lower limb to the gunman. I had him in my sights but didn't pulled the trigger quick enough. The choice to kill was a bigger issue then. The job was keen to prosecute at the twitch of a trigger finger. Now that the terrorism is at the highest alert state, they've had to realise you need to feel supported to react to any hostile threat.

I could clearly see my assailant but his pistol was down as he was coming out the jewellers. I saw him raise his shooting hand but didn't react quickly enough. He got a shot off first and my shin took the bullet. He went down without getting another chance and didn't live to see a courtroom. The saving to the taxpayer in court time was offset by the public enquiry over the lawfulness of the kill. We won in the end. It was clear-cut. I got compensation, which was lucrative but not enough to ease the loss.

I sit back and take in the moon through the gap in the curtain. It sits above the top of roofs owning the night sky. I take heart at my insignificance on this planet. I unload four Tramadol from their plastic coffins and down them with scotch. It doesn't take long for each poison to take effect. The moon turns to darkness.

12

Holiday Inn – 24-hour service station off M25 – 8th September, 2020. Small meeting room, tea and coffee facilities only, water available. Plain, nondescript walls. Room rate ninety-nine pounds.
Persons present:
DCI Winter
DI Hudson
Alex Kennedy

DCI Winter: Good morning. You know A/DI Hudson from the last meet.

Alex Kennedy: Morning.

DCI Winter: Tell me what you learnt from last night at the Ace Cafe.

Alex Kennedy: They were all there. All chilling out, laughing, joking, looking at all the bikes and having fun. No drama at first. All very relaxed.

DCI Winter: What about this person? (Shows photo of DS Batford)

Alex Kennedy: Oh yeah, he was there all right (emphasises by tapping image with index finger of right hand). Made a fool of himself and nearly got a good kicking for it.

DCI Winter: Tell me what you heard. Anything that may be of use to us.

Alex Kennedy: Nothing. It wasn't that kind of meet up. They were relaxing and enjoying some down time amongst the bikers. That was until he came along.

DCI Winter: What happened?

Alex Kennedy: The guy in the photo covered Snowy in a load of drinks. Snowy got the arse and went to batter him. The guy remained cool, though. Snowy had him by the throat. The guy was telling him to put him down and let go but Snowy wasn't having any of it. Razor said the same but Snowy didn't listen. Then the guy just took Snowy out. He got out of the hold and sent him into Razor's bike. Snowy and the bike went over. Razor reacted but it calmed down as the police arrived.

DCI Winter: We know what happened when the police got there, but what happened after they left? What was said?

Alex Kennedy: The guy in the picture got a wad of cash out. Looked like five hundred in twenties from the size. He gave it to him and told him he'd be good for the repairs. Razor took the cash and the fella's bike as security. They swapped numbers and arranged to meet tonight at Razor's club. Razor's expecting two grand in cash to cover damages and the guy gets his bike back. If all is good, he can stay and enjoy the party.

DCI Winter: Did the man in the photo give a name at all?

Alex Kennedy: No.

DCI Winter: Okay. I need you at the club tonight. Here's two hundred.

Alex Kennedy: Two hundred? You're way off the mark with that kind of money. This lot aren't small time; they're big. Two hundred will get you a cheap bottle of champagne. I need a grand, minimum.

DCI Winter: That's all there is. Sign here on this receipt. Call me as soon as you can to let me know you're out. A/DI Hudson will make arrangements for our next meeting.

Alex Kennedy leaves the room and is seen exiting main building.

DI Hudson: Anything else for this evening? Thought I'd see the wife for lunch.

DCI Winter: I didn't know you were back together. Of course. Go, but make sure you get everyone up to speed about tonight's deployment. I want the outside of the venue covered. Foot capability and one vehicle if they all leave together and only if Batford's with them.

Hudson acknowledges the request, grabs his coat and leaves. Winter remains to make notes.

13

Decision log entry, 8th September, 2020

A good start. Contact has been made and Batford's got himself noticed by the criminal network, albeit by unorthodox methodology.

I am aware that police property has been appropriated but this is a Met Police problem.

I have conducted a consultation with a band E lawyer within the Crown Prosecution Service. They have advised to continue the operation despite Alex Kennedy being present and handling money during a drugs supply. There is insufficient evidence to arrest Detective Superintendent Hall at this stage. To arrest Alex Kennedy would disrupt the investigation and hinder any chance of a successful prosecution.

I am overjoyed my intuition has proved correct.

I am of the opinion the involvement was minimal. I will worry about this issue later.

For the first time, I feel I may have misjudged DS Batford. He's certainly unorthodox in his approach but to date has not been caught with his hands in the till.

I remain open minded. I have found him more approachable on this operation despite his disregard for authority or rules of any kind. Approachable doesn't amount to warmth.

Entry complete.

Klara Winter DCI
National Crime Agency
Senior Investigating Officer
Op Kestrel

14

The concierge to Mike's Thames-side apartment building nods. It could be by way of recognition or out of politeness. I don't know. He doesn't ask questions as I move towards the lift. He's paid enough to keep his mouth shut about who visits the building. Mike has invested in a flat whose opulent facade contains celebrities and lawyers who have made enough to afford such luxury and location. Mike has one of the cheaper flats but that's what you get when you invest dirty money in an area beyond your reach.

Mike's called the meeting on. I'm hoping he's brought enough cash to cover me for tonight's sojourn. I explained on the phone it wouldn't be cheap. He knows the kind of money we're talking when I say that. The job isn't keen on handing out charity for cops like me to go and be entertained by criminals, but hey, it's part of my role. In the end, the Commissioner wants results to feed to the Home Secretary, who in turn feeds the Prime Minister, who then throws the scraps to the public by way of false promise backed up by dubious statistics. It also helps to remind the Home Secretary that criminals have expensive tastes and good staff doesn't come cheap. The security of the country isn't a raffle, more of a lucky dip. So to send me out with two grand and some spending money is small change in the end.

I reach Mike's floor. The female lift announcer's automated voice purrs my arrival. The noiseless metal widens. I check left before turning right towards the flat door. Mike hates me calling it a flat. He refers to it as his London residence or *The Residence*. He can be such a cock. When I arrive, his door is open. I hear Mike on the phone. I wait and look through the two-inch gap. He's pacing around like a circus bear. His voice fades in and out as he goes in different areas of the living room floor. He's had a few – there's a half bottle of scotch on the small bar and a pool of spent drink at the base of a glass tumbler. Nice to know your cover officer is fit and prepared to back you up when you're out on the plot.

He has yet to be called upon by me. That's more my choosing than his. I want to leave each contact with the enemy alive. Not having to think about him on exiting. He was good in his day. His day has long gone, and the dark side has him in its cloak of fame and misfortune. He finishes his conversation and throws his mobile on the new three-seat leather sofa. I can tell it's new: the receipt's on the bar. The sofa was delivered today. The cost is irrelevant. What is relevant is that he paid on a card. He's losing his grip on the realities of his situation. A card is a tracing device where cash is king. It's criminality for dummies and Mike should be way past the first chapter by now.

He goes to the bar and gets me a glass. I'm okay for one. I don't intend on driving tonight. I'm a law breaker but some laws I have respect for. "So who was that on the blower?"

"Fucking Winter. That's who. Here, take this." He hands me a good measure and we move to the balcony. The doors are shut but the view towards Battersea Power Station is spectacular.

"What did she want?"

"To know if I was alright with tonight's deployment and if I would be out too. I set her straight as you heard. She asked if you'd mentioned the two grand you'd need for tonight and that it would have to come out of the Met's covert policing budget. It was a statement more than an ask. I told her it was all good." I can see from the way he knocks back his drink that it wasn't.

"Where's the money then? I've not got long. I went to the street the club's in today and had a look at the area and surroundings. Smart place your mate is running, very smart. I'm surprised you haven't stuck some money in it."

"What do you mean by that?" He's not looking pleased. All flared nostrils and mono-browed. "I know Sullivan as a snout and nothing more. What he does, he does and what I do, I do. Here's your cash for tonight and flash money." He hands me an envelope. I make a point of counting it in front of him. It's a thousand short.

"Are you having a laugh? Fifteen hundred quid? I told you two grand for the bike repair and a grand flash money and you give me enough to get a good kicking and a bus home. What's with this? Oh hang on… You're having a laugh. Very good. I've bitten. Now give me the rest." Mike's silent. His head's down. He's staring into his drink as he swirls the ice around with the rotation of his wrist.

"The Commander wouldn't authorise any more. Trust me, I was practically begging, which isn't me, as you know. She says you shouldn't have got yourself in that position and you were lucky to be staying on the job after the show you made. She's refused to pay the bag of parking tickets you submitted, too. You'll have to cough for those yourself. Where's the bike, by the way?"

"Pay them myself? Fuck's sake! The tracker still shows where I left it. At the Ace Cafe. They wouldn't know how to ride it anyway." A smile forms on our faces and Mike relaxes. The beauty of an adapted bike. "Go to the kitchen, in the top cupboard is a box of cereal. There's two grand of mine in there. Take it and have a good night out. I want to know what Razor is up to in addition to what he's telling me. Must be something we can spin to our advantage."

I do as instructed and find the packet of Honey Nut Loops. Mike would never be a porridge guy or a fresh fruit man. I take the cash and dust off the extraneous sugar. It's the amount he said it was.

I come back to the lounge to notice the city lit up like a

birthday cake. I've always loved London at night from up high. Seen it many a time in this state and I never tire of the view. I feel safe surrounded by the plastered breezeblock and steel beams that entomb Mike's world. He's sat reclined; he remotely slides back a false wall that reveals a 105-inch Samsung TV. He has his back to me in a cinema chair that's fit for a king. I check my phone. I have an hour to get to my destination.

"Where's the clobber for tonight?"

He doesn't turn around, just points with his scotch glass towards a spare room. He's been good enough to leave it hanging. I may be mistaken but it looks pressed. It's a two-piece that will fit well with a pair of handmade shoes to match. I don't do off the shelf. Those days are gone. I'm good to go. I remove my leg and hop into the shower, leaning against the wall for support. I make sure I don't cover the jets that are inset to the wall. I sit on a stool and relish the comfort the water brings.

I have time to think, consider my options and get in role for the evening's entertainment. I never go in with a plan or a preconceived notion of how the night will play out. The shower TV shows me the time. I kill the jets and get up. It's slippy and I don't wish to go to ground.

I lean against the mirrored mantel tiles and for a moment, take stock of my fading body. The tattoos, once pristine, are beginning to show signs of decay. I see the back piece in the rear mirror and the dark priest stares back at me through hooded eyes. The cigarette burns and belt welts are still reminders of my youth. The depths of the burn scars differ as to how long my foster father held them down for. The welt marks from the belt show the same signs of ferocity and the buckle chips of skin display small indentations that could be mistaken for acne pockmarks. I wear these badges knowing all too well how they were earnt. It's not the only thing to catch my eye.

Specks of white powder dust the surface of the black marble sink surround. I know Mike isn't a talc guy. He doesn't cut the stuff either; he just moves it on. I make a mental note. I'd be surprised if he's had anyone back here to party and more so if he'd let it snow. My thoughts are shattered by the sound of gunshots. They're coming from the living room. A steady rattle of automatic fire and smashing glass. I hit the floor. My breathing rapidly increases. The blood pumping in my ears. I roll away from the bathroom and into the bedroom and remain on the floor. I grab the clothes I'd laid out on the bed. I'm not getting dragged out in my birthday suit. I get fully dressed as the shots continue. The noise masks any I'm making.

It's gone quiet. I can't understand where the gunfire could be coming from as we're too high up and not overlooked for someone to use an automatic weapon. I may have missed the flat's door opening when I was in the shower, though. I stand and press myself against the wall and listen. It's then that Mike enters the bedroom. "What in the fuck are you doing?" I look blank. We enter the living room and I see *Call of Duty* on the big screen. "Aren't you too old for that shit?" I'm relieved.

He has the kind of smile a drunk develops as the alcohol permeates the veins and enters the brain's synapses. He puts both hands on my face and pats my cheeks. "Looking smart, my son. You look the fuckin' part and more. You need some gold though; this lot like a bit of bling. I'm thinking nothing fancier than this neck chain. He puts the chain round my neck and it hangs appropriately just above my upper chest. "Now then, let's take a look at you." He steps back, nodding his head in approval and moves back towards the bar. He's swaying slightly and would be described by a probationer as unsteady on his feet and smelling of alcohol. He's pissed and he's my cover for tonight.

"I'm using my own pseudonym. I don't give a shit what the Commander thinks. She's not out there. I am."

Mike turns towards me and takes a sip from his fresh glass. "You what?" He's not impressed. But neither am I.

"You heard. If Big H wants to come for me, then let him

come. Winter can take him out and all ends well. I'm not running, Mike. Big H needs to know that. It won't look good if he suspects I'm a cop and having him hear I'm back will help that. Anyway, the chances are slim to none, so that's my decision."

"Don't forget who you're talking to. You don't have the right to make those kinds of choices! I've got limited numbers of undercover officers all over London running from north to south and back again, all fucking night long, and you're playing the biggun?" His voice is raised. He's now a drunk looking to fight. Raised voices in this block will result in police being called. Neither of us need that. His face is flushed crimson. He's breathing heavily. I watch him as he stops leaning on the bar and starts towards me. I know he's my Superintendent but right now he's a threat and being a prick. I choose a pre-emptive strike and Mike goes to the floor on the first punch to his kidney. He starts to rise again and another punch to his temple renders him useless.

I check his pulse. He's still breathing. I drag him to his new sofa and put him in the recovery position. His shirt is undone around the neck. I stick a large, Indonesian wooden salad bowl on the floor under his mouth in case he vomits. I feel better now. If anyone finds him dead, then they'll think he's choked on his own spew. I hope it won't come to that. I like the man. I make a mental note to call him during the night. I leave his work phone on the loudest ringtone under his ear. He grumbles as I move him to position the phone. I take that as a good sign.

I take the glass tumbler he used and put it on its side on the floor under the hand that's dangling off the edge of the sofa. There's no blood. The police won't even consider forensically examining his flat if he dies. They'll see the white powder marks and put it down to misadventure. Toxicology will be so high for alcohol they'd consider topping it off with a cherry and an umbrella. Anything else will just be gravy, as they say. It won't do me any harm to have been here. Aside from the block's CCTV, there's the concierge and he'll sing like a canary if it all comes on top. I check my appearance in a floor-length mirror before I leave.

I struggle each time I appear, as I'm not. Although I relish the role, it's not conducive for someone who struggles with their own identity.

I do a last check on Mike; his chest is rising and lowering and he's snoring like a gorilla with a cold. That'll do for me. I've seen worse in custody. They survived the night in a cell. Not on a sofa in a London pied-a-terre. I exit his residence and the door automatically locks behind me. A female occupant of advanced years meets me. We exchange pleasant nods of greeting as she heads for the same lift. I don't, as a rule, enjoy the company of strangers in such a confined space.

We wait outside the lift door and I dutifully press the button. It's rising from the ground floor so will take a short time to arrive. The woman reapplies some dark lipstick in the mirrored lift door and I do my best to ignore her. It's to no avail.

"I haven't seen you about here before, young man. Are you new to the block?"

"No, just visiting. How about you?"

"Lived here for five years now. Bought one of the first ones off plan and so glad I did. Most wonderful people here, so polite and courteous. Most are out all day and rarely cause a nuisance at night." The lift arrives. I proffer her in ahead of me. She accepts with a gracious nod and turn of her head. She has to be in her seventies, hasn't succumbed to surgery to maintain her physique and skin clarity. She clearly works out and from the muscle tone, I would say a regular yogi. She has a calm presence. Nothing more is said as the lift glides down. The floor stops moving with a light bump. The voice announces our arrival and indicates the doors are about to open.

"Have a lovely evening." It's all I have to offer by way of goodbye as the lift doors open and she strides out into the foyer.

"Likewise. Enjoy your night clubbing." She gives me a sly wink and the concierge opens the main door. I follow her and see she's heading for a taxi across the street. "Would you mind if I took your arm? I'm not as steady in these shoes as I used to be but still love a heel." I can't refuse. She takes my arm. I feel like an escort.

My attire is fitting the occasion. I smile at the concierge as we exit and head for the taxi. It's pulled up near the roadside, four ways flashing. The passing over-ground train echoes in the distance. The traffic is stationary as we begin crossing the road towards the taxi. As I approach, I ask where she's going so I can tell the driver. I near the car and turn to the driver's open window. Car horns become lively.

The headlights of the approaching car is the first thing that alert me to the outside world closing in. The second thing is that it's on the footway. The vehicle careens straight through the old dear. I instinctively roll over the cab's bonnet. There's screaming, chaos, people running down into the tube station. I'm on the road. I see reverse lights heading towards me at speed. I roll under the taxi as the lights become blinding and collide with the cab's bonnet. I carry on rolling and exit the underside of the car and into the road that's now congested.

The ramming car has left. It's back up on the pavement and away. I get up surrounded by a crowd. No one is helping me. All eyes are on the lifeless body of the woman on the pavement. I see blood, lots of it and a bare foot. The other encased in a heeled shoe. I move away. My body aches but I'm unhurt. My clothes have taken a beating but that's just the jacket. Sirens echo. Time slows. The doors to the MI6 building are locked down. I know this wasn't a terrorist attack. It was meant for me.

I have to leave. If the police link me later, I'll claim shock. I'm guilty by association of helping the poor woman to her death. I buy a bottle of water and snap out four more Tramadol. I down them all. I check around me. I need to move away from the area as cordons are being thrown up. A black cab is turning. I hail it and he pulls over. "Euston, please."

The cabbie stops at Euston station. A nearby club has an AC/DC tribute band on. 'Let There be Rock' is reverberating around the bar. The alcohol is making my head feel light but still in control of all my senses. The band is good and the air guitar playing from a corner of the room is being gratefully received. The Angus Young wannabe has the shorts and school tie with no shirt and curly hair. He's good enough for me to stay for 'Whole Lotta Rosie', another scotch and a drink with a bar leaner. My phone vibrates. I check the screen. Razor's number is up. I press green and step outside.

"Yes?"

"I take it you don't give a shit about your bike? I've arranged for its crushing in the next twenty minutes unless you appear with the cash. What's that shit in the background?"

"Keep your hair on. I keep my own time. I'll see you in ten. Make sure your door goons don't wind me up." I kill the phone, finish my drink and say goodbye to the company at the bar. She smiles and turns back to the band. I don't blame her. Where I'm going sounds like a right barrel of laughs. I know where my bike is and it isn't at a scrap yard.

15

I get another cab to drop me at the venue. The driver's thankful we've reached the final destination after my insistence at random stops along the route. Nothing was behind us to arouse any suspicion. As long as he gets paid, he doesn't see any issue in stopping where I ask him. I alight into the shops whilst he waits. He has no intention of leaving me as I've paid upfront and he likes the look of the notes. I take out my phone, back everything up to the SIM card and ensure nothing is left on the handset. I wipe all my messages and call logs, then reset the phone to factory settings. The cab driver pulls up outside a red door. I look over the cab's roof at a tasteful neon sign announcing the club's entrance. The driver wishes me a good evening and leaves to fleece another fare. I knock on the door and Snowy greets me.

He's dressed in the standard issue black shirt, long black coat and black gloves of a door operative. He's not smiling. It's his door and domain to police. I give him the satisfaction, on this occasion that is. He invites me over the threshold. Once inside, he indicates I raise my arms. I make a biblical cross for the obligatory pat down. He only does the top half and waist. I haven't called Winter. I'll do that when I get the opportunity. Her team will have seen me in the door, though. You couldn't miss me, as there was no queue to talk of with the club's entrance being in a side street off the Euston Road. You'd have to know about the place to bother checking it out.

The entrance hall is deceptively wide with one entrance in and out at this level. Snowy leads me down a flight of stairs to a relaxed drinking lounge. The clientele are wealthy and well turned out. The decor is tasteful and not what I expected from Razor. There are no pictures of motorbikes but framed mug shots of visiting celebrity attendees. It oozes class. Long sofas of red leather line the room walls with low drinks tables in front. The wooden floor is varnished oak that clicks as the high heels of the female waitresses stride over the boards. The table service is conducted by the kind of people you'd expect to see in a fine art gallery – well turned out and knowledgeable in their craft and trade.

The bar complements the room's minimalist style. No beer pumps here. Clearly not a drink of the trade. Champagne, wines of many denominations and liquors are the drinking person's beverages of choice. I'm struggling to see Razor with any links to this venue, let alone owning it. He would suit a bar in the East End and not appear out of place. Snowy nods towards a connecting door. I follow his lead. No one glances in our direction or has any interest in who I am. If you're in here, then you're meant to be in here and that's enough for them.

Snowy pauses at the door and presses the intercom twice before entering. The door is soundproofed. If police were to raid this place, you'd need the rapid entry team to mechanically force the doorframe with the giant can openers. I follow Snowy in. Razor is sat in a brown leather regency-style chair, smoking a cigar. He's dressed in a smart two-piece suit, open neck white shirt, gold neck chain and watch to match. He's increased the jewellery on his hands but hasn't gone overboard to give the appearance of being common.

He nods towards an identical chair opposite him. Snowy remains at the door. The room is as big as Mike's living room. The street entrance deceptively denies the volume of space behind it. Razor has a private bar area and staff. The staff are motioned to leave. "What will you drink?" Razor's up and behind the bar, sweeping his hand along a host of shorts on display.

"The Dalmore, straight, no ice."

He finds the bottle, dispenses a decent measure of the twenty-four-year-old single malt into a crystal glass, and hands it to me as he sits back down. He says nothing of my choice. I can tell by his face, pouring that hurt.

Razor's in good form. "It's a good night to be here. Nineties music night, love it!" He's smiling at me. I raise my glass in acknowledgement of his hospitality. My options are limited here. I can't get out any other way than the one I came in and that's blocked.

Razor nods at Snowy. Snowy hesitates before leaving but gets the message and does one. Just Razor and myself grace the room now. I say nothing. I was always taught it's impolite to break silence. The other person may be deep in thought and wouldn't be appreciative of the invasion. It also gives me time to mull over various strategies for the evening. The female who'd been sent for drinks at the Ace Cafe isn't here. Razor breaks the silence. "I didn't think you'd have the bottle to show. Do you have the money?"

I remain impassive and twitch my upper lip towards my nose. "Yeah, I have the money. Do you have my bike?" He throws me the keys and I catch them. He's added a key fob with the number of the club on it. Tasteful.

"It's out back. I'll have one of my lads stick it in the van and bring it back to you."

I wait until he's finished his drink before replying. "I want to see it before I give you the money."

"Fair enough. I'd be the same in your position, especially as you're sat there like a cocky little cunt thinking it's never moved." He's got a smile on him that would make a Harley Street dentist orgasm. He's swept the bike and found the tracker I placed under the seat. I focus on my breathing, remain calm, assured, and wait for him to confirm my thoughts.

"We found a tracker under the seat. Shitty little device you can buy online. What interests me is why you'd have it on there. If I were in your position, I'd have one the police could access remotely to find where the bike is, or better still just get a new one. So, what's the deal?" He chugs on his Cuban and smoke swirls around his assured, over-confident face.

I get up and walk to the bar. He indicates with a nod that I can help myself. I do just that. He places his hand on top of his glass. I wander over to a signed picture of Liam and Noel Gallagher with Razor. Razor's in the middle with his tongue out, arms around them both whilst holding two bottles of beer.

"Nice picture. They were good back in the day, shame they turned out to be such a pair of dicks. I'm wondering if that's what I need to do once I've finished this drink and your hospitality. I came here to honour a gentlemen's' agreement, not to be questioned as to how I keep tabs on where my transport is." Razor's by my side. He guides me to another picture. This one's of Lemmy, a decanter of whisky in his mouth like a baby's bottle, winking at the camera.

Razor continues his guided tour "Those little fuckers didn't know how to party like that man. Now *he* knew how to have a good time. Him and his band drunk me dry but what a night. Club was packed out, floor took a battering, bar took a restock I haven't seen since he died. He would always come here when he was in London. It was a place he could relax, be himself and get wasted. Now I know a man who knows what he likes when I see one. You had bottle to take on Snowy at the cafe. It didn't go unnoticed. No man who's a pussy would do that or have two grand ready to offer at short notice unless he had a decent income stream. So take the plug out of your arse, let's introduce ourselves properly, and I'll show you your bike. You can stick the two grand behind the bar and have some fun."

Razor has his meaty hand on my shoulder, patting it like he would a dog. There's presence in his application of skin on fabric. I turn and face him and hold out my hand, "Sky's my name." He has my hand in a shake. Both of us apply enough pressure so as not to intimidate but try and find a level playing field. He could have had me robbed on arrival, beaten to a pulp and dumped as a lesson. He hasn't. I take that as a good sign. "Friends call me Razor on account of me always having a close shave." His head rears back as he belly laughs at his own joke. I smile in reciprocity

"Right, then. Let's go and party shall we, Sky?"

"Yes, Razor. Let's do that."

Snowy opens the door and I follow down some carpeted stairs towards the basement. A code activates one set of doors and the sheer weight of them opening provides a suction that you'd expect on a vault. The door closes and I can hear music from beyond another door at the far side of a clean, white-seated area we've entered that mirrors the bar upstairs.

This area is slick and designed as a place to kick back. Orange pod chairs with sofas to match and his favoured small drinking tables are the only furniture. The bar is white with a marble top. You'd expect it to feel cold, but the decoration gives the illusion of being underground in an ice cave. A fleet of women all dressed like they've stepped off a Paris catwalk greets Razor. These aren't staff; they're here for the fun.

Razor walks towards the bar, leans over to the barman and speaks into his ear. I notice the barman glance over to me and nod. He reaches down below the bar and brings up a small steel box, which he hands to Razor, who brings it over to where I'm sitting. Razor joins me and the barman follows shortly after with a double Dalmore, as I like it. Razor has straight vodka. I watched the barman make the drinks and there was no sign of foul play. Nevertheless I swirl it and sniff before I drink it. Razor notices, smiles, raises his eyes and pushes the box towards me. "Stick all your phones in here. House rules. No signal down here and no photos are allowed for your Facebook wall. You keep the key and get it when you leave. The box is kept in a safe in my office."

I take out my only phone, break it open and keep the SIM card. Everything is stored on there. I put the broken up phone in the box and put the card in my wallet. Razor doesn't break a smile. He hands the box to the barman who goes to the door to take it upstairs.

The doors to the main floor open and there's the girl from the Ace Cafe. She strides over to where we're seated, nods at me and bends down towards Razor. After a brief conversation, for his ears only, he gets up and adjusts his jacket.

"Right, son, let's go and have some fun." I get up as he pauses at the door. The sound's dim. The opening bars to 'Fuckin' in the Bushes' fill the auditorium. Razor strides in and starts shaking hands with those who reach towards him. Others are pumping the sky to the beat of the track whilst Razor is busy nodding his head to the rhythm as he enters his arena like a gladiator. Kat is at his side; her eyes scan the room as she pushes people aside and Razor makes his way towards a sectioned area at the far side of the room.

The music is bouncing off the acoustic foamed walls. I have never experienced anything like this before. There must be three hundred people dancing, jumping and partying. The dress code is relaxed. Drug taking is open and evident. It's a blizzard in here and no one gives a shit, as they're all stoned or getting that way. There's a staged area that hosts the DJ. She's swaying her headphone-adorned head like a hippy in a trance. 'Fuckin' in the Bushes' slips into 'I Am the Resurrection' and a party of blokes that could have fallen off a rugby pitch lifts Razor into the middle of the dance floor. The atmosphere is energised. The room is a swirl of lights and flowing fabric as bodies move with the music. I join the party now the Tramadol has taken hold and the alcohol warms my blood. For once I feel alive and go with the flow. I need to be trusted and pissing off the host acting like a prude won't achieve that. I have no idea of time and don't care. I need to shake off the shit and bathe in the city's sweat.

'Hindu Times' bashes my brain. My voice croaks the lyrics with Razor as the surge of the dance floor swells with heat and tears. The air-conditioning does a job and as the start of 'Fool's Gold' fires up, I'm lost in a haze of ritualistic energy and delirium. I manage to remain standing. The crowd aren't boisterous enough to knock me down. I feel someone's arse against mine. The touch is brief. It's Kat. This time she's dragging a comatose guy out towards a set of doors at the back of the dance floor. The doors are flung open and he's transferred to two minders. The doors shut. A separate pair of door hangers blocks the exit, fingers pressed against their earpieces. No one alters what they're doing and carry on dancing or imbibing in their drug of choice. Razor waves at me to follow him to the side of the dance floor. The people part. I follow behind him and we enter a glass room. The volume subsides to a level where it's easy to speak.

A different barman appears. We take a seat and look out on the crowd. Same drinks are left with a bottle of water and a menu. I take the menu, as does Razor, and we survey what's on offer. There are others in the booth: a young Arab and a couple of henchmen who drink orange juice and water and enjoy watching the show from the confines of the glass cell.

"So, do you like what you see?"

"Yeah. It's a great place. You've done well." I'm conscious of the company we're keeping to have any fruitful conversation. I sense Razor takes a guess at my thinking.

"Everyone here has a secret. They pay two grand a week membership to come here and indulge that secret. I have three rules: no weapons, nonces or phones. There's a diverse cross section of society who enjoy the ambience and relaxed atmosphere. What goes on here stays here. Any loose lips get dealt with accordingly. I'm making you aware of that now so there's no misunderstanding when you leave."

"Understood. So what's with your woman there, the one who was at the cafe? Is she your wife, mistress?"

"Kat? Neither. She's head of my security. Fucking good at

the job, too. Stunning and cunning all in one beautiful package. I have enemies, plenty of them. You don't get this far in life and make none. Now you've asked a question, it's my turn. What's your business?"

I take a sip of water and maintain eye contact. "I'm retired. Took a hit in the army and got paid out. I invested the money well and live off the returns." He's not convinced. I don't like the way this is going.

"Don't bullshit me, son. I've been around the block more times than a blind sprinter. Your return would have to be fucking high to be able to blow two grand just like that. You approached for a reason yesterday. You either come out with what you want or I'll see you out myself." He motions to Kat who comes into the room. He whispers in her ear and she goes to the Arabs. They vacate the room without hassle or argument.

The clear glass turns opaque as Kat presses a button near the door. She shows the men to another member of staff and remains in the room stood at the door. I notice she's wearing an earpiece. There's little option available to me. Either I try to leave and the whole job is blown, or front it out and see how we go. I choose the latter.

"The truth? I like your bodyguard and followed her into the cafe to get her attention. What happened after that was an error on my part for which I'm here to apologise."

I open my jacket so he can see I'm reaching for the money. I bring it out and place it on the table. "Two grand, cash, as agreed. What I've told you is true, although I'm always on the lookout to top up my pension with private work. I'm flexible, skilled and discreet. I'm good behind the wheel of a car or bike if you need extra outside staff." Razor motions for Kat to come over. She does and takes a seat at our table. She sits back and crosses her legs. She's paying no interest in me despite my fake revelation.

"Tell me, Sky, does she look like the kind of woman who'd be interested in the likes of you? You couldn't keep her in a week's wages. You've got an interesting name, one I've not heard of. That can be a good or bad thing. I need to do some asking around. I make it a rule to do my own referencing of potential recruits. You understand it pays to be careful in my game?" He's finished and looks out towards the dance floor. The food arrives and he starts eating his rare steak burger and fries. I opted for the same. Kat must be on a break as she joins us with a mixed fish salad, no dressing. Her eyes meet mine as she eats and she offers the glimpse of a smile.

Razor breaks the feeding. "I need to make a couple of calls. You stay here with your dream. I'll be back soon." He motions for a barman who comes in, picks up his plate and follows him out of the room. I sit and eat, hoping the food will soak up the alcohol. I don't feel safe at the present time. I feel like a prisoner on a cell visit left with the gaoler. I've no idea why he left when he did but have to take heart that I'm still in his club and in an exclusive area. If he didn't trust me, I wouldn't be here. Either that or he's making arrangements to have the situation rectified by his bodyguard who's sat opposite me.

I keep fit, train four times a week at the gym and feel confident in my physical abilities. Edinburgh, and the hit and run earlier, have unnerved me though. Kat stepped in quickly at the Ace Cafe. She had no idea how I may react. I've seen her work the floor here and the male who was escorted out didn't stand a chance, despite his size. She's martial arts fit and has confidence to match. Kat breaks my thoughts.

"So, do you like the place?"

"Is that the best chat up line you have?" I smile at her and she looks straight at me, her large eyes reflecting the main dance floor lights. She's stoic in her response.

"Funny. You're not my type. You were lucky last night he didn't floor you. We've been sat here for a few minutes and you haven't given me the courtesy of a thank you at saving your arse from a certain kicking. I see men like you every evening. Flash your cash, wear a sharp suit and chain to match. You reckon you're God's gift. Well, you're not. You wear your ego like a Whoopee cushion just waiting for someone like Razor to sit on you and laugh as the air gets released."

She finishes her speech and having put me in my place, stares out towards the dance floor. The opaque glass is one way. View out only. Razor clearly feels no trepidation at leaving her alone with me. He's chosen his security well and feels at ease in this environment. His shed. His lair.

"Must be a bitch to work down here? It's like a tomb with atmosphere." A weak attempt at deflection away from me but I need to get some rapport back from where I'd left it – high and dry.

"Money talks. It pays me well. He has a way with money like all men in his position. Why did you turn up here tonight? Fool's errand, if you ask me, unless you've got something he wants."

"I gave him my word. What more should there be?"

"Something about you isn't right. I don't know what it is yet but I make it a habit of knowing who's sniffing around looking for work. You don't look like you'd know your way around a bar." She turns back to me and her eyes are wide, conveying her message. I sense this won't be a tale of unrequited love. I get up and look out the window.

"Just remember, it was your boss who invited me here. He could have organised a courier for the money and handed me back my key but he didn't. You could be wasting your breath as this may be the first and last time I'm seen here."

She remains seated and responds. "I hope you're right because as of this moment, he's making a call. The person he's calling knows everything about everyone. What he doesn't know he can find out. He never does that unless he's thinking he has further use for someone. What that could be with you? I don't know. What regiment were you with?"

"That's none of your concern. With the greatest respect, I'll talk to the organ grinder, not the monkey. You've made your position clear." She shrugs and turns towards the door as Razor returns. His face is relaxed. He's smiling as he dominates the dance floor over to my holding cage. His bald head is glistening in the lights. As if he's read my mind, he takes out a handkerchief and wipes the top of his head. The handkerchief is floral; I'm guessing a Japanese designer. He enters the room and comes over to Kat. She stands and he leans into her side. I can see speech but can't make out what's being discussed. Kat leaves the room.

"Everything alright?" I ask. Razor sits. I feel like I'm in an interview room with me as the suspect, unrepresented, with no custody time limit. Razor stands and begins pacing the room. Each step definitive and with purpose. Like a cat with a cornered mouse.

"I've made a call. You've not been telling me the complete truth as to your employment. This concerns me. Your motivation for attending has become, let's say, questionable." He doesn't look at me but states his case. I swallow and maintain my composure. The trick in this kind of scenario is to ensure your legend is good. Stick to it in the event you're fronted out as an undercover Old Bill. I don't believe for one minute he suspects that but preparation prevents piss-poor performance.

"Word is you're a bit of a legend of the North? North London, that is. Not the kind of legend you'd want, mind you, being on the mob's most-wanted list. Dusty, they're calling you, as you've a reputation for taking out the trash. Last person I knew who worked the bins was my old man. He was as straight as they come. But you're far from it. Last bit of trash you're rumoured to have disposed of was another man's gold or 'ice' shall we say. Now you're here in my club drinking my best whisky and eating my food. So I think to myself... what would you want from me? A place to move some of the gear you're alleged to have nicked from one of North London's top villains? You like my company so much after one meeting you'd like to become best pals? Or simply you're an arrogant, jumped-up prick that has come to me for protection? So, Sky, which one is it? If you fuck me about further I will hand you over to the Italians and they will reward me handsomely."

He's sat down. He's not going to top up my drink. I've no idea who he's spoken to but whoever they are, they're spot on. They certainly know me. This isn't good. I thought I'd done well enough to be on the radar but as a weak blip. Intelligence didn't show any firm links with others I'd come up against through work. I have two options here: Deny everything or go with it and try and make a silk purse out of a sow's ear. I decide on the latter.

"You're right. I'm here partly for protection and partly for work. I've heard you have something in the pipeline and you need another party to make it happen. Now, I'm not saying I know what the job is, but I do know that whatever you have planned, I will be of use to you. You've referenced me now. You know what I'm capable of. For the record, I didn't have anything off from the Italian. He settled that score when he slotted those two on the Barnsbury. I get why he's pissed, though. He hasn't got his gear back and is down on his bank balance. I can't help him there. That knowledge died with the two he had executed. I need money and I'm for hire. That two large was part of a drying pot of cash. In return, I want to know you have my back as far as the mob is concerned."

Razor gets up and goes to the door. Kat opens it and a few seconds later returns with an open bottle of whisky and two fresh tumblers. Razor puts the glasses down and pours two. He picks one up and starts drinking. I take the other and do the same. "Why should I do what you're asking? Put my club at risk from unwanted attention just because you chose to work with a bunch of foreigners with long memories? You're nothing to me."

He drinks some more. "I have your number. I'll be in touch. Now drink up, it's time to leave." I take that as a positive, down the whisky and salute him with the empty glass. I grab my jacket from the chair at my side and put it on. Kat opens the door and acts as my escort across the club's floor and up to street level. She hands me my bike keys and phone. She points across the street to where the bike is. I have no helmet. I'm drunk. I turn towards her. I hand her the lock box key. "Until the next time then."

She says nothing. Returns inside and shuts the door. The early morning air is cold. A breeze displaces road grit and dust as I walk towards Euston station and find a taxi home. I've seen the car Winter's outside team are in, but for once I feel comfort in that. For a fleeting moment I realise someone has my back. They must have been through different emotions not knowing what was happening. It's oh four hundred hours and they'll be as tired as I am drunk. I put the SIM back in the phone. I'm not being followed. The streets are deserted. I try Mike first. My conscience seeking ease at the situation I left in his flat. The mobile rings out and sounds loud in the relative ease of the city at this hour. Lights are on in some windows. Workers getting ready for an early shift or those who enjoy London's entertainment returning home. Eventually Mike's croaked voice comes through and I breathe a sigh of relief he's alive.

"It's me, Sam. How are you?"

He's awake. He coughs violently. I hear phlegm being projected from his fat-filled, nicotine-invaded throat.

"Where are you?" He obviously doesn't wish to share his current health situation.

"Making my way to Euston. You?"

"You know where I am, you overzealous twat. The same place you fucking left me for dead."

"Let's not get too dramatic. You were conscious and breathing when we parted. I even put a cover over you, you ungrateful bastard." I wait as he begins to wake up.

Mike comes back on.

"Listen. Get home and we'll meet again soon. What was the outcome?"

"To wait until he makes contact."

"Okay. That's a good sign. As much as we could have expected tonight. You got in and stayed a good while, so he must think you're all right. Have you phoned Winter?"

"Not yet. There's something else we need to discuss but not here."

"I'll call her. Meet me for a drink, later, the usual place."

I acknowledge and end the call.

I try Winter's number but it's engaged. I figure the outside team are letting her know I'm out and leave it for a respectable hour. I know I should speak but my mind isn't in the game for what detail she will require. I turn my phone off, hail a cab and head to Watford. The Commissioner won't be happy at this expense but needs must to keep up appearances. Tradecraft has no cost in my head.

16

The Italian espresso attacks the back of my throat like a lover's tongue, awakening my brain, clearing out the previous evening's debris. Mike hasn't arrived yet. I look out of the coffee shop window at the entrance to Cobalt Square and view the minions going into work. Slaves to a wage with little return. I remember the vibrancy the place once had. Detectives buzzing in anticipation at the next job, overtime was healthy. There was a lust for work and getting the job done was the only food everyone wanted.

Times have changed. Office space is sparse and units fight for computer terminals and vehicles to do the job. There's no overtime and the work is dictated by those above who are driven by the Mayor's needs and what the media perceive to be issues that need policing. Meanwhile, those like Razor carry on exploiting the current times, making sure their vaults are filled before the tide turns and they become the next best project. The mediocre one percent bung the government threw two years ago has bitten the depleted cash pot, taking a chunk that won't return.

I feel different to Razor. My motivations are self-serving. I too have used austerity to my advantage, but I trample on the pond life to reap my rewards. I don't exploit the workers. I get the job done the police want but not the prosecutions or seizures they always hope for. The cat has to have its cream.

The coffee house owner doesn't care. Whatever the

financial situation of the country, people always find the money for coffee. His is the best. I see Mike as he crosses at the lights in front of Cobalt Square. He doesn't wait for the lights to tell him to precede, he just weaves his portly, Barbour-clad frame through the stationary vehicular commuters, pushbikes and pedestrians.

He pulls up his coat collar and has his head down as he comes towards the coffee house entrance. He sees me and enters. The owner gives him a smile and a nod. Mike's a regular here. His habitual drink of choice arrives shortly after he's sat down and removed his coat.

Traffic becomes a slow-moving vista framed by the large wooden window of the coffee house. The windows don't steam up here, strictly continental breakfasts and fresh coffee. Mike has the appearance of a man who's ended up at the end of the line and just got off the first train back. I know because it's been a habit of mine in days gone by. Days I rarely visit now due to my reluctance to socialize with those I occasionally have to work with.

By *those* I mean police colleagues, not criminals. There are so few undercover officers left, and spread so thin, we no longer know if the other still exists or if we've gone onto other things. Mike sips his coffee and nods at his cup out of appreciation of the content's effects on his alcohol-addled body.

"You took your time."

Mike looks up. He isn't in the mood for smart quips. "I had a rough night as you well know, so what happened?"

"Well, I can't say my night was much better. I was trapped in some kind of underground bunker your man calls a club, after giving up my phone and any means of communication with the outside world, aka, you."

"Boo, fucking, hoo. You're a grown up now and can look after yourself. You've been doing this long enough and never had any problems…death threat aside."

"Word of my worth is out on the street. Razor made a call, away from me, and fed back the fact I was on Big H's most-wanted list. He also established I have a reputation for *taking out the trash,* as he put it. Now forgive me, sir, but I have a slight cause for concern and feel justified in using my original legend. If he were to find out the opposite it would have been game over. He wasn't buying my initial story. It's also good for me to know how credible the threat still is. He's using it to his advantage and holding it over me like a loose hood." I keep my powder dry around the other attempts on my life.

"Relax. He's doing what any good criminal at his level does. It's his way of getting a reference. If he still wants to talk, then the reference's good. I'll make sure the line room know and check with them if they heard the conversation."

He sips his coffee and looks out the window. Life outside hasn't changed but he has. He's not the same man that took me under his wing as a DC showing me the ropes of the undercover world. We had a laugh and some good jobs off, then he went and took promotion and I didn't like the next man I had to work with, so I did the same. Mike went higher. I could too but will wait and see how this game pans out. It too could be my swan song if my hit man has anything to do about it.

My phone vibrates. I let it ring some more then show Mike the number. Mike recognises it and nods. I pick up. Mike gets closer to the phone so he can hear. I can't go hands free; it's too busy.

"Yes?" I'm hoping the caller will recognise my voice.

"Meet me at the club in an hour, bring your bike, I've got a job for you." I recognise this voice. Brusk and to the point. Razor.

"I'm busy right now. What's the urgency?" I never give the appearance I'm at any one's beck and call despite the wish to infiltrate his domain. To appear hasty would smack of desperation and be out of character.

"See you in an hour. Whatever you're doing can wait. I can't." He's hung up. Now I should put a call into DCI Winter but as I'm sat opposite my cover officer I'll leave that to him. He won't bother. Like me, he wants to be selective with what her team knows. Right now she doesn't need to know. I down the coffee.

"The elderly gentleman will settle for the drinks." Mike spits his coffee out and the owner smiles, nods and continues drying a freshly washed cup. The last thing Mike hears is the jingle of the bell above the coffee house door as I exit towards Cobalt Square and the underground car park for my bike.

17

National Crime Agency, briefing room, 08:00

"Right, listen in. I need everyone to focus. Shut down the computers and take the phones off the hook. I know it was a long night for some of you and I appreciate this is a reasonably early start. DI Hudson, an update on the events last night."

The team turn, all eyes on DI Hudson as he shuffles in his seat and grabs a blue A4 book he's made notes in. The dark skin under his eyes tell the team his focus may not be on top form, so it's hoped his notes, however brief, have been made at the time and not post the event.

"All I can tell you is that he entered the club and was seen leaving at oh four hundred hours. He took a cab back to Watford and a residential premise. The address you confirmed as safe, ma'am. He made no contact with us and hasn't since he left."

Murmured voices intersect across the briefing room and DCI Winter breaks the debates with a cough.

"I too have had no contact with him, but after our conversation, DI Hudson, I'm happy he got back safely. I tried his number last night and it was turned off, as was his cover officer's. I will pick that up after this meeting. I want a full research package on the venue, associates, social media chatter, the works. Any other questions? Good. DI Hudson has your actions for today and we go live in an hour. I will be in my office."

The room echoes with sound of speech and laughter as the team break in to their respective factions. Phones are replaced in their receivers and the computers turned back on. New radio batteries are exchanged for old and camera batteries are renewed. A DC is sent to ensure the observation van is on charge and appropriately equipped. DCI Winter closes the blinds to her offices and picks up her landline phone.

"Commander Barnes, please." The PA accepts her call and puts her through.

"Good morning, ma'am. Deployment went ahead last night, just awaiting contact from Alex Kennedy, our CHIS. I will establish if they were there and any update on the evening's events. Batford left the premises at oh four hundred hours and was seen to enter his safe house, alone. I've had no contact from either him or Superintendent Hall."

"Well, that's to be expected. The main thing is that Batford has established contact. We will take things one stage at a time, Klara. Knowing Batford as we do, things normally hot up from here. Your team must be alert and in a position to deploy at a moment's notice. We're both on the same page. We will get the result we need from this."

"As soon as I have anything, you will be the first to know, ma'am."

18

Decision log, 9th September, 2020

I have heard nothing from either Batford or Hall since the deployment last night. My team confirmed the motorbike Batford had given over to the target has been recovered.

The bike was left at the target premises in Euston. I am making no attempt to recover this item and will leave that with the Met to sort out.

I will need to establish from Alex Kennedy (CHIS) who was present at the venue to ascertain whether Mike Hall had arrived before the static observation point for the target premises was put in place. Mike Hall was not seen leaving before or after Batford. From this I believe he wasn't there. I don't have the resources to keep Detective Superintendent Hall under surveillance at present.

I know it's early days in this operation, but I feel positive the outcome will be different form the last foray with DS Batford. There will be a prosecution and the right offenders incarcerated.

I have further meetings with the Met in place and will explore other covert options should they be needed.

My main priority is establishing a criminal link between DS Batford, Detective Superintendent Hall and Razor.

At this stage, I intend to keep outside resources at a minimum to give a false impression to DS Batford that he is being given a free run as he requested.

Batford will not be running free for much longer if all goes to plan with this operation.

Klara Winter DCI
National Crime Agency
Senior Investigating Officer
Op Kestrel

19

Traffic's light across London's' warren of streets. Light for a bike. Not so for a car. I called in a favour and got the bike scooped up from the club and delivered to me. Surveillance motorcyclists love the chase and thrill of getting in and out unnoticed. More so on an adapted bike. She was from the Special Projects Team and felt a buzz at the chance to develop her training.

London is welcoming as I enter her embrace. The bike feels solid beneath me. The engine copes effortlessly with the endless gear changes. Razor's astute to call me on for a job after such a late night.

It feels like a test to assess my availability at short notice, as well as my ability to perform a role with little rest or food on board. After a lifetime of varied and unsocial hours, I consider myself a veteran in this field. I know there's nothing he will throw at me that will faze me. I move over to the kerb as a fire engine bulldozes past me then comes to a halt at a set of lights. I look over at Mount Pleasant sorting office at the phone box where I'd had Stoner meet me first time. She's in there with her back to me. Then she turns and winks with her good eye.

The lights change and the cars in front jostle for position after the fire engine forced them either side. I've moved to the front of the pack and waste no time in leaving them as I head towards Kings Cross and Euston Road. I'm checking my mirrors. No obvious vehicles follow behind me. I'm aware that Winter will have upped her game plan and will not be telling me everything, as I won't be telling her.

I have a strong sense of solitude and self-reliance; I know I'm being watched.

I do an immediate right at the back of the fire station and come out in a loop towards Holborn. The post office is in front of me and I swing left. I pull over at the kerb side a short distance up and stop, engine running. I can see The Griffin from the junction with Clerkenwell Road. I smile at many a good night in there. I don't wait for the lights to change. I go on red through static traffic and ignore the next set of lights and bank right towards the city. There's no one following me.

When I arrive at the club, I see one bike outside. It isn't Razor's. It's Trigger's. I make a mental note of the index plate in case I ever need it, or Winter does. The streets are alive with pedestrian traffic. I pull up behind his bike and put mine on the kickstand. A borough traffic warden approaches, nods and walks straight past. We're both on double yellow lines but he ignores this. Razor must have the wardens in his pocket. Anywhere else our bikes would have been ticketed and lifted. I can do without any more fines. They reveal location and create a hole in your pocket.

The morning sun rises above Razor's cash cow and makes my eyes squint behind the dark visor. I take some breaths, remove my gloves and when I'm ready, unclip the helmet strap and remove my lid. I wear a balaclava underneath. I'm prepared and in role. My time in the police is limited. The clock is counting down. I need to make hay whilst this glorious sun beats down on my world-weary body.

It's not that I hate society. As a rule, it operates pretty well, but my kind of society has blurred lines. Lines that are self created. A need to expunge the sections that do no good and promote those that do minimal harm. I can't say no harm, as I supply a class A commodity that does grievous bodily harm even though it's by choice. I don't supply those that can't afford it. I supply Mike. He does the rest and I get my split per kilo. We supply what society considers the elite: bankers, politicians and diplomats. You get the picture. They like to party and party hard. I have nothing against this.

My role is to facilitate their perceived happiness. I see myself as an expunger of the greedy, the truly corrupt elements sat at the top of the London hierarchy feeding off the poorer masses. It's the top of the food chain preying on the ones below and causing more misery that I hate. If one topples from above as a result of a bad line, then the world's a better place.

By expunging I don't mean killing. That would involve cutting the gear with substances like anthrax or fentanyl and such like. I don't cut. We just move the kilo on, as is. I haven't paid for it after all. The door to the club opens and Trigger nods me in. The same charade of searching is limited to a basic pat down. We make our way to the first floor bar area that is being cleaned by a guy who's meticulously wiping down the bar and tables.

Trigger offers me a drink. I decline. He pours himself a Jack Daniel's and proceeds to cut a line of powder on the bar's newly wiped surface, much to the disgrace of the cleaner. Trigger does the line, wipes the under side of his nose and continues another sharp inhale. I do nothing more than watch the floorshow and wait for him to make the next move.

"You want one? A line, I mean."

"Too early for me. Where's Razor?"

"He's engaged so he asked me to meet you. We've got to visit a fella called Polish, then rock on to a home visit." He downs the JD and puts the spent glass under the bar whilst taking a cloth and wiping the bar's surface of extraneous coke. He's prepping himself for work. I've seen this so many times. The courage of powder and a short before the work comes on.

It gives a false sense of security for when the work turns dirty. Me? I never touch the stuff. Never consume what you deal. It leads to an income drain and high medical bills when it all comes on top and the creditors want their return. I prefer the low-key approach. Other than being on a hit list by a hotheaded Italian, so far, so good.

"Right, let's go and see Polish." Trigger is keen. I'm not.

I want this done and done swiftly. I need to get in with this firm, and quick, before I've got the Italian – and Winter – breathing down my neck. Trigger looks up from his domestic duty.

Trigger dictates. "I'll lead, you follow. He lives on the Kingsmead Estate, Hackney. When we get there, we park up in his garages and go on foot. I hope you can keep up." Trigger is smiling, which I take as a good sign.

"What's the job? I want an idea before we leave so I know what I'm walking into. It's a rule of mine."

Trigger's head throws back in an overzealous laugh. "There's no time for your rules here. You do as Razor asks and when he deputises you, listen to the Sherriff of the day, which happens to be me. Polish is like Jewson's tool hire. He supplies the tools for the work. After we've seen him, we go and visit the site manager who hasn't been paying his workforce at the agreed rate and time. Think of it as a wealth and safety check. Is that enough for ya?"

He's come from behind the security of the bar and stands too close for comfort. "Here's your radio mic. We keep in touch on the move." I take it and motion with my left hand for him to lead the way. He walks first and grabs a plain black motorcycle jacket from a coat hook. He's wearing leather biker trousers and boots. Plain, nondescript and fits with most motorcyclists in the capital.

Our little convoy starts out and heads north towards Holloway. He rides well for someone who's smacked up. Good control of the bike and weaves neatly through the congestion. Keeping up is easy, though. I decide to bait him over the radio. I have my reasons for this and hopefully it will pay off.

"Is it today or tomorrow we're due there? I've barely changed out of second gear." The radio mic clicks off. I await his response. He takes the bait quicker than a carp. I see his left foot work the gear down. The bike pulls away in between a bus and a lorry. He gently banks the bike from left to right and narrowly misses the sides of a bus's mirror.

"Catch me if you can, mother fucker." The cocktail he'd imbibed earlier is doing its job. I replicate his move operating the gears by hand and keeping him in constant sight. A couple of car horns sound off but more in frustration at the lack of movement than our riding. We're approaching the lights at Pentonville Road and Penton Street. He banks left without indicating, taking the bike in a low position into Penton Street, passing the black cab offices. He revs the engine and banks right into Chapel Market, which is empty. He finally turns right onto Liverpool Road towards Upper Street where he stops at the lights. I casually roll up alongside him. He remains stationary. "Still here?"

I notice a marked police car join our queue. The driver is interested in Trigger and edges up closer. He'd led us down the one-way into Chapel Market. Unwanted attention has been drawn. The operator is looking at Trigger's index number and writing it down. The advantage of a dark visor. My eyes are nothing to them but see everything. We're in a position of potential compromise as Trigger is stoned. Trigger is aware too. "Shit, it's the filth." The radio mic kicks in and cuts.

"Stay calm. It maybe something or nothing. The cop shop is a stone's throw away." The driver blips the two tones and indicates for me to move up. The operator's window is down. He indicates for Trigger to park up around the corner. If Trigger gets taken out now, then I have no way of learning who Polish is or who owes the big man money.

I also need my methodology to come to fruition and make Razor think I'm God's gift to his firm. I activate the mic "Leave this with me. Meet me in, Burder Road, thirty minutes. Don't be late."

"You what?" I don't engage in further conversation. The

police car gives another agitated blip of the siren. I get out of neutral and into first. The driver won't be able to see my gear change, as I don't use my left foot and just sleight of hand. The marked police car is edging closer to Trigger. It's time to make my move. I do the red light at speed and bank left onto Upper Street.

The marked car has been given no option but to pursue. Pursue he does with relish. I know the feeling when a bike or car goes from zero to extreme. The adrenaline buzz kicks in. Its purity is greater than any druggie's high. I can't let them have a long game of chase with me though.

"November one, active message."

"Control to November one. Go ahead."

"Motorcycle failing to stop for police. Upper Street towards Holloway. One rider."

"All received stand by for link with main control room."

"November India, you're through to the main channel. I understand you have a vehicle failing to stop. Upper Street towards Holloway. November one, continue commentary, over."

November one: "Rider approaching zebra crossing, bike slowing for pedestrians, now accelerating. Forty miles per hour in and out of traffic, request helicopter."

Met Police Command and Control Centre: "Received. India nine nine, are you airborne and available to assist November India section, vehicle making off from police, over?"

Helicopter: "India nine nine, taking off now, expected time of arrival, three minutes."

November one: "Control from November one. Vehicle still not stopping, standby…pulling over Essex Road junction with Upper Street. Cancel any other vehicles and helicopter."

MP CCC: "All received. I'll break the link now and leave this with local units. Out."

They come to a rapid stop in front of me. The driver has the pursuit car at an angle and the operator's out. I show him the keys and he grabs them. He takes my arm up behind my back and gets me off the bike. I'm thankful I had the forethought to put the bike on its centre stand. The driver's out and removes my helmet. I kick off the conversation.

"I'm sorry to have to do that to you. You were about to compromise a surveillance operation that has been running for a year." Both officers look at me with doubt. The driver is of a level of service to recognise I may be talking the truth.

"I just want you to continue talking with me as if it were a routine stop and look like you're checking the bike and writing a ticket. Anything that makes this look genuine as the team we're after will be watching and it could arouse suspicion if you just let me go."

The driver pushes his flat cap up his forehead and stares me out. He isn't sure. I've no doubt this is a new experience for him and he can't dismiss the possibility out of hand. My arm is released. It's a good start.

"Show me some ID." The operator has a black notebook out and looks convincing enough. "I don't carry ID with me. You can call this number ask for Mike; he will vouch for me."

"No ID? Ask for Mike? You're having a fucking laugh, mate. Stand over there." I do as directed. Trigger isn't anywhere to be seen. I'm conscious he could be observing. I know I would be if I were in his position. My phone rings. I reach to answer it. The driver reacts.

"Keep your fucking hands where I can see them. Let that ring out." I move my hand away from the phone, raise them both in the air and smile as I lower them again. The operator had moved away to listen to his radio and has now returned to where we are. The driver moves a short distance away from me. He can tell I have no intention of making off on foot. He leans into the driver and whispers in his ear. They come over to me and the driver leans in as he speaks to me

"I hope we're right on this one and you're not having us over?"

The driver looks into my eyes and I his. A look that says *can I trust you right now?* I do it all the time. You can never be certain but must make the choice based on the other person's reaction and your gut. My gut is telling me I'm almost home and dry.

The standoff is broken by the sound of the helicopter above. It's low enough to be filming this stop. It hovers briefly and the driver gives the pilot the thumbs up. It banks and leaves the scene. I know the pursuit, although brief, has been called in. Other units will be making their way out of curiosity more than anything else. They may have linked Trigger with me. Eyes of the thin blue line will be everywhere. I need this wrapped up quicker than a last-minute Christmas gift.

"Check my phone – dial the only number in it. Ask for Mike, he's my Detective Superintendent. Tell him what's happening."

He's heard enough. "Okay, get on. I can't be arsed to carry on with you anymore. Good luck with whatever you have on." He nods to the operator and they both get back in the car. I wait for them to go and the small crowd that have gathered disperse.

People were on phones recording the scene. The voyeur culture in full effect. It will be on YouTube before I've had a chance to get back on my bike. Nothing to see here. Move on. I put my lid back on, don the gloves, check over my right shoulder, head into the traffic and set a course for my meeting point with Trigger.

My heart beats rapidly. I keep a watch in my mirrors, stop at the roadside frequently, wait, then join traffic again. I'm satisfied the drama is over. Hopeful we can get back on plan. Trigger's at the meet point. He's off the bike and pacing. His toot has lost its volume. Not a good sign. The Dutch courage is wearing off and that leads to volatility. He sees me, throws down his cigarette. The butt rolls away, flicking remnants of hot ash away from his bike, a potential incendiary device. I kill the engine and get off.

"What the fuck happened there? Why'd you pull that stunt, you stupid bastard!" I have my lid off and place it on the ground, saying nothing in response to Trigger's diatribe. He's not happy at a conversation with an elective mute and comes closer. In basic training, one of the first rules you learn in any potentially hostile situation is to defend your personal space. This amounts to creating more space by moving away or using a pre-emptive strike. I choose the latter as I've had enough of the morning already and he's killing my enthusiasm for getting this job done and put to bed.

My head connects with the bridge of his nose. He turns around, head in hands. He's silent in his pain. I put this down to shock. As he's bent over, his right hand reaches for the inside of his boot. The flash of a blade appears as the switch is pressed and the blade is activated, making an unwelcome appearance. I position myself in a side on stance and watch his eyes as he tosses the knife between his right and left hands. I've kept my gloves on. I'm aware that the gauntlet section will provide some protection. He's towards me now. Both arms out at the ready. Blood streaming out of his nose. Not a pretty sight and not one I want causing any undue attention from the public, who could put a call in to police. I got away with it once today and that was my luck up.

I maintain my gaze. Keep my body in a loose fighting stance. My left leg out front. He can take a low stab at that all he likes. I only hope it isn't above the knee. I wait for him to decide his next move. I know when that will be, as he will feel the weight of the blade in his hand before striking. By a way of reassurance, he still has it in a firm grip before taking the swipe. The other rule you're taught is to verbally tell your assailant that there's still time to put the weapon down. In training, you shout a bit whilst weighing up the asp or baton, or going for the spray or a Taser. I'm without a weapon and only have my hands, which I like and intend to keep scar free. I prefer my own verbal enthusiasm in these circumstances:

"Put the fucking blade away, you stupid cunt. Let's grab a drink and calm the fuck down. It's getting like an episode of *Strictly*." It's not having the desired effect I'd hoped for.

"We've got a job to do and this ain't helping." He's not interested in this approach. His first swipe is wild and falls way short of the mark.

"You're a wrong un. I never knew why Razor took you on but I'm done with pissing about. You're gonna suffer for what you just did." He's got streams of snot and blood running from the base of his nostrils and over his top lip. Drips of claret are marking the road surface where we parry. There's no doubt in my mind he's lost the plot. I'm hoping not enough to induce excited delirium. I've taken enough and need to kill this quickly, and quietly, as curtains are beginning to twitch. He continues to pace in a circle. I replicate his movement but still keep side on and wait.

He takes an ill-thought lunge. He's over stretched and off balance. I use his forward momentum to my advantage and move as the knife hand shoots forward, taking his arm and pulling him to the floor. At the same time I invert his wrist, showing his palm to the sky, and bend it towards his face. His grip on the knife is still there as the blade edges closer to his eye. An increase of pressure forces his wrist down towards his face. He screams in pain, drops the knife and rolls onto his front. I make sure he stays down, pushing his now straight arm and shoulder into the tarmac, exerting pressure on his wrist to the point where it would be easy to break. He turns his head to my left. His cheek grinds into the street's surface.

I put the toe of my boot into his mouth to stop him

screaming and muffle his addled cries. It's time to give him his caution. "I'm in no mood for a Ceilidh and we've got a tight schedule. Now you've got two choices: I let you up, we shake hands and get the fuck out of here. Alternatively, I just break your arm, leave you here and tell Razor you bottled the job and I gave you a kicking for my troubles. Either option's good for me."

The corner of his mouth that isn't eating tarmac moves. "I'll take the first, I'll take the first." His breathing is exasperated with the floorshow he's performed. I pull him up. He bends over, spitting blood from his mouth where he hit the floor. He holds each nostril in turn and blows through each, expelling the remnants onto a parked car. I can tell he's had enough. "Just follow me. We'll get that drink at Polish's gaff." We both hear sirens in the distance, waste no time leaving the area and head towards our first meeting.

20

The entombed garages echo with the sound of two 1200cc engines. Our lights are off as we glide to a halt. Trigger finds the garage we want. A lank-haired estate rodent is waiting in the shadows. This one's five ten and wearing multiple tops. Easier to change description if you leave a crime in a hurry. He opens the door. We park the bikes inside and leave the helmets on.

"Who's the feral-looking youth four units down? He nodded at you as we came in." I need to know. To lose the bike here would be careless.

"Don't worry about him. He works the cellar at the club and's a runner for Razor. Razor doesn't supply here but devised a youth training scheme for when he needs things watching or moving. The bikes will be safe with him there."

I follow Trigger up some stairs that lead us towards the block that houses Polish. Kids are out playing. Residents are smoking. Grime music can be heard coming from a balcony. As we climb three flights of stairs littered with spent works. A child of five passes us. Her street evolution has taught her to avoid the sharps. We find maisonette twenty-two. The entrance door is obscured by a large and thick expanse of steel. I've seen weaker doors on a tank – a clear sign visitors are by appointment only. Trigger rings the bell and looks right. The camera light above the door blinks red. The camera moves, there's a loud click, and Trigger pulls open the metal security door. The main door opens and we step in.

We take our helmets off. Trigger dispenses with introductions. We move into the main living room past the kitchen where meat is boiling in a pan with onions and a scent of garlic. Our host notices me looking. "You like food?" I nod to the negative. His was an offer more than a statement. He motions with his hands for us to be seated. A woman enters with three mugs and puts a plate of biscuits down. The mugs contain strong black coffee, the type you could stand a spoon in. Our host decants four sugars into his and sits back. Once we're alone, business begins.

"So, 'ave you got what we asked for?" Polish sips his coffee considering Trigger's request.

"You know, you come here and drink my coffee, eat my biscuits, but you never call me by my name. My name is Adok. It's because of people like you that I have big metal security door now. Ignorant English who think I take jobs and claim benefit. I do none of these things. I work hard for a living to support my family."

Trigger spits his coffee out in laughter. "Bollocks! It's because you went from cleaning offices to metal work, that's fuckin' why."

Adok smiles and strokes his goatee, the only hair he owns. He's in his fifties, has a wiry build and from his handshake, he would be a sure bet in a fistfight.

Adok chuckles and smiles. "So, before we do business, let me tell you story."

Trigger groans. "Not another of your poxy tales from the riverbank."

"Yes. So I just got back from trip to Poland, see my friend. We're at my family home and he say, 'Adok. I need help with puppy. I get him from Russian guy on market.' I tell him, of course, I help him. My friend, he say me, 'Adok, I have many dog but this one is fucking bastard.' So, we have few drinks and after I say him, 'Let's see dog. I try and understand why he being bastard.' He drive me to his house and we go to back garden. I look out at garden and back at my friend and ask him, 'Where is dog?' He look at me funny and say, there at end of garden! I say him, 'That is not dog! That is bear!'"

Adok looks at us both. A grin stretches across his animated face. His shoulders move as he laughs. He's slapping his leg as he recounts the story again in his mind. We say nothing and wait. "Is my English not good? See! You have problem, not me. I go get what you need." He leaves the room. I smell the coffee first before drinking it. After a short break, he comes back in with a Makarov pistol. A newly rolled cigarette perches in the corner of his mouth. He shows it to Trigger who dismantles the weapon with ease. It's become apparent where he gets his nickname. He middles the guns for the syndicate. I don't touch it. This is Trigger's party and I'm not holding the drinks.

"I have stripped and cleaned it. It hasn't been fired and my supplier is good for this type, as you know. You like?" Adok squints as he lights his cancer stick.

"How much ammo?" Trigger demands, as he looks down the dismantled barrel.

"Ten rounds." Adok hands over a small canvas bag. Trigger nods and pulls an envelope from inside his leathers and slides it across the table. Adok takes it, doesn't count the money. A trusted arrangement. We finish our coffee and leave. Once we're down in the garages, I front Trigger.

"Okay, I'm going no further unless you tell me the fucking job. I'm no patsy. I want to know what the game plan is. Your shout." He sits on his bike. I mirror him. The garages are deserted, save from a tired looking moggy that's seen better days. The lookout is AWOL.

"Fair enough. A Turk's behind on the rent, well behind. Time's come to settle the debt. You don't need me to tell you the Turks can be a bit testy when it comes to family. This fella's been disowned. The nod's been given to Razor, by the head of the family, to deal with it as he sees fit. Today is a frightener unless he kicks off. Then he's dead. I go in, you wait outside to pick me up. We come back here and go our separate ways back to the club for champagne and charlie."

He makes it sound like a trip to Tesco. I have other ideas, namely: I shouldn't be here, yet I am. He has a gun and is off his head enough to use it. I would be an accessory to murder and have little chance at getting off at court as my bike's been stopped and recorded by police. I'd bet my pension someone would clock us at the address and note our presence. Neighbourhood watch has much to answer for. I don't reply immediately. I need a course of action with minimal collateral damage.

"No. We both go in and deal with the problem. You don't know how many are in there or whether the family have changed their mind about your VO." A visitors order is used in prison but it may as well apply here, as we're likely to end up on C wing if this all goes tits up. He's not impressed.

"I do the fuckin' talking and you do as you're told. It won't take long but we do it my way." Trigger's visor is slapped down and he's already striding his bike. I take that as an agreement. I can deal with Trigger when we're at the venue.

We set off in a loose convoy. I make sure I can see him but not close enough that cameras would link us. I have no idea where the hit is and haven't had the freedom to call it in to Mike or Winter. I know I won't get the opportunity. I hope to fuck the venue is a home address and not a work premises. I don't know the name of the target or anything about the background of the family. Turks have a strong family bond. They don't fuck about. I doubt permission has been given to slot a relative.

Family is family. The Turks look after family themselves and don't tend to sub contract the work. I have no family to attach myself to other than the police family and that relationship is weak to the point of divorce. I'm the one who's over the side with a woman called Desire, and desire for what I can have is at the forefront of my mind. I'm a lawyer's wet dream. My position is beyond defending but I know a couple of bent briefs that would take a punt at the job.

I look ahead and see Trigger turn off into a side street in Green Lanes. I'm back in familiar territory and feel naked without any backup. Big H's accountant, Hamer, was a regular at a club here and Big H had interests in the area too. I keep the visor down and wait for Trigger to kill the engine. The bikes are parked up facing out into the main drag and opposite is a small cafe. Trigger has his visor up and looking directly at it. That's the premises. The target must work there. He's waiting for confirmation he's in. I see a male come through a door to the rear of the counter, grab a tray of pastries and go back through the same door he came through.

Trigger nods at me then sets off at a pace across the main street. Cars are at a standstill due to lights. I'm conscious that this area has monitored and active CCTV coverage. Everyone makes it their job to notice what's happening here. The cafe certainly does and the camera twitches as Trigger approaches the door. There's a room at the back and that's why he took the food out there. Unless he's got an addiction to cake, there must be more than him on the premises. I hear shouting. Trigger's made his entrance.

I notice a small alleyway adjacent to the cafe and take this. On cue the first of the party is over the wall and away along the alley in the opposite direction to me. Another follows but it isn't the target. I'm at the section the jumpers have taken and put my back to the wall. My visor is down. I'm aware of trying to look as though I'm meant to be here and not alien to the area. I don't feel confident I've achieved my aim.

A set of feet comes over. I see the bottom of chef's whites. The same guy that Trigger had taken an interest in. I grab the feet and pull him down over the wall. He lands on his arse and tries crawling away like a crab in the direction of his compadres. I put my foot in his balls and apply pressure. Not enough to make him scream, just enough to ensure he's got the message not to move. He stops and lays on his back, muttering in Turkish. He grabs my leg and pleads for me to stop. He's young, around twenty-five and from the look in his hazel eyes, is way out of his depth. He's strayed outside the family to start his own racket and now the next players want the court. Game over.

I lean down and grab his collar, heave him up and slam him against the wall. I don't have much time, as Trigger will be over any minute. "Listen up. There's a guy coming over that wall any second who has a bullet with your name on it. I'm the only one who can stop that." He nods frantically, glancing from me to the wall. I look like one of the troop of Daft Punk. He can't see my face, which is how it will remain. He has sweat forming on his forehead and I feel the same inside the helmet. I need us both away from here fast. "Where's your phone?" He nods to his pocket. I take out an iPhone. "Not your friends and family line, don't fuck about." He nods towards the shop. "It's in the shop, it's in the shop."

"What's the number?" He doesn't hesitate and vomits the number to me. I've had so long at this game; memorising numbers has become second nature. "I will call you at seven pm. You'll meet me where I say. Bring enough cash to keep us off your back. If you don't, you're dead. We know where you live. Doing this will give you more time, now go." He breaks free and runs. As he gets out of sight, Trigger appears round the corner having exited the shop. He raises the pistol but doesn't fire. I feel relief. We get back to the bikes and head back to the club.

21

Razor has a face like a revenue officer whose most wanted has been given a rebate. We're in what I have come to know as the bunker. It's his den. The same one I was in earlier this morning. This time the air is thick with the fumes of disdain emanating from Razor's pores. He's pacing like a caged lion awaiting his midday feed. He stops, goes behind his desk and takes a seat. A house butler hands him a cigar box. The nicotine feeder appears as tense as a porn star's cock. Razor takes a cigar and leans in to the proffered lighter. He takes a lungful and expels the smoke, his pursed lips disingenuous to the gathered crowd. It's as if a faulty smoke grenade's misfired enough for a weak effect. Trigger has said nothing. The bike's radio mic was killed on the way back. Snowy and Kat have their respective places in the room. I feel like a spare prick at a wedding. I'm done with the games and kick things off.

"I don't know about all of you but I've got plans. Let's get this done and dusted." As anticipated, the fuse was short enough to let Trigger explode.

"Get things done and dusted? You stupid cunt! You fucked everything up out there and you know it. From the off you had the filth on you. You wouldn't fucking listen to common sense and let me handle it. To top it all, you let the Turk go. Now your plans can go fuck themselves, sunshine, because you've cost us big time."

He sits down after his speech. His shirt collar is open at

the top button. He's left room to breathe. I lean on the pool table as a cue is on the surface and I may need it. Snowy is at the door; Kat is sat close to Trigger. I've had worse times in the dock. I know my notes for this jury. I intend to present them leaving His Honour, Razor, in no doubt as to where the guilt lies.

"You done? Now let me explain how I see things. I got here as I was told to. I was met by Trigger and waited whilst he did a drift of snow and a double of club scotch before being told to follow him on the bike." Razor's eyes shift to Trigger. His lips tension on the tight rolled cigar becoming more pronounced.

"I follow him whilst he draws attention to us by doing childish moves through traffic that only a novice on a job would pull." Trigger takes the bait. Before he can get up, Razor waves him to remain seated. I carry on regardless.

"He gets the attention of plod at a set of lights. I know he's going to get a tug and would get nicked because of the entire toot in his system. I make off and plod go after me. I lose them. I had to create a diversion, as Trigger was the only one who knew where we were going and what the job was. I get away with my ruse and we then link up. Trigger fancies himself as Bruce Lee and decides to pull a knife on me, so I take him out. With me so far?"

Razor is up. Trigger shifts in his seat. Razor's assistant pours him a double scotch and Razor moves towards the pool table and me. I remain where I am. I was about to continue when Razor picks up the cue, lines up the white and takes a shot that breaks the pack. I say nothing. He's heard enough.

"How did the Turk get away?"

Razor is looking at Trigger but the question is directed at me.

"Trigger went in the premises the Turk was meant to be. He told me to wait for him to leave. I did what he asked. I saw a load of people come out the back and away. I had no idea who was the one you wanted. That's it. I did my job. He fucked up. End of."

I look at Razor. His round blues pierce mine. He's looking to see if I'm lying. He knows Trigger; he doesn't know me. He doesn't know that I'm sponsored by her majesty's government to lie for a living. I'm very good at my job. I maintain his stare of indifference with mine.

"Trig. Come up here." Trigger gets up and appears happy with himself. I may have misjudged the situation and brace myself for what's to come. It's not the first time I've been subject to a kicking. I feel confident my presentation was convincing. I hope so as I'd engineered the whole job to cause a rift between the group. Trigger is the weak link despite his ability to handle a weapon.

Trigger approaches Razor. Razor smiles for the first time and opens his arms in preparation to embrace. Trigger has the same intuition and goes in for the man hug. I move away. I need distance if this is to come on top for me. Bromance is not my thing. The cue is gone. Razor had predicted my move. I'm left with bottles and a cue rack that's out of reach. No phone signal and no phone as it's in his deposit box. I'm fucked. My luck has run out. I remember the Army training and the advice we were given if we were captured: if you're breathing, you have a chance.

No one suspects me of being police, just a criminal who's rained on their parade despite me thinking I'd saved Trigger. My thoughts are shattered as the cue Razor is holding twirls like a majorette's baton and he smashes the handle into the side of Trigger's temple. Trigger drops to his knees at Razor's feet and blows rain down on Trigger's body.

"You. Don't. Do. Gear. On. My. Watch. Or. Drink. My. Fucking. Scotch. You. Piece. Of. Fucking. Pond life!"

No love is lost. Each word is emphasised by the cue impacting with Trigger's body and hands as he cowers in defence. His next move is his worst. He reaches for the pistol in the back of his trousers. As vainly as he tries, due to the energy weakening in his body, Razor pulls a 9mm from underneath the pool table and places it at Trigger's head.

Trigger takes his hand away from the gun and his shoulders move in rhythm with his weeping. I hope to whatever God there may be that he doesn't execute him here. I don't believe he will. He knows the clean up will be enormous and the risk of detection too great. Razor maintains the pressure of the muzzle as he gains control of his breathing. The prominent vein at the side of his head slowly pulsates and dissipates as his control returns. The cigar steadily drops ash over Trigger's blood-spattered shirt.

"No one tries to pull a shooter on me in my premises, especially not someone I thought I could trust. If you're gonna kill me you fucking look me in the eyes before you send the bullet. Get up and get the fuck out of my sight. Leave the piece with me. You. Sky! You have till midnight to sort this mess out and finish the job. The Turk knows what's mine and he'll pay up. Take Kat. Don't come back unless you have the money. You'll get Trigger's share for your troubles plus a bonus if the job's clean. Now all of you fuck off out of here."

Speech over. Summing up done. The defence win. I step over Trigger on the way out. I don't like doing it, as the man is in pain after a severe beating but I'm in role. Like a dog, I've been elevated in the pack and must respond as such. It's my job. But it's the harsher side. My work here is just beginning. I have a Turk to visit who will settle his payday loan.

22

Undisclosed location – meeting minutes – confidential, not to be disclosed
Persons present:
DC Kearns, Intelligence Unit: minutes taker
DCI Klara Winter: National Crime Agency lead
A/DI Hudson: National Crime Agency
DI John Cooper: Professional Standards Pro-Active
DI Ken Aldridge: Intelligence Unit lead

DCI Winter: This meeting is to update each other and allocate any actions we see fit as a result. I will state what limited information we have so far and then hear from you, John and Ken. I'll hand over to DI Hudson who will explain what we've ascertained so far.

DI Hudson: As you are aware, this operation is in its early stages but has been productive. DS Batford has gained access to Razor's club. As far as we are aware, Batford is still in contact with him and his associates. Alex Kennedy our CHIS has corroborated this. I've taken a call from Alex prior to this meeting and they've stated Batford had left the club this morning and returned later where it was reported a knife fight had taken place involving DS Batford. Also a chase where Batford was stopped by police and let go. Alex wasn't in a position to say much more and sounded muffled. They reported they may be away for a day or two but weren't certain.

DCI Winter: I've tried contacting Batford. He answered but said he would call back later as he couldn't speak. He sounded calm and coherent, and gave me no immediate cause for concern. He's his own department's responsibility but I am joint managing the threat too.

DI Aldridge: We've run our daily check on Batford's bike index number. He was stopped yesterday in Essex Road N1 by an area car unit. It's been marked up on the Computer Aided Despatch system as a satisfactory stop and words of advice given. Nothing more to say about that.

DI Cooper: We won't be speaking with the officers involved in the stop, as we don't wish to show out at all with this enquiry. We will covertly obtain any bodycam footage and dashboard camera feed. We know who the officers are and will speak with them in the future should we need to. There's nothing to suggest that will be required, at this stage. Other lines of enquiry regarding Detective Superintendent Hall and DS Batford are negative at this time. We are leaving any outside surveillance with DCI Winter until we feel we must engage in joint covert work.

DI Aldridge: As to the threat to life against Batford, I can confirm it is still live but remains at the same low-risk threat level. As you know, but aren't supposed to know, we've got Razor's phones hooked up. He's in contact with Detective Superintendent Hall. We believe from the conversation that this is a long-standing arrangement. Hall has informed Razor that Batford sounds like the man he needs and that he's dispensable. He hasn't alluded to him being a police officer but this connection, and using Batford, could be indicative of more sinister things. Razor would have no other reason to speak with Hall.

This call was made when Batford met Razor for the first time at the club.

DCI Winter: You're suggesting that Hall and Razor have known each other for some time, and that Hall has instigated this operation to feed Batford into his inner circle for their own benefit?

DI Aldridge: I cannot assume anything from a few conversations. All I can tell you is that Hall and Razor are known to each other. I would suggest they have been for some time prior to this operation being effective. We conducted some historical checks but nothing came up on our systems. It would be likely they met off the books. Furthermore they are due to meet at 'the usual place' in two days' time at seven pm. Reasons for the meeting are unknown, as is the venue. That will be for you or DI Cooper to ascertain via conventional methods.

DCI Winter: How do you know Razor is talking with the Superintendent? It could be someone else with the same first name. All the Superintendent's phones have revealed nothing. That's what was said earlier in this meeting.

DI Aldridge: Not all the Superintendent's phones were disclosed to police. Human Resources records showed old personal numbers. He no longer lives at the address shown either. We went through his expenses receipts and there was one with a different number recorded to all the rest.

It would appear he's been careless or greedy in his petty cash claims. Either way, we benefit. The number is unregistered and not police issue. He's using it to contact Razor and that's the only number appearing in his call data. If we're lucky, he'll keep this number for the duration. If he drops it, we're screwed. We can't ask Batford; he'll smell a rat.

DCI Winter: Agreed. As operational lead, we will let things run as they are. Any other news from your side?

DI Aldridge: Razor has been in contact with a man he refers to as Polish. We can't work off this as it brings back too many hits. Whoever this man is he clearly had a package that Razor wanted. That package may be what Batford and another were going to collect. That would confirm what Alex Kennedy, your CHIS, was saying about Batford being sent out.

DCI Winter: Very good. Keep monitoring this angle and feedback anything you find. As for us, we will continue working with Batford and Mike as we are. I am fully aware that the methodology they're using is skewed. If I kick up now, it could ruin all this work. I also have to consider the threat. If I can nail Big H for attempted murder, then that's all good too. I just hope it isn't more than an attempt and the full offence. I have my Armed Operations Unit and Armed Metropolitan Police Surveillance and tactical team support. I know from recent experience Batford and guns go together. I'm on the end of the phone and ready to react to whatever presents itself, gentlemen. Let's make this joined-up approach work.

23

The outside greets me with an unwelcome wash as the rain pounds my face. Within seconds I'm wetter than an otter. I start up the bike and head for a link up with Mike. I have to lose Kat. I don't want any baggage on this job, whatever Razor may have in mind. There's a decent wad of cash to be collected and I'll have a big enough holdall and transport for my share. I picked a WhatsApp message up from Mike when I surfaced. I have plenty of time to collect some alternative transport for this evening's foray. I've exposed the bike to local police. I need to change it. Razor will see it as good skills and hopefully build on my purported reputation for ensuring client security and job satisfaction.

I call Little Chris in transport. He has a car lined up and can swap the controls over onto another bike whilst I'm out tonight. As for Winter, I've promised to call her back and will do so once I'm away from here. As I check the rearview mirror and ride away, I see Kat standing, arms in the air. All dressed up with no place to go. That's a problem I'll deal with later. I've no time for it now. I've taken enough shit for the time being and need some respite from the criminal underworld.

Mike's drinking, penchant for the white and association with Razor are making me nervous. I have no idea what Mike thinks is so special about this opportunity. How we could gain from it, especially after such a good hit on Big H. It reminds me my accountant should be in touch soon.

I've taken a risk with the money, a big risk. It's distributed across different self-storage places. We're not talking a few thousand pounds; we're talking a million. Mike doesn't know where I have it and as far as he's concerned I've invested it in multiple properties rather than the one he stuck it away in on the banks of the Thames. You'd think I should be overjoyed at having such a vast sum of money but the fact is it's a burden.

I don't need any more yet I feel compelled to play along. Maybe it's the extra buzz on top of doing the undercover work or I'm just so fucked from life I use it as my drug of choice.

In the better days, life was easier in this role. There were more willing combatants to spread the work around and the odd social back at a covert flat. Now there's no wish for it. The people are burnt out, deflated and don't want the role. Times have changed. Direct entrant detectives have watered down the pool to choose from, as they're ring-fenced for borough work and nothing else unless demands dictate. I can't say I blame them when the flavour for this kind of work is diminishing.

The role sounds great and glorious on paper but in reality it's a mare's nest of a shit storm with little reward. Unless you're like me, then the rewards come with the level of risk. Why do this when you can do a straight eight and be home for tea? I still do it because I don't fit the mould anywhere else. I'm a pain in the arse to work with, as Razor will be slowly realising.

How much he needs me will soon become apparent. He will either bin me to Big H or cut me in on the real work. I'm certain Trigger is off the team sheet. He'll be grounded or dealt with in a more permanent way. I should feel for the man, but I don't. He's just one more walking disaster the world can do without. I'm conscious I'm thinking of myself in the same equation.

I weave through the traffic over Lambeth Bridge head straight over the roundabout and then first right. As I approach the garages I get waved through the barrier and back into the soft, warm belly of my police family. Little Chris has done well and left me the keys to an Audi sport. I leave the bike and deliver the keys in a drop box outside his office. I know he'll have it ready for me once I return the car tomorrow.

I sink into the black leather sports seat, adjust the steering wheel height and select the auto sports mode on the gearbox. I turn on the engine via the push button key and opera blasts out at full volume in my ear. I kill the music system and laugh as I select reverse and manoeuvre out. The music joke was an old one from the uniform days. As radio operator, at the end of nights, you would turn up the main set volume on the area car at the end of a shift. When the new radio operator arrived, a loud noise would deafen them as they turned on the police main set. The volume was set loud due to the noise of the two tones and the need to hear the police radio over them. It's the small things that kept us going. That and discreetly turning on the driver's heated seat in summer.

I head out towards Blackfriars Bridge. I feel a fool still wearing leathers but will have time to change once I'm back at the flat and collected some items for this evening's work. Not the standard wallet and keys anyone else would take but binoculars and a clean phone. The top half of the leathers are rolled down. My black T-shirt is all other drivers can see.

It's wet from the ride but needs must when Sheriff Fatman sings. I find a meter near the Tate Modern and head for the restaurant and my debrief with the said Sheriff. As I approach the entrance, I see Mike in a window seat talking on the mobile. He's animated and by the low head position, swearing quietly to whomever he's talking to. He sees me, nods and terminates the call. I go inside and sit opposite him with a good view out at the entrance.

I had a clean run in. I'm as happy as I can be that my route was clear of unwanted attention. "So how are tricks?" Mike's casual comment matches his clothes, which is unusual not seeing him in a suit.

"As good as can be expected after a trip to an armourer and a fight with a knife-wielding fuckwit. You?" I get a menu and scan the lunch page.

"Been at the factory doing some paperwork and smoothing things over with the Commander. I've got to update Winter after this so we need an agreed course of action as to what you have and haven't found." He checks his watch.

"There's no hurry, is there? I thought we were good for a couple of hours?"

"Something's come up but I've got time for lunch. Always time for lunch." He's shifty. He's never been good at hiding it completely with those he's worked closely with. "I don't know what the main job is yet, do you?"

"Of course not – that's why you're deployed to find out." He sips water, ice and no lemon. "You must have some idea, Mike. You wouldn't be going to so much trouble engineering my deployment on an NCA job. Let's cut to the chase. I'm in and need to know where I'm being led – you owe me that much."

Mike looks out the window and rubs his chin. He's wearing a pair of Tom Ford frames. He takes them off his face and rubs his eyes before putting them back on. The attached cord hangs down his back. It either acts as a reminder he's wearing them, or the noose he feels getting tighter.

"Truth is, there's not been much contact from Razor since you joined. My money's on the fact the bit of work he's got planned is looking good and ready to go live. When I last spoke with him, he was banging on about a Turkish network who import coke and heroin. Razor's done business with them before. Razor wants to take control of the whole route into the country. The operation is small but turns over good money and most goes through his club with some being taken up country to Inverness. That's all I know from conversations we've had in the past. I've had other pro-active units take out most of the competition from information he's given. No one knows where the information's come from as I've used your crime-stoppers rouse and told them. That's why you're in because it'll be big and good for us." He takes a look around and leans in.

"We can have Razor taken out by our lot, then control the line ourselves. It'll be a piece of piss. We've got the ability to flag the people we deal with on the systems and see if they're being looked at. We classify the information reports under National Security and make it go away. There will always be people talking but we know how to hunt them out and take care of them. No one is any the wiser and the job gets put to bed early." He moves back as the waiter approaches and we order. I'm not entirely convinced of his logic but it's beginning to make more sense as to Mike's interest.

"So where does the Commander really sit with all of this, then? She's changed her tune since the last job. What about Winter? She's going nowhere and we seem pretty keen to play with her mob at the moment and not our own. They must know there's no intelligence of any armed robbery?"

"Where there's drugs of volume, there's guns and you just said you went to an armourer. Guns have to come from somewhere. Any that get taken out in joint work with the National Crime Agency and us always looks good for the top brass. You know the state the country's in. No one's got a pot to piss in anymore. Terrorism is a top priority. We get most of the work where guns are concerned whether it's got an armed robber attached to it or not. What's the fella's name you saw?"

"He's got a street name of Polish but he said his first name's Adok. Lives on the Kingsmead Estate. Large metal door, camera above. He had the gun in the house. I could see a bunch of keys on the kitchen table as I walked past, so my bet is he's got an offsite storage facility somewhere. The pistol's a Makarov. He claims he got it from a trip to Poland but he clearly knows Russians from what he was saying. Razor had it in his club when I left this morning. I don't know about now." The waiter brings our food and leaves. Other diners are engrossed in their own meals and no one is sat in front or behind us at tables.

"Good work. Leave the Polish address with me and I'll feed that back to the Commander and Winter. They need to know there's a gun address. Could be useful in keeping them occupied with that and away from Razor for a bit. Let me know if you see the gun again. Carry on staying on his good side and don't go nutting anymore of his players." I smile and he grins. It's the most I'm going to get out of him and part of me knows he's holding back.

I can't do this completely alone. I need someone to work with who's close to Razor. That person is the one I deserted in the street earlier outside the club. I'll have to make it up to her once I've taken care of tonight's work. As for Winter, Mike will cover that call. We finish and Mike waits whilst I leave and head back to Watford for a bath and a change of clothes. This could be a long evening.

24

Meeting room – basement – Central London hotel
Persons present:
DCI Winter: NCA
DI Hudson: NCA
Alex Kennedy: covert human intelligence source (CHIS)

DCI Winter: I thought we'd meet and find out what you've seen and heard since we last spoke. We understand Razor may be getting busy and beginning to set in place what he has planned. What's your take on this?

Alex Kennedy: He's getting busy, that's for sure. He's losing his temper with everyone at the club. The club's split in two. Basement is used for to- end clients who pay a weekly retainer and can do whatever they like there. Coke, heroin, whatever your fancy. Only rule is you don't bring your own drugs as Razor supplies it. He has people posing as dealers in the club and if he were raided, he would be nowhere near it. Thing is, the kind of people who go there value discretion and it's run like a dream for a few years now. Top bar is used as a front of house for those who don't want the frenzy of downstairs.

DCI Winter: The picture I'm showing you now, have you seen him at the club?

Alex Kennedy: No. That's the same guy you showed me a picture of before. No, he hasn't been in. Not when I've been there anyway.

DI Hudson: Where are the drugs coming from?

Alex Kennedy: Razor has a couple of lines running. One is with a Turk who supplies the heroin. He owes Razor and there's been feelers put out to get what he's owed. Nothing's come of it yet, though. He's got another line for cocaine but I haven't heard much about that. I know he's taken on a big supply though as it just keeps coming. It could be that it's running out now, but like I said, I don't know.

DI Hudson: What about firearms? Does he have access to these?

Alex Kennedy: Oh yeah! He's got access to guns. I don't know how many but he has one around him just in case he needs it and will call one on for a job.

DCI Winter: When will he be acting on what he has planned?

Alex Kennedy: You're kidding me, right?

DCI Winter: No, we're not.

Alex Kennedy: He's on it now. He has been ever since the other guy you showed me in the picture turned up.

DCI Winter: Okay. Thanks. Keep in touch daily from here on in and let me know when you're with Razor or any of the others.

Alex Kennedy: Of course. Just make sure you've got my

back. I'm relying on you.

DCI Winter: Your safety is my main priority above this operation. Here's a hundred pounds to cover your expenses. Sign here.

Meeting concludes and Alex Kennedy leaves building.

Winter turns to Hudson. "So we now know Razor has access to guns, where he supplies the drugs from, and there's a Turkish connection and another unknown for cocaine. We also know Mike hasn't been seen at the club as Alex Kennedy didn't identify him from the photo we showed."

Phone rings. Winter answers:

"Winter."

"It's Mike. Can you speak?"

"Yes, what's happening?"

"Batford's had a meeting with me. Job's looking live. Razor has sent one of his men to get a firearm from a guy called Polish. We're getting our teams to research. Initial intel is suggesting the Kingsmead Estate. Get a team in that area and get ready to place a camera in an observation point once we've identified it. Address has a large metal external door. Your guys may see it before our methods kick in. I'll update you once I've heard back from Batford. He will be out of contact most of the time as the team are tight on him and there's a no phones policy in the club."

Winter pauses briefly before replying. "Very well. Thanks for the update. I'll get some people on it now. It's going to limit me with staff for covering Batford whilst he's out so I will leave that with you to manage."

"Understandable but we have to prioritise the firearms. Leave Batford's outside cover to me."

"Keep me updated with anything else Batford finds out."

"Of course."

Conversation finishes.

Winter dials another number into her phone and awaits a

connection. It's answered on the third ring.

"I've just had a meeting with Alex Kennedy, our CHIS. They've identified Batford being at the club but not Mike. Mike has just phoned and spoke of a possible gun supplier he's trying to get my team to flop onto, leaving Batford uncovered whilst deployed. It stinks. Get your team out and I'll do the same. The cover must be loose. Batford is skilled and has blown my team out before. If he sees any of us, the job's sunk. Once I get a positive address for the gun premises I will cover it with an observation point. If I get intelligence a gun is in there, I will have to react. We're time limited now. All work must concentrate on Mike and Batford. Where they are, Razor will be. Where they are, the job will be."

DI Cooper pauses before replying. "Agreed. I will arrange a briefing immediately. I suggest you do the same. We know Batford is back in Watford; he's triggered a remote camera. He arrived on foot; we don't know where his bike is. I will arrange the briefing at your base so your surveillance staff can be present. We're getting closer to nailing this team, Klara. I suggest we use your operations room to cover the deployments from here."

"Agreed. See you and your team in an hour."

Hudson grabs free biscuits and a handful of boiled sweets, and they leave.

25

Decision Log

Further to my earlier entry, I have met with colleagues in the Met involved in intelligence and Professional Standards. I am satisfied that Detective Superintendent Mike Hall is corrupt.

I understand the hesitance of the others with this regard, but I don't have their weakness to be pessimistic in this area.

Detective Superintendent Hall is making attempts to distract my team away from the lead enquiry by revealing a tenuous intelligence report concerning a firearms address occupied by a male called Polish.

I have responded to this, as it doesn't take the effort he implies at identifying a fortified address on a named estate.

I will be keeping full surveillance on both Hall and Batford despite my claim otherwise.

Alex Kennedy (CHIS) is gainfully employed and they have provided actionable intelligence. My concern is to ensure I have enough evidence to successfully prosecute all offenders within the remit of this operation.

The crown prosecution lawyer agrees that any intelligence must be assessed individually and be reacted on according to the needs of the investigation. Any intelligence that is deemed life threatening MUST be reacted to accordingly.

So far no intelligence has come to light that requires immediate action.

I will continue with my team conducting outside surveillance. Met resources will not be required outside at this time.

It is my opinion that the drugs from Big H that allegedly went missing in the last operation are being sold to Razor by Batford and

Hall. Why Hall should want Batford in the syndicate is the issue bothering me.

To date, no intended crime has been revealed.

Batford is a thorn in my side but he is no fool. It hasn't escaped my attention that Hall is apparently absent from the club.

I will update the log as and when new intelligence is gained or a reaction to it is required.

Klara Winter DCI
National Crime Agency
Senior Investigating Officer
Op Kestrel

26

I duck under the, warm, soothing water, place my heel on the edge of the bath rim near the tap. Sound is negated to pulsation. My stump is enflamed but not as bad as it was before I invested in state-of-the-art prostheses. They say crime doesn't pay but it pays me well. I feel a sense of worth reinvesting in technology that enhances disability research and my ability to stay gainfully employed.

Having money enables me to adapt regularly as science evolves. I'm embracing the Terminator option providing me with greater movement and comfort for longer. The advances have meant my limited nerve endings can communicate with the prostheses, which has its advantages in terms of stability and natural movement.

As I lean back, I lay submerged and allow my mind to wander. I have a theory that your shit should be let out. That's why I'm such a car crash when it comes to interpersonal behaviour and ethical boundaries pertaining to matters of law and relationships.

An old DCI once asked me where I saw myself in three years' time. This was on the first day attached to a Robbery Squad. Truth was, I had no idea where I would be. I hadn't even thought of why I was there in his office. I was in my mid twenties and had had enough of uniform. I lied and said I saw myself as a career detective. Where? I didn't know. He could see I was lying. He set me straight.

"I'll be the judge of whether you make the grade or not. If

you're still here on this borough in three years, then we both know the answer." I was rotated around the various squads, Burglary, CID, Domestic Violence and Sexual Offences. Then came the Crime Squad and that sealed it.

I applied for central pro-active roles and jollied with the Flying Squad, Projects Team and Firearms. The idea was a plain clothes tactical response to back up those central units tackling armed criminality. The day I got shot changed me for life. It wasn't just the loss of a foot but the loss of identity that went with it. I was no longer fit for what I loved despite the reassurances from the hierarchy that it would all be okay.

The Independent Office for Police Conduct investigated. The robber's death was a clean shoot. A lawful use of force. No police charges would be sought. I rehabilitated quickly and responded well to the prostheses. The same DCI suggested that I should apply for the national Undercover Officer Course as my condition could be accommodated and used as an asset.

That DCI is now Detective Superintendent Mike Hall. The same Mike who took me wherever he went in the Met. The same Mike I'm beginning to doubt.

The corruption started years before when we were both out on active jobs. Money seized didn't all arrive in property and drugs went missing. We had the contacts, through work, to move gear on. It seemed so easy. Mike knew you had to be amongst it to benefit. That's where the undercover role came in. He would look at the jobs being proposed and no matter what the remit fit me in.

I passed vetting to the highest level without issue. I had no debt; I rented the same place I had for years and never defaulted on payment. I had little in the way of a social life due to the long working hours, so outgoings were slim or paid for on expenses. Relationships were brief to nonexistent for the same reasons. I never wanted to be the one rushing off a job because of kids or outside pressures. I lived and breathed the work.

There's a saying in the police that the 'job's fucked'. It's banded about like a fable. Truth is, it is. The focus changes from day to day as more people leave and more are forced to go due to the cuts. Criminals know this too and reap the rewards of slack borders and over stretched forces. Direct entrant detectives now back fill posts that were a result of cutting numbers and losing skill. I use the term force as I've never believed in the police as a service.

I surface, and the water drains from my face, the realisation dawns that I may be the prey amongst this pack and need to watch the pecking order closely. I have no intention of becoming the next meal. Someone on the inside is feeding the assailant. He's clearly not going to stop hunting me until he's had his hunger satiated.

I pull the plug and watch the polluted water drain away. Safer for me to exit an empty bath. I get out and hear my phone. It's the Razor phone. I wait a short period then answer. I sit on the edge of my only lounge chair, water slowly evaporating off my skin.

"Yes?"

There's a brief pause then the caller identifies herself.

"Where in the fuck are you? Why did you piss off when we were supposed to be heading out together?" She's not happy. I wouldn't be if I'd been treated that way.

"Kat, I'm sorry. I had to run. I got a call from an old client."

"You have one client now and he's wanting a result tonight unless it slipped your fucked up mind. He was asking why I was still here and I told him you'd gone to change and would be back. Get your arse over here and let's go." She's very persuasive. I tell her I'll see her in two hours. I terminate the call.

She's waiting outside the club like a courier with a no show. She knew I'd turn up on time. She looks at her watch. Her eyes widen in a way that say *what the fuck* rather than *come over here*. "I'm here aren't I? No need to be uncivil. We could have a long night together." She sits side on to her bike. I step closer. I know how cautious bikers can be around their rides so keep a respectable distance from the frame.

"How was the main man when you left him?" I need to know.

"By left him, you mean when he was happy he didn't need my protection for the day?"

"Exactly what I meant."

"He's good. He filled me in on what he wants and he doesn't want any blood spilling tonight. He just wants his demands heard then we're out. Where's your bike?"

It had felt strange getting the train carrying a crash helmet but I was glad to be out of the leathers as the underground was stifling. Jeans, plain black tee and leather jacket will work just fine for this job.

"Let's say it's attracted enough attention for one day so we're both on yours. You'll have the bars; I'm on pillion."

She rolls her leg over the seat and leans down and grabs her lid. A few basic rules are needed before I go anywhere and she needs to be clear around those.

"Before we go, you are there to back me up and me you. I will deal with the Turk. You will be my shadow whilst I do what needs to be done. I've had one outing today with a lone ranger and that's been enough. If you can't handle the arrangement, just say, I'll go and you can tell Razor I fucked you off en route. Your call."

She looks up and stares at the sky whilst breathing deeply. I know the technique – it's a basic human one before we explode or remain calm. "Okay, hotshot, we do it your way. Razor wants it done at the home address. He wants a strong message despite the lack of firepower this time. We're not alone though and that's tough shit."

She nods in the direction of a saloon with blacked out rear windows that's just drawn up. As she does Snowy and the butler from Razor's pied-a-terre appear and get in. I have no choice now – the job's on. "Very well." I put on my lid, as does she. She flicks the dark tinted visor down and nods that she's ready to leave. I hang on to the sides of the frame. To cling to her would appear needy and I'm anything but that. The temptation's great but resistance must be the priority. I move my left leg onto the rear footrest and grip as well as I can with the right.

My left thigh will do a job but how well depends on her riding. I have the feeling she'll be slicker than an oil spill. I'd made the call to my friendly Turk and the meet is set up. I just hope he comes alone. I'll know if he doesn't. I'll be watching him and he knows he can't set off until eighteen forty hours, so Razor's wish fits with my way of thinking, albeit he'll be coming out before I can get in, which suits me. I don't like confined spaces to conduct business.

Mike ensured the intelligence on the cafe from earlier was done quickly and an image was sent to my secure laptop at the safe house, which resulted in a positive identification of the Turk. Everything else fell into place after that, including his current home address. He lives with family. He's the last sibling left at home, no pets. I'll know if Kat takes me anywhere different. The calm of the street reverberates with the firing up of the engine and with one last look over her left shoulder, I tighten my grip and we head off.

27

NCA offices Spring Gardens

A phone rings on the melamine office desk of DCI Klara Winter. She takes off her glasses, rubs her eyes and places them back on as she picks up.

"Winter."

"It's Cooper from Professional Standards."

"Hi, John. What do you have for me?"

"Mike and Razor met earlier today. We don't know where as we don't have people out covering either of them. We need to go fully operational outside now. The loose arrangement following our briefing just won't work. My gut's telling me they are close to their goal."

"I can't go on gut, John. I need something definitive before I commit outside surveillance. These targets are not stupid and very surveillance aware. I'm going from experience here. The last job, Batford caused a bomb scare on a train to expose a team. If Batford's close, then they will be too. Batford will be on high alert and could be wrapped around the other two. I can't get hold of Batford as his phone is off and Mike's being helpful, which causes me concern."

"I hear everything you're saying but I have to justify not reacting to the information I'm getting in. Phone taps aren't easy to get and have continued. I have my own aims here and a pro-active team ready to respond. I'm sorry, Klara, but you have your resources and I have mine. I've held back, but now I'm ready to deploy my teams if I get further intelligence regarding these two meeting. We're missing a trick here and the opportunities may cease if either drop their line."

"If you deploy without me knowing, there will be hell to pay. I may not be in the police but I know the protocol all too well having spent a significant time doing your job. It may not have been on a Professional Standards team but it was still targeting National Intelligence Model, level three criminals. I thought Batford and Mike would be the tough ones to work with so don't let me down here."

"I've said my piece. I have the backing of my Command. You do your job and I'll do mine. We will work together but you have to be flexible. The Commissioner is sighted on this operation and has a clean record on winning high-profile corruption cases. She won't take kindly to further joint work if we lose this one."

"Is that a threat? The National Crime Agency has operational lead here and you will be mindful of this. I expect continued support. We'll meet face to face tomorrow and discuss further. Any fast-time operational decisions, you call me and we talk them through. My vetting level puts yours to shame so you can discuss anything with me. Speak later."

"As you wish."

Call ends.

28

Kat sticks to the road like a ballet dancer commands a stage. The bike effortlessly glides in and out of traffic leaving the shadow car as a memory. We're heading in the right direction, according to my information. At this pace we'll make it in time for my pre-meet sit-and-wait point. The two hours had bought me enough time to check the location and find a suitable place to plot up before I step into the unknown.

The target's house is detached in a nice part of Highgate, a Victorian with an electric gated front entrance. The driveway is large enough to accommodate three vehicles. A swimming pool sits serenely in the back garden complementing the neighbour's. I couldn't see any cameras and can only think they're covertly situated for the residents' piece of mind. Cold callers, of the leaflet dropping kind, aren't this family's concern. Cold callers like me are.

I hang onto the back of the bike and lean in with Kat where required to maintain the bike's balance. We stop at lights on Holloway Road. The shadow car is six cars back. Snowy is in the driver's seat and made good progress to catch us up. Kat puts her foot down to steady us and flicks up her visor slightly. I do the same, just enough to hear and speak but not enough for a camera to pick me up. She's adopted the same approach, which calms my nerves. Travelling as a passenger is never my ideal but feels worse when you're on the back of an enemy's transport having not been told where you're going despite having knowledge from other sources.

"Still with me then?" She's smiling beneath the lid and I relax slightly.

"Is that the best you can do? Feels like a Sunday ride to me." I return her smile and she laughs.

"If I wasn't trying to draw attention to myself, you'd be begging to get off and chucking your guts up by now. Feel free to hang onto me if your arms tire. Don't get any ideas mind, you'll be disappointed." There's warmth to her tone that's been absent. Away from Razor, she's more relaxed but still remains committed to the course of action.

The lights change to green, her left foot knocks it down into first, and we're away with a brutal flick of the accelerator. I wait till the bike slows into its own rhythm. I place my hands at the base of her waist and leave them on her hips. I use the time to focus on the job ahead and avoid this brief feeling of human warmth as a distraction. I struggle with any feelings of attachment to another human being let alone the one sat in front of me now. I'm at work. That's all that matters to me. It's the way I am. There will be losses. Every job I enter into ends in loss.

Loss of freedom, property, cash and commodity. I lose friends faster than a tourist loses cash in a casino. I make connections along the way, as they're not all bad, just people who've taken a different direction in life, as have I. I know I'm one of them. I've crossed the line.

I'm a pawn in a game of chess, playing for each side. I hope to be the major winner despite my small status on the board. Like the pawn, I have limited moves. Each one I make must count. If I get to the other end of the board, I get promoted; I become of value.

I have no idea how this will work despite me playing out possible scenarios in my head. Each one comes with an exit strategy that doesn't involve anyone else with me. Last thing I need is two stooges getting in the way, let alone Kat, as she's so close to Razor. I know she's watching me like a hawk, as are the others. She won't want to take a back seat but she'll have to.

The new addition of butler boy concerns me. Throwing fresh meat into the arena well before the first bite appears extreme, but what am I to know. I'm the new boy and this is the way it is if I want to appear like I have a need to belong and climb the pecking order. My goal is to see this job through. In order to be there, to cash the cheque, I have to show I'm worthy of running the errand.

I check my watch. By my reckoning, we're five minutes out from the address, giving me another ten to get in place. Holloway Road has become Highgate village. We approach the uppermost part leaning left at the very top and head towards Kenwood House. As we approach the side of the estate, we pass the entrance to the target street. She pulls over and we wait for the others.

A film crew have wagons out along the road for actors and staff providing a neat line to tag on to. The car arrives and Kat goes over and tells them to sit tight. The windows of the vehicle come down and smoke emanates out polluting the pavement. The stop was welcome by all concerned.

Kat and I stand by the bike, keep our helmets on and raise the visors. There are no overt CCTV cameras where we are. Opposite us is a school playing field for the privately educated elite. I bring my mind back to the job in hand. A quick scan of the area shows no immediate concern in terms of Winter's team or my hunter. Obvious points to stop are empty and where we are, the film crew wagons provide good cover. Kat breaks my concentration.

"We're ten minutes away. It's called Fairways, in Sheldon Avenue. You'll have time to get down there and back out. The guys will back you up, no arguments. They'll be sat up with me further down the road. Once the job's done, come out and walk towards the A1. They'll pick you up, take me to my bike, and we're away."

"I'll meet him away from the address. I don't like confined spaces to conduct business. When the Turk leaves, you watch me and follow me on the bike. He'll have what's owed. If he doesn't play ball, then I'll deliver a message to Razor's satisfaction. Now I'm running out of time. Tell that lot and leave the rest to me. You'll have to drop me one street down. The rest I'll do on foot."

"Those two know the drill. They'll follow me, get on."

I get on the bike. She nods to the follow car; the engine starts and she moves off and heads towards Sheldon Avenue. I take a deep breath and close my eyes. Sweat is forming on my back and my neck tenses. I tap her shoulder and she pulls over into Denewood Road. I get off and she leaves.

Nothing more needed to be said. I leave my lid with her and take out a baseball hat from my jacket pocket along with a pair of Ray-Bans. I appear like anyone else in this area. I turn into Sheldon Avenue and cross the street from Fairways, my target address. I know where I'll be watching for my meet as he leaves his house. He'll be out in three minutes. Although I'm cutting it fine, it works in my favour not to be exposed in this area for too long.

Eighteen fifty-eight hours. I hope he keeps strict time. A motorbike engine breaks the street's silence. I see a headlight coming away from the bottom end of Sheldon Avenue towards me. I stop and bend to tie my lace as the bike draws to a stop opposite Fairways. It can't be Kat unless something's gone tits up. I see the rider's boots. It isn't Kat. The rider is of the same height and build as the Turk. The gates to the entrance are shut and the rider approaches and presses the buzzer. He has a messenger bag over his shoulder and starts looking up at the windows of the house and steps back into the road to get a better view.

His lid is still on. The visor is up, but from where I am, my view is poor. I remain as I'm fiddling with my laces and look up at him between two parked cars. The gate begins to open. I see my meet coming out. He's shifty, looking back at the house and at the rider. He starts waving his hands in a gesture to go away. His eyes are surveying the street like a startled lookout. He's carrying a holdall. I see, as he exits the gate, it's full.

I lean back against the car to get purchase as my leg's giving me pain. I lean into the boot of the stationary vehicle I'm behind, and the two subjects are on the opposite footway looking away from me. The rider has his hands up in the air and is pointing at the house. The Turk is agitated. "Not here, not here! We agreed away from here." The first thing that drowns the conversation and the cosy serenity of the street is the sound of a large engine vehicle tearing up towards them. By the noise of the engine, I'd guess three litres, and the acceleration would suggest turbo.

I move farther back, catching my jacket on the index plate, and hope I don't set off the car's alarm. I stay low. The engine is the only the sound increasing in volume. That tells me it's getting closer. A skidding car tyre connects with road grit. The vehicle comes to a harsh stop. The smell of burning brake and tyre rubber follows. I look under the car I'm against. I can see the feet and lower legs of both the Turk and bike rider. This is my last image of them alive. The sound of automatic gunfire penetrates the air and their bodies. The motorcycle rider's upper torso hits the tarmac. His hand is covered in blood and limp at his wrist. There was the briefest of screams as the force of the bullets tore through both men, putting pay to any voice. The Turk's head explodes off the tarmac and his bullet-riddled body lies motionless.

Masonry from the wall that houses the gates peppers parked cars and glass sprays from nearby vehicles. Cordite enters my nose as spent 9mm shells litter the tarmac. Glass drops around me from a shattered windscreen. I have nowhere to go. I'm cornered and hope the occupants of the car don't feel the need to check the bodies before leaving. Forensics is the last concern of the vehicle's assailants. The desecration of targets is the primary objective. I stay crouched by the rear wheel hoping it will offer protection and pray the bullets haven't ruptured the lining to the petrol tank.

A door slams shut and then another. There are two occupants. By the cross over of sounds, both were shooters. The vehicle J-turns kicking up gravel and cartridge shells like a matador uses his cape against a defiant adversary and heads towards the A1. I don't look back. I've seen enough from under the car. I have no index number and no description of occupants. To look up further would have meant certain death, and there's been enough of that in this leafy suburb today.

I know they're dead. The lack of sound and large pools of blood are my indicators. No one would have survived that ferocity of firepower at such a close range. I also know from the wheels of the car it was a saloon. My breathing quickens as I get up and look for a way out of the street. I head back towards Denewood Road. Front doors are shut. There are no window twitchers. The house's occupants are taking a safe approach and staying clear.

Two tones are dominating the air as police units are making their way towards the scene. Neighbours calling it in from the safety of their rear rooms. I make it to the relative solitude of Denewood Road. With my hat pulled down and shades on, the sun beginning to fade, I carry on along the street moving through people who are now venturing out once they realise it's not on their front door.

My phone goes. The Air Support Unit's engine breaches my addled hearing from the sound of gunfire. The helicopter must have been close. Its search light floods Sheldon Avenue and lights up the macabre scene on the roadway. I check the phone. It's Kat. I blank the call and don't turn the phone off. I want them to think I'm dead. I have a surprise for them once I've got a change of clothes and calmed down.

I feel bile rising in my throat and try and find a secluded spot to throw up. I find it and for a brief time empty my stomach of its last meal. I wipe away the remnants of bile with my hand and regain my composure. A cat looks at me from the top of a fence that lines the alley that's provided me much needed cover and a rest point from the carnage a street away. It doesn't stay and I don't blame it.

My mind races with the fact I'm a witness to a double murder. Although my evidence is weak, I believe the car was a saloon from the brief glimpse of the wheel arch and wheel, possibly, occupied by two people and provide an account of how the biker was when he arrived at the address and the interaction with the deceased Turk. It's the last thing I need.

I think of calling Mike but decide against it. I'm in no fit state for conversation. I'm dazed, disorientated and out of my comfort zone. The sounds of gunfire and helicopter noise echoes in my head. I conduct a brief body check. I'm fine. No shrapnel or ricochet wounds. Glass is in my hat and I know it will be infesting my coat. I have to ditch the clothing and fast. Police units will be locking down the area very quickly and this vicinity will become one large cordon until they can establish a route in and out for the bandit vehicle and the victim on the motorbike.

I know the route and could save them time but I have other pressing priorities. I no longer feel safe amongst these people and that needs to change in my favour and fast. I let go of control with Kat and her cronies and that will be the last time I make a fool's errand with this mob. Blue strobes are bouncing off house walls as I move down the street. A searchlight illuminates gardens as the light is fading. To try and flee now would be fruitless and add suspicion.

I take off the shades as they're no longer of use and continue towards the marked Armed Response Vehicle. I concentrate on each step and focus on my breathing to calm my mind and give the appearance of someone who's meant to be there. The driver is looking at me and as the car gets closer, the driver gets the searchlight from the passenger and aims it in my direction. I decide not to stop unless directed.

I draw level with the driver and the light cuts through me. There's radio chatter from inside the car. It's all concerned with setting up a forward rendezvous point for all emergency vehicles, as armed response vehicles search the immediate area first. The cat from earlier darts from a hedge and across the road. I freeze in the light. The driver brakes for the cat and the light drops inside the car. The driver remarks to the operator it was just a cat that made the bush move. My phone goes again. It's Mike. I ignore it. I need to get away.

I surface at Kenwood House. The film crew's catering unit has now been taken over by cops' blagging tea as they wait for further instructions to deploy after the armed response vehicles' sweep. I move behind them. No one turns and looks. All are concerned with making the most of the commandeered facilities before the show's over. I carry on walking and begin to regain composure and thought. I know Kat and the team will be well away from here, at least that's my hope.

A mini cab pulls over and a fare gets out. I jump in the back before he's had a chance to complain. I tell him to get me to Hampstead as I'm late for a meeting and show him a fifty-pound note. He nods, moves out and I sit back and take a moment to relax. The driver drops me where I ask and he gets the money promised. I see a decent clothing shop. I'm thankful for its late opening hours. I come out with a new set of clothes and the old in bags.

I see a charity clothing bin and deposit them in there. The clothes are good aside from the glass and any other forensic deposits. It's a risk dumping them but I have to take it. I just hope the bins get emptied before police link me to the scene and then to the clothing bin. It's a long shot but realistic in these days of private CCTV and nosy neighbours. After the brief sojourn, I head down into the depths of the underground. I need to get back to my place of safety and evaluate my next move.

29

I look up towards the summit of Mike's block. Lights are on in his flat. I grab a drink in the bar below. It's tough going up against your Superintendent even when he happens to be your partner in crime. I check my watch and give myself time for another scotch before I hit the lift and confront my cover officer. I ask for it straight and the barman obliges. The Thames is displaying her finesse this evening with a rolling tide that isn't too sharp. The lapping against the barrier wall soothes my addled mind.

I lean against the wall and set my glass on top. I'm outside the pub boundary but some rules are there to be broken. The banter is good and lively as the city dwellers unwind after a day's raping the economy. The drugs business makes more than any of them could dream of. Okay, the risks are greater and staff turnover is an issue, but complaints are dealt with swiftly and there's a no-return policy on all products. Caveat emptor the only legal advice needed. Whilst these high flyers fiddle the numbers and drink espresso for lunch, somewhere in the world a boat or plane is being unloaded with a parcel that will contribute to a multi-billion-pound industry.

All I see amongst the throng is a group who are epitomising the Dunning Kruger effect. It also applies to my Superintendent. I down the drink and place the empty glass on the table. I pick up my messenger bag and make for the block's entrance door. I had an access card away last time I was in his flat. I let myself in the main door and call the lift. The lights count down without sound until the lift hits the ground floor and the doors soft glide to open. I check my appearance in the mirror as the doors close and the lift rises towards Mike's floor.

The lift arrives and I exit as a lady in a white poolside dressing gown and matching white fleece slippers enters. Her brunette locks are high in a wooden clasp. She smiles and I reciprocate. I wonder what it would be like to live in a place like this with only the gym, sauna, restaurant and pool to think of. Mike refers to the block's eatery as a restaurant. I see it as a posh cafe with a licence to sell alcohol.

I listen outside the front door to his flat. I hear the sound of the television and one-sided conversation. I knock, as is customary, and wait. I don't want him to know about the access card and thankfully the concierge wasn't on point when I entered. I hear Mike's dulcet tones approaching the door and take a step back. Racks of locks are disengaged and the door opens. His eyes raise, and he looks at what was my watch and lets me in.

He motions to the bar with the phone and indicates two with his left index and middle fingers. I take that to mean a double. I grab two whisky glasses and fill them appropriately. I lay off the ice, take the seat overseeing the city and wait for my host to terminate his call. Unusually he's moved into his bedroom and shut the door.

After a brief interlude the bedroom door opens and Mike emerges. He's still in his work suit. The knot from his brown tie is approaching the top of his sternum. He takes the glass I offer and sits opposite nursing the crystal. "What's with the evening visit? Invite only here. You know that." He speaks evenly and calmly as he takes a slug of his drink. He takes off his suit jacket and rolls up his sleeves. From a glass box on the coffee table, he picks up a cigar and doesn't offer me one. I say nothing. Let him have the floor and the false feeling he's in control. In my mind it does me no harm to make him think so. Works to my advantage and always has.

"Can't drop by on a mate now?"

"This place is my bolt hole and off limits to all coppers unless invited by me. I'm your cover officer and senior and you'll be minded to remember that." He lights up and sits forward. I mirror his move.

"You're only my cover officer because the job doesn't see fit to find a replacement of a suitable rank. You're my authorising officer too which goes against the grain of the Regulation of Investigatory Powers Act. I'm a mere detective sergeant following orders, sir, and will stick with that line if I'm ever questioned."

He's taken the bait, stands up and leans over me. "Don't think you'll EVER come out on top if this goes sour. We're in the same ship and I fucked the lifeboats off before we set sail, son. Now drink up and get us another and we'll start again." His stentorian voice has mellowed. He sits back down holding out his now empty glass. I've left mine and fix him another, bringing back the bottle.

"I'm staying here tonight. I can't be arsed to head back and your place has more creature comforts than mine." I throw that out and he acquiesces with a shrug. "Who was that on the blower? You looked pale when you answered the door, everything okay?"

"Yeah, yeah. My mum's not been well; it was the hospital. Another reason for the last hurrah. If I get nicked it will send her off. I don't want to be responsible for that." He sits back and flicks a switch to his seat and it starts reclining, raising his legs. He nods at mine and I do the same. I'm hoping the warmer setting will calm his demeanour and he'll open up about his relationship with Razor. I need some tablets. I up end my bag on the coffee table.

The box of Tramadol spills out along with a pen and a Moleskine notebook. I leave them there, knock out four Tramadol and down them with whisky. I offer the pills to Mike and he bats them away. "I don't take that shit." He gets up, goes into the bedroom and comes out with a gram of white powder, or 0.0357 ounces if you're that way inclined.

All I hope is that he's paid me for what gear he's kept back from the end recipient.

He clears a prep area and moves the powder around like a seasoned addict. No wonder his office visits are getting less and less. Remote working on a secure laptop is his preferred method of housekeeping. Again he doesn't offer me any, as he knows I don't partake. His lifestyle is out of control. His out-of-office email responses will be wearing thin for some. You don't get to his rank and responsibility and not turn up for the occasion even if it were one you'd rather avoid. That privilege is destined for people of my rank who care but want a proper wage for the consideration.

Why work your arse off when the prospects of promotion have gone? Inspector rank is there if you want to work shifts in uniform but detective ranks are dwindling. As the cuts have developed, the career path has gone. If you've been in London three years and have a degree, you're deemed fit for the rank of detective. You can detect in uniform and do that whilst on shift dealing with everything else.

My career path is still required but only to justify the legislation and the powers. I see Mike has relaxed some and my mind returns to where I am, rather than the lucid dystopian thought patterns that inhabit my brain. "You probably need to know I nearly got shot and killed today."

Mike spits out his drink and sits up, wiping his shirt and finally taking off his tie over his head. "Come again?"

"There was an execution in Highgate. The Turk and another got spread all over the tarmac by the occupants of a saloon car and some automatic weapons." I take a pause and study his face. He's a seasoned player and if he does know anything about this, he's keeping a poker face. He speaks the word 'on' and the TV comes to life and when he asks for Sky News, the channel appears.

An overhead shot of Sheldon Avenue fills the screen and highlights a forensic tent and cordon tape that fills the street like satanic bunting. We listen to the commentator who reports police are appealing for witnesses and that no arrests have been made. No CCTV is shown or trace and eliminate photos. Eliminate from the enquiry as a witness rather than the type I witnessed. He stares at the screen and orders the television off once it's finished. He grabs the bottle and tops us both up.

"Who was it? Do you know?" Mike is keen to establish what I saw and who else may be aware of my presence.

"I saw nothing other than the vehicle colour, tyre and type of shell casing. I was behind a car taking cover once I heard the tyres arrive. What's come across your desk?"

"Nothing has. It's the first I've heard. Were you alone?"

"No. Kat dropped me off and there were three of Razor's cronies in a shadow car but I couldn't see them. What if it was Razor trying to take me out?"

Mike swiftly turns away from his drink and his rodent eyes fix mine. "No way. It wouldn't be them; it's not his style. He's not against using a threat or a shooter to reinforce his point, but not a drive-by. He'd want to know if the Turk would pay up. Why gun a guy down who could have what you need?" Mike organises another line but doesn't take it.

"I need to know, Mike. This shit is getting serious and neither of us need the heat. You can pull me out of this and you know it. What's so great you need me in? You owe me the truth on this one so I can prepare properly. Another few minutes and it would have been me hitting the dirt."

Mike gets up, starts pacing, running his fingers through his hair and slapping his forehead with the palm of his hand. I leave him to it as it could be his way of psyching himself up for a big revelation or just trying to get his drug-fuelled sponge of a brain together to make sense.

"I know as much as you right now. Razor's always been straight with me but now he's going cold. I know he's looking for a good payout and from what you've just told me, so is someone else. My money's on two firms wanting a bite of the same apple. Have you seen any of them since the shooting?"

"No. I need to know if it was them or not, Mike. If it was

a setup, then I'm a marked man and I'm not in it for that."

Mike nods. I allude to nothing more.

"I've bought another phone for you to get me on. Drop your line, Mike. It's time to up the game plan." I pass him a burn phone all charged and ready to go. He puts it on the table and the screen gets dusted in white powder. He shakes it off and puts it in his trouser pocket. I down the drink and go to the bar. I take the pen and pad as I don't want them becoming contaminated. I leave the pen in a steel holder next to a blank pad by his landline. His are old work biros not fit for purpose.

"You're a good bloke, Sam. We've worked well over the years. Had some great jobs off. It's a shame times changed us. I wanted you to know you're a good operator and that's another reason you're on this and not on some poxy estate infiltration. Don't get me wrong – I'm proud of my service but things have changed too far. Policing boundaries and remits blurred beyond focus. Not like the bad old days of this kind of work, eh? Mixing it up with the higher echelons of criminality, having a blast, then screwing them over whilst watching their empire crumble. Only to be taken over by a younger family member on instruction of the main man from prison."

Mike pauses and lights up another cigar and this time passes the box. I take two. One for now and the other for appearances when I meet Razor at his club tonight.

"Very touching. I'm off to Harvey Browns and a reintroduction. Let Winter know I'm out before you're completely wasted. I'll be in touch once I know where we're going. I'm going to mix things up tonight, clock's ticking. I'll make my own arrangements for sleeping, no need to wait up." Mike raises his glass and I check out of his regal tomb. I go to his room and change clothing. He's allocated me half a wardrobe. I appreciate this is as far as his cover officer role extends. I check the clock in the hall. I make a mental note I need to eat. Time's against me. Sustenance will have to wait.

30

The phone in Klara Winter's office rings. She puts down the file she's scrutinising and checks the time. She hesitates, then answers, hoping for a wrong number. She's disappointed.

"Winter."

"Klara, it's John Cooper, Professional Standards. We've had a breakthrough. I need to meet to brief you."

"Shit! Of course, where are you?"

"Front reception of your building."

"I'll be down to escort you through." The line goes dead and Winter leaves to collect what she hopes is the best news from a phone call she didn't wish to answer.

Once the necessary visitor passes have been issued and the phones locked away, both Winter and Cooper enter her office.

"What do you have for me?" Winter grabs her pen and sensitive decision log and both sit down in a small meeting area.

"We've had Mike's secure laptop hooked up as well as his office terminal. He hasn't been using the terminal for anything other than email response, when he's in. Having the secure laptop gives the appearance he's working in the building but without going into too much detail, he's not been using his office recently."

Winter takes that to mean his office is wired for sight and sound. "Go on."

"He requested his intel section run a check on a Turkish male called Kemal Ahmet. There are no links in the system to this request and the name hasn't come up in this enquiry until now. The Turkish male was executed today in Highgate along with what seems to be a random motorcycle courier. The courier would appear to have got the wrong address and got caught when the purported target came outside. The address is linked to a prominent, Turkish organised criminal network involved in gun running, drug importation, kidnap, extortion, you get the picture. Background work on the male shows him to be linked to a cafe in North London. There was an incident recently where a man with a gun wearing motorcycle gear entered the cafe. CCTV shows another male outside the premises also wearing motorcycle leathers. This male is seen on camera talking to the victim before the victim runs."

Winter stops writing and puts her pen down. "You're thinking one of those people was Batford, aren't you?"

"Yes. Yes, I am. The intelligence is circumstantial but the methodology for asking for the name enquiry on Kemal Ahmet is covert."

"I see what you're saying, but the very nature of their work is covert. Mike is authorised to work remotely from this laptop, isn't he?"

"Yes, he is, but has he told you about why this check was requested?"

"No, but it could be from another job that's he's overseeing."

"We thought that too but then we worked up a subject profile on Ahmet. Lo and behold, Razor's name has come up as being an associate of the head of the Ahmet family. The head of the family has been known to frequent his club."

"Well, that changes everything. It's time to go fully operational, John. We'll have a joint briefing in the morning and bring both of our teams up to speed. I will arrange a meeting with Mike and establish what updates there are. That way I'll know if he's holding back. Whatever the outcome, I have to react to what you've presented and the timing of it couldn't be better."

Business is over.

31

There's an ethic that echoes through criminal society: never weaken. To show weakness is tantamount to death. I need to show Razor I'm very much alive and kicking and that he needs me more than I need him. I remember the first thing I was taught as a trainee detective constable: Assume nothing, believe no one and challenge everything. ABC of detective duty.

I'm in no doubt that hit was for me and the motorcyclist was a clear case of mistaken identity. Whoever conducted the hit thought the motorcyclist was me. Did Razor set up the hit with his own firm? If he did, the cover car's crew would have been told him I wasn't wearing leathers, and my description would have been conveyed to the shooters.

I know Big H holds the scythe and has every intention of executing my death warrant. It hasn't escaped me that the provenance of my whereabouts, earlier today, was only known by a handful of people. One of them happens to be my boss and Razor. Both happen to be in the same bridge club. I could be jumping to the wrong conclusions. It could also have been Trigger seeking revenge for our previous altercation and his ensuing justice.

There could be a grass amongst the trusted. All I know right now is that I've started a job and I intend to see it through to a satisfactory conclusion for society and my own personal gain. I am a serving detective sergeant, after all, and the public deserve to feel safer on London's streets. I intend to give value for money in the taxes that contribute toward this ultimate goal.

As I exit Euston station I check in a coffee house window and see if anyone's paying interest in my movements via the tinted windows reflection. I double check by going in and standing in the queue, waiting, then just as I'm about to be served, I leave. No one's followed me in. The architecture that would be used to camouflage a surveillance team appears clear. The outside scene is uninterested in my movements.

I turn up the collars on my Tom Cridland thirty-year jacket and adjust my grey flat cap. Mike's idea of a joke with the jacket. He knows it would last an ecologically minded person thirty years but with me it may only last thirty minutes. I like it though and intend to hang on to it for as long as operationally possible. It's also a way of him saying I'm sticking around. At least I hope it is. I could be reading too much into a single article of clothing. My phone rings and I feel the vibration in my jacket pocket; it's Mike.

"Holy shit! Have you suddenly become concerned for my welfare? I was only thinking what a great boss you are."

"No. Some things will never change. I've had Winter on the phone. She's arranged a meeting at her offices tomorrow, oh nine thirty hours, before morning prayers. You know, the briefing of events that happened overnight. Commander is coming and we're expected to make an appearance. Show yourself alive and well tonight at the club, then fuck it off early doors. I need you at the meeting tomorrow. Can you hear me?" I pause for a moment, consider hanging up and claiming my battery died but think better of it and stick with the status quo.

"Yeah. See you there. I'll crash at yours tonight after all. We can grab breakfast and come up with a game plan. They must have intelligence by now and it would be good to know what that is."

"Good. Make yourself at home later. I know you've got my spare access key so let yourself in." He hangs up. I now know he has his flat wired. A wise security option. He won't have sound though, just vision, and he's obviously conscious of unwanted attention. I may have underestimated him but my gut says I haven't. It will be a basic optional extra when he bought the flat. I smile at my reflection in the phone screen and head towards Harvey Browns.

London's evening sky is pockmarked with the ambient glow of differing wattage bulbs. I enjoy the comfort it brings of not feeling alone. I wonder, after twenty years, how many years I have left in me to carry on doing this job. No one wants a person of my service and it's only the disability that keeps me here. Not that it would prevent me getting another job outside but it could never match this one.

As I approach the club's entrance I notice the outside camera move towards me. I know I'm being watched, as the street is dead. I know everyone's in as all the fleet is parked up outside. I pull on my collar, turn my head left and right to stretch my tense neck. Sky is back, fucked off and ready to roll. The door opens as I approach. Snowy steps out and stands blocking the pavement.

I take a step forward and head butt him. He goes down, clutching at his nose. His black gloves take on different shades as the blood emits from its fracture. I know it's broken, as the crack was audible as my forehead connected. I'm in control. There's no red mist. This firm has to know I mean business and unless I'm threatened with a gun anyone is game on.

The next adversary is the bar boy who approaches and has both hands out in a gesture that indicates I'm to stop. I ignore this and send my prosthetic into his balls. The aircraft titanium shell on skin will have hurt and his moaning indicates its effect. I step over him, take the key card from the waiter's pocket and hold it against the entry pad to the door to the downstairs club. The door clicks. I pull on the handle and drop the card. I know it will be evident to Razor and Kat that I'm in. I hope they're making significant preparations for my arrival. It's at times like these that any police training pertaining to use of legal force goes out the window.

The Met wouldn't consider my tactics authorised officer safety techniques unless the circumstances justify the force. I say they're lucky the people are able to get up. I'm in a different world now. A world that collides with my own and the lines are blurring faster than a set of headlights on a slow shutter speed. I'm not here to gather evidence. I'm here to establish my longevity and need with this firm.

I'm in the bar area outside the club. I can hear the thump of a bass line emitting from behind the doors. Light rays fan out from the ceiling and it sounds in full swing. A petite Titian-haired lady is sitting at a table smoking a joint and drinking a short. I approach, give her a smile, and she reciprocates and glides over on the Italian leather. The seat is capable of accommodating two and with her small frame, an easy third. I have no intention of taking a seat or sharing a smoke. I hold out my hand and motion towards the clubs doors. She takes a last drag of the joint and stubs it out, downs her drink and takes my hand. I lead her towards the music and a date with hell.

The barman has a nervous look. He's on the internal phone; an empty steel box that should contain my phone is ignored. As we enter the dance floor I take her waist and draw her close, her pert arse grinding into my crotch as she reaches up with her head behind my neck. I have a view down her front that punters would pay for. An old school club night is in full swing with Faithless's 'Insomnia' the current tune of the evening. I steer her towards the other side of the dance floor and towards the private booth.

The one-way glass system is active. I know Razor will be in there. He'll be entertaining another rich dick or looking for me. I don't care either way. I know my options. The options are curtailed as I feel a pressure on my back. That pressure increases as the contact pushes harder sending my synapses into a threat reaction. I have no way of spinning round as the petite one is hanging on with little intention of letting go.

Whoever is behind me has my false leg pinned in a way that means my balance is compromised. I stop. I feel breath near my right ear. I recognise the scent. It's Kat and she's ascertained my intentions.

She raises her voice above the music and issues her ultimatum into my ear. "Don't be a fool. Let go of the girl and walk into the room. It wasn't us. Razor's glad to see you're alive, as am I." I hesitate, for effect more than drama. I know she's right. I'd seen the saloon the others were in and it hasn't been cleaned. The saloon that housed the shooters would have been covered in claret, skin fragments and stone chippings. Razor would have given instructions to lose the car. I extricate myself from the dancer and she gets swept away with the music, oblivious to me. Kat escorts me towards the entrance to the booth and my meeting with Razor.

As she presses an access card against the door panel, she hands an ordinary dinner knife to a waiter and smiles at me. The handle felt more ballistic than innocent. She motions for me to raise my arms. I oblige as she carries out a body search. She retrieves my phone. She can keep it as my preparations have been done prior to my arrival. I stare ahead and let her do what she needs to. She activates the booth's door and enters first. I follow taking in the room as we enter. The door shuts behind us. Razor is on his own peeling an apple with a lock knife and motions to a chair for me to sit down. Kat leaves and a waiter enters with a hostess trolley that contains food and drink. Two place settings only. He's been waiting for me. His reluctant dinner guest.

"Good to see you alive, although I don't fuckin' appreciate the way you entered my club and treated my staff and punters."

"Drink?" He motions to an open bottle of champagne. I nod in agreement.

"I was on edge. I thought you'd organised a hit and wasn't best pleased." I take the offered glass and wait for him to take a slug before drinking mine.

"You could've phoned." He carries on eating and sits back, wiping his nose with the back of his hand. "Kat tells me you would have seen it all. I need to know who it was. My contact has been spread all over the road and I'm still down half a million."

"Well you're out of luck. I was too busy on the tarmac making sure I didn't get shot. I saw nothing other than the aftermath. It wasn't pretty."

Razor doesn't react. "I've put the word out but no one's talking yet. A rumour of a firm of Lithuanians getting ripped off by the same family, but that doesn't sit well. Someone's talking and I don't know who. It ain't you as I reckon you were up for offer. It ain't me, as I need the money and the business. I've had the head of the Turk's family on the blower and he's spitting feathers. I don't blame him. I've got a war I don't want. It needs cutting off at the pass. What I need to know is, are you still in or out?" He lifts a plate off the trolley and passes it over. Pie, mash and liquor. How traditional. He doesn't have the look of a troubled man about him.

His club is open as usual, security remains the same. His fleet is outside where it usually is. He's either lying about something or has an arrogant self-confidence that his empire is indestructible. He's a tough man to read. I know from our brief time he's a player at the top of his game. I also know that he's a grass and that he'll have been feeding Mike whatever he saw to get the heat away from his area of work. What I hope to find out is why he thinks he needs me and what I can bring to the table.

"That depends on what you need doing and what my cut would be."

Razor looks up from his full plate. "The job earlier was more of a pimple on my arse than a full-blown boil. I can't afford to take a knock on half a million. I won't appear weak. The Turk's family has a long history of good-quality heroin. The best in London and they know it. I want his line. The only way I'll get that is by having the main man taken out of the equation. It's not a bad thing now his son's gone as there's no one else to take over the family firm. I want you to pay him a visit, offer my condolences and an offer of joint working. If he refuses, I want him dead."

He looks out over the dance floor. I down my drink and help myself to a top up. I refill his glass at the same time. A contract to kill. Now that's heavy shit. I'm not wired and it would be his word against mine. I dispense with the open questions of how, where and when and concentrate on the what. "So, what's in it for me? You could get someone much cheaper, I can assure you." He cuts into his pie and the gravy leaks out and intermingles with the green of the peas. Two elements joined together through a cut. I need to know he's serious and not just bluffing to see my reaction. If this goes down an evidential route, then I will need to know his true intentions.

"I could do it myself but I'm a busy man. I can afford to outsource my work to the right person. I know your capabilities. It comes with being wanted by an Italian mobster. I also know it takes balls to walk back into a den you think you're no longer welcome at. I'll get your debt written off and you'll be free to go wherever you please."

"Very generous. I'm already free to go where I please, as I've demonstrated. I've no fear of Big H or his cronies. He's looking for the wrong man, but I don't intend on telling him that face to face. I appreciate your generosity but it isn't worth a man's life."

I sit back and mirror Razor's breathing. He says nothing and rubs the inside of his thumb with his index finger. His eyes look up to the right as he leans forward. He's thinking of his next move. "Very well. There's a shipment of brown on our soil making its way to the capital. Arrangements are in hand to take possession of the said load. Half will be yours on the condition I move it through the club. You pick up the cash once it's done. You're looking at coming out with half a million. In addition, you come on board here as my business advisor. I like you, you fit in well. The Turk needs a quiet departure, if it comes to that. If he comes on board and gives up the money he owes, you get two hundred and fifty thousand and still have the option to join. You won't get a better offer. You'll be earning more than you could dream of. You'll have my security as far as Big H goes, too. The Turks' line is huge. Once it's under my control, we're laughing. The stakes are high; I need the best for the job. None of the goons I have are anywhere near capable of this. You've got twenty-four hours to come back to me. If it's a no, then we part here."

I have Mike's words in my head and take the opportunity to vacate the premises. "I'll be in touch. Thanks for the hospitality." We don't shake hands. We have no agreement. I fasten my jacket and pull it down. The shadow at the outside of the door opens and music fills the void. Kat lets me out and escorts me across the dance floor, this time by linking arms. Once we're out in the quiet bar, she unlinks. She smiles and smart cards the next internal door. Snowy is at the other side and ignores me as we both walk past and up to the upper bar where the barman is vacant.

"What did he have to say?" I look at Kat. She's leaning on the bar, her body open towards me. Not in a sensual way. She's never sensual. Always in control of her environment. Her posture is her way of telling me she could take me with a sweeping kick. She stands up and steps closer, her face close to mine. I feel her hand enter my back pocket and my phone slides in.

"Like you said, just wanted to make sure I was alright." I smile and leave.

32

"Operational Control from Alpha one, we have no sighting of subject, Batford, at home address."

"Operational Control from Alpha two, we have subject Batford leaving club premises on foot. He is alone. Eyes about. We have door view and limited street view at present. He is out of street and east towards Euston."

"Operational Control from Alpha three, we have eyes on him towards underground.

"Received. Continue as per briefing. Operational Control out."

The cool night drizzle embraces my neck like a lover's hand exiting a shower. I move towards the underground and I feel my muscles tighten. My eyes itch. A side effect of the opiates. My stump is chafing against the prostheses despite the best America can offer in technology and fitting; it still has its moments. Money bought me the best limb and treatment. I used legal tender from my injury payout as I needed to be sure I could evidence the purchase and trip if I'm ever financially investigated.

I was paid well, from my health insurance, but no amount of money will replace my lower leg or compensate for mental anguish. The power pack that helps the fluid movement of the leg vibrates and reminds me it will need topping up at some point soon. I have no intention of going back to Mike's place. In light of the early start, I make the decision to collect the bike from Lambeth along with a new set of leathers and a lid. From there it will be back to the Watford safe house. Little Chris had covertly left a message on my phone. I know the keys will be with security.

I descend the steps carefully. Many feet have carried the street's wet debris and deposited it on the surface, creating a slip hazard a yellow warning sign does little to combat. I look behind me as I take the first few steps and my gut senses a presence. I double back to the annoyance of those descending and wait at the surface. No one comes up and no one at the top disappears or moves into view.

I wait for a few more people to come along, then join them again and move towards the tube and my journey towards home. I feel like a suspect on an old-style, group identification parade but the charade is necessary to keep me on game. I'm looking forward to another bike and the freedom of the road as the volume of people carries me through to an overcrowded stop and inevitable tussle for domination of a fixed point amongst the hordes. It's late and everyone wants to be home.

A guy in front dominates a zone of platform. He stands tall, arms folded in front of him. His black leather, three quarter length, coat stretches across his broad back. He's not going anywhere but through the first available door despite other passengers' wishes. I know I'm like him in many ways. I have a job to do like he feels he does. That job is getting in people's way to get what you want and achieve your goal.

I see my job as a public service despite my skewed boundaries. His is just plain aggressive and not altruistic in any way. I can't do with that right now as I, like the others behind him, just want to get home. The peace of the platform transforms into a violent wind as the tube emerges from the tunnel and the sound reverberates off the metro-tiled walls.

Those wearing head gear hang onto it and others turn their

faces away from the dust storm the train kicked up. All those other than Mr High Almighty I'm Getting on this Train. The train stops and the doors arrive in the exact spot he's occupied. The position now is a standoff as the passengers on the train can't get off due to him wanting to get on. I wait as the doors part. He steps up; I knee the back of his leg and he stumbles forward.

As I expected, no one reacts to help. The throng of people surge forward and begin moving around him whilst we watch him flounder like a beached whale. The masses behind me begin their push forward to get in the carriage. The momentum means the guy begins to get inadvertently trodden on as the physics of the surge takes over and the only way is forward.

As he tries to get up, shouting and swearing, he's ignored and pushed through and back out of the door with the crowd. The beep sounds as the doors close and catch him in his rib cage as he's on the carriage floor. I lean against the joining door to the carriages and watch from a distance as two British Transport Police, who must have been called to the platform, help the guy up. As they remove him from the doors, his anger takes over and he lashes out with fists and feet. The doors open then close, and as we move off, my last vision is of the man on the floor attached to Taser prongs and writhing as fifty thousand volts surge through his Herculean body.

I feel nothing. A slight feeling of guilt at having started the whole event off but then it eases as quickly as it arises. The train rattles through tunnels towards my penultimate destination and as I scan the carriage for any plain-clothes Old Bill, I relax and lean my weary head against the window and wish for home.

33

Decision Log, 9th September, 2020

Today has been long but productive. Intelligence has come in quickly and links have been made between Razor and associates that also include Detective Superintendent Mike Hall.

An execution has also taken place in a London street involving a prominent associate of Razor's. I am in contact with the Senior Investigating Officer for this offence to further any links with my operation.

Full surveillance is now in operation and as of twenty-two hundred hours I have Batford and Razor together without my knowledge. This is exactly how I saw this operation playing out. Batford clearly underestimates my ability and that of my team. He will rue this day.

He is fully aware of his role as an undercover officer and the condition to maintain contact with the operational lead. This was made clear in the beginning and this is not being adhered to.

This will be the last entry for this day.

Klara Winter DCI
National Crime Agency
Senior Investigating Officer
Op Kestrel

34

"What will it take to make you realise you're a joke? A nobody who no one will listen to or have any respect for?"

I try and turn from the smell of his putrid, alcohol-addled breath as his mouth emphasises each point and spittle spatters my face. His grip on my cheeks prevents my head turning. I have no way of moving. I'm in a chair and he's in front. The room is bare save for a few personal effects; photo frames of distant memories capture my mind and help me focus on something other than the fat twat's lips that invade my personal space. I plot; I wait for my time to come when my world will invade his like a savage army of hate and bitterness. My army will rip his throat out and have his tongue as a trophy.

"Are you listening or lost in that fucked up, useless world of yours?" There's a bang at the door. He ignores it. My heart rate has increased. I'm tense and wait for the next slap, punch or worse. He's looking about the room. He's after an object of retribution. He'll be lucky to find anything of worth in here. As a prison guard, he's destroyed all I've ever had that would warrant keeping, apart from one framed photo. He looks at the photo and back at me. I can't hold back my feeling of attachment towards it.

He sees the reaction in my eyes and moves towards the broken chest of drawers it rests on. He picks it up and looks back at me. He's smiling now. The only time he smiles is when he knows he's got me. He's found my trigger point. He holds the ammunition and he makes a low-throated growl as he coughs up phlegm, then gobs it all over the photo and throws the frame down with such force the glass smashes, and he grinds the remaining pieces of photo and frame into the floorboards with his boot.

I no longer feel fear. With a battle cry that echoes from the bare walls, I launch at the callous bastard and prepare to take the punishment. Any other ten-year-old would do the same if their foster carer destroyed the only image they had of them as a baby.

It's morning. I'm unsure if I'm fully awake but it feels as though I am. I've no idea why the memory has arisen, but it has. I'm in Watford but I'm conscious we have a meet. My head is still woozy. At the end of the bed sits Stoner. She's crying. Her face is as I last remembered it. "I never knew you were treated like me. I suffered at the fists of every man I ever met, apart from you. I didn't listen and I paid the price. You should've been there, babes. I was so alone. Now look at ya. You're all on your tod with nowhere to turn but over your shoulder every time you leave your house. Now you know what it was like for me every time I had to call or meet you. Watch yourself, lover, or you'll be joining me." She blows a kiss and fades. My eyes snap open. All I see is the ceiling and the glowing flicker of a dying thirty-watt bulb.

I knock the thumb switch out of neutral and beat the traffic across Pentonville Road as I head towards Smithfield and a meet with Mike. The chosen cafe venue's quiet. I park the bike near the ambulance hut where I can watch for any unwanted attention. I insist on sitting facing out the window with Mike opposite. Any attempt on my life here and he'll provide me with some ballistic cover. Mike's upbeat. An unusual trait for such a miserable bastard. He's ordered the coffee. He knows I'm a stickler for punctuality.

The bitterness of the first sip catches my throat and reactivates my mind. We waste no time bringing each other up to speed. Mike will take the lead. I'm just for decoration. Pointless two mouthpieces spoiling the environment especially when one is prone to making feelings known that have no place to be aired. When we're done, we leave separately. I go first making sure I've enough time to get to the meet destination. Mike gets a cab.

"Operational Control from Alpha one. Subject Hall and subject Batford have left cafe venue separately. Will update further as route progresses."

"Received at Operational Control. All Alpha teams are advised targets are mobile. Operational Control standing by."

35

Waiting in the Commander's pre-meeting room is like waiting for the head teacher but without the same fear and trepidation. I say this because the job is moving forward and she can't afford to pull the plug on the whole thing now. It would be like writing a book, getting ninety thousand words in and going fuck it. Pointless. The personal assistant has changed and a new breed of hungry, mad, by-the-book wannabe sits in the chair. This one's male, always been in uniform by the looks of his crisp ironed shirt and suitable tie. A level transfer into the world of specialist policing but only for the Commander's ear and experience at management.

Yes, I'm bitter. Yes, it could have been my choice at some point in my fucked up career but I chose the dirty path and have no shoe polish or need for an iron. We check in five minutes before our allotted slot. Mike has a fresh suit on. He must have gone back to the flat before getting here, which also means he wasn't at home last night. I lodge the thought. I'm dressed in jeans and an AC/DC European tour T-Shirt. Like me, I can't believe they're still going and not thrown in the towel. Will the Commander mind? I'm beyond caring. Besides, I'm operationally deployed and may need to leave at the drop of a text.

Don't get me wrong, she's one person in this screwed up force I have the most respect for. She's been there and got the T-shirt. A seasoned detective who decided to take the glass ceiling and bulldoze the thing to the ground to make her own panoramic office windows. She takes no shit and I respect that. Mike checks his phone and turns it off. I don't touch mine. You can never underestimate the urgency of others' calls and the required need to respond. I have my own force response criteria and that amounts to when I choose to answer the call. The phone goes on the PA's desk. He gets up, opens the door and ushers us in. I put in my first request. "Black coffee and two packs of biscuits."

His face doesn't even break a smile as he leaves the door for me to shut. The room has a more authoritarian tone than her last office. Since the Yard moved, she chose to have her office in the new building rather than offices south of the river. A uniform Commander occupied this one and she clearly thought her presence was better suited as it overlooks the Thames. A leather-topped writing desk that would appear to be a permanent feature dominates. We occupy the two remaining armchairs. DCI Winter and DI Hudson are present.

In better times we had a closer relationship with operational teams. We'd all go into a Commander's meeting knowing we were singing from the same hymn sheet. Now there are no hymns but the sermon remains the same. Get the job done and put to bed spending the least amount of money. Terrorism is becoming the job of the spies and we get the doors to go through and the follow-up investigation. I'm a dying breed in the field of intelligence led policing. The Commander opens the meeting just as her PA brings in a round of tea and coffee and places it on a side desk designed to receive such a gift. The Commander begins.

"Good morning. I will dispense with introductions and move onto the updates for my knowledge and oversight. Before we begin I expect the contents of this meeting to be accurate and *all* information shared, where appropriate to do so. We will break with tradition and open with your side of the house, Superintendent." She looks away from Mike. I nudge him to look up and to tell him he's on.

Mike shuffles in his seat and leans forward. "Very well, ma'am. DS Batford has done an excellent job gaining access to the group. He has been accepted as a criminal. Batford reports Razor has done his own homework and believes DS Batford is on a hit list by our friend Big H. This hasn't altered my assessment of the threat. I am treating it as independent corroboration; it exists and the threat level remains at low." Mike pauses and no one interjects. "DS Batford has established the group have access to guns and this information has been passed to DCI Winter for information. At this stage it is evident Razor has a criminal plan. DS Batford believes this will come to light imminently." The Commander isn't impressed.

"Nothing you have said leads me to believe he has any plan in place. Yes, we have the gun angle and that can be dealt with conventionally without further need for DS Batford. You updated Klara on this and she has identified the premises and has an observation point in place. What is this 'job'? I have to justify my covert resources, Superintendent. Why can't we react to the flat that has the gun provider in and move on?" She looks at Mike, her threaded eyebrows raised in anticipation of his response.

"We need more time to establish if there are any matters that would cause a national security concern, ma'am. The guns may not be at this address. At present it is unknown where any more may be."

"Don't start with the national security bullshit, Mike. At present there's been a gun and no mention of others. Now you've mentioned national security! I know you're doing your best to bolster a dead duck of a job." Mike looks aghast.

Winter chips in. "Ma'am, if I may come in at this point. We may be able to add more intelligence that has come to light as a result of our work. We were running a profile of Razor on our systems and established a list of known associates. My team has been monitoring reports of a select number of these associates. One came up in dramatic circumstances yesterday. A Turkish male by the name of Kemal Ahmet was gunned down in North London. I have spoken to the Senior Investigating Officer for the murder. He has told me there are no leads at present. Information is coming in that may be of use to us. I have requested I be kept up to date with the enquiry. In return we will provide any assistance the Met may need in terms of research or analysis. The line is still live on Razor but nothing has been reported from this to DI Hudson. In light of this, the NCA feels the enquiry should continue until we are satisfied there are no links between our operation and their investigation."

"Yes, I'm sure the National Crime Agency would love to have Met resources for as long as possible but the link is tenuous to nonexistent. So an associate has been shot and killed. But there is no further intelligence linking Razor to the shooting." The Commander is succinct in her summing up.

"That's correct, ma'am. Unless DS Batford or Detective Superintendent Hall have anything further to add?" Winter pauses and looks across at us. The Commander has her head down and is writing.

"First we've heard. Rest assured we will report back anything we may pick up our end." Mike is even quicker. The Commander looks up and we all look in her direction. I attempt a slug of coffee but it's cold and the timing isn't good for a refill.

"You've got twenty-four hours. That's sufficient time for each side to come up with a substantive investigation other than the gun angle. If nothing has changed in this time, then I expect the gun address to have a warrant executed. I know my surveillance authority has more time but I don't. The Commissioner wants swift action. Gone are the days of long, protracted operations. Unless this government comes up with more cash and detectives in the next twenty-four hours, then that's all the time you have. I have a limited budget to manage and different priorities to address. That's all, thank you." She nods at the PA; he opens the door and ushers

Mike and I out. Winter remains and the door closes.

Phone rings in the Commander's office. The Commander listens then turns to Winter.

"They've left the area. It's clear to me, Klara, that from the briefing you gave me before they arrived, information is being withheld. You have my full support for this operation. I have spoken with John Cooper at Professional Standards and our Intelligence Unit. I expect they will have new information within the twenty-four-hour time frame. If they don't, then I'm sure you will. Be prepared that Batford and Hall may choose to react within the time frame given as they need the cover of an authorised operation for them to execute whatever plans they may have. Speak with your CHIS, Alex Kennedy, and let's add meat to the bones."

"Yes, ma'am." Winter leaves.

36

"Klara!" Mike shouts across the canteen. Winter nods and indicates with her index fingers the letter T. We hold our cups up and she knows we're good. Rude not to get her one in but we thought she might be a while longer. In truth neither of us had the money for three and nothing runs on tick in a Metropolitan Police canteen. She comes over weaving through tables, her large handbag slung over her left shoulder.

I draw a chair out beside me; she sits down placing her drink on the table, always a takeaway cup. We never sit for long. "Jesus she was a pain in the arse today, eh? Twenty-four hours to wrap this job up? She's having a laugh. I did my best afterwards but she gave me a pill and sent me away." Winter stops and drinks.

"We won't let it die an early death. Razor's a shrewd bastard. He'll want things moving if there are any legs in what you were saying about this shooting. Just seen a bit on the news. Shocking it could take place on London streets in broad daylight." Mike pauses for effect but Winter carries on drinking.

"You can't tell me that you know nothing of this? Batford, you're in his club, there must be some talk?" Winter has to rope me into a dull conversation.

"Everything I know has been passed to Mike to deliver to you. I have nothing more to add. Razor's ready to move on something, though. I just need more time to find out what."

"Well, we've all heard her highness. We have a day and the clock's ticking. It's down to you now, Batford. You're the closest thing we have to him. If he says or does nothing then I do a firearms warrant on a Polish man's door and hope for a decent result. Mike, I need you on speed dial now to make this job work."

Winter gets up and Mike raises his Styrofoam cup in recognition of her request. She says farewell and exits the area.

"Well, sir? What the fuck do you have in mind now?" Mike picks up his cup and motions for me to follow. I follow him out of the building and we cross and lean on the embankment wall.

"It'll happen within twenty-four hours. He called me last night. We had a few beers at a local near him. He has a shipment in his sights but he's said no more than that. Says he'll tell me when it's on the move. The idea is he'll let it run then let us know when to hit it. Spend more time with him from here, Sam. Let me know what's happening. I'll call Winter after this and make sure you're covered outside. I can't take a risk on guns. Maybe this one was never to be for us. Win some, lose some, eh?"

Mike screws up his cup and lobs it over the wall into the Thames. I say nothing, just nod and leave. Someone is yanking my chain and I need to know who.

37

China Town, London
Persons present:
DCI Winter
DI Hudson
Alex Kennedy (CHIS)

DCI Winter: I wanted an open meet, somewhere you'd be comfortable, as will we. Order what you like. I'm paying this bill. It's busy enough that we can talk freely without our conversation being picked up. It's a shame you couldn't get here earlier than midday but I understand why. You are pivotal to the success of this operation. Without you we're struggling to understand what Razor is planning and more importantly when and how he proposes to execute it.

Alex Kennedy: It's not been easy getting close to Sky. Last time he was in the club it nearly kicked off. What I do know is that Razor needs him. The job is big. Razor needs a guy taken out. A Turk. This Turk runs a large family who import heroin and Razor wants the line for his club. He'll deal it and launder the money through the business. The club has a great turnover. Razor has an accountant who's a tight manager of his finances and that's the way he likes it. He was inspected by HMRC a few years back and nothing came of it. Everything was accounted for down to the last straw and cocktail umbrella.

DI Hudson: We need you to get closer to Sky. We need to know what he's up to and how he's spending his day. You know the limits you can go to and that hasn't changed. From here I want updates regularly.

DCI Winter: Bottom line is we have twenty-four hours grace to know what's happening and when. The clock is counting down. The longer we're here, the more time we lose, so eat quickly. This is ramping up and_so must you if you want to see this to the end and you can leave the firm with no problems.

Alex Kennedy: Good. I need a new start, well away from here.

DCI Winter: In this newspaper is an envelope. In the envelope is five hundred pounds. Put your mark here, below your name, on this paper. I'm not concerned about receipts. It's all there; I counted it before we came. A result is what I want from this and the right people banged up for a long time. Be careful though. Don't be foolish. They'll be getting twitchy the closer it gets to any off and you must keep your wits about you.

Alex Kennedy takes the newspaper and leaves the cafe.

Hudson leaves the cafe with Winter and phones the operational control room.

"We're live as of twelve thirty-two hours. All updates of targets through me, and I will be with DCI Winter. We're coming back to the base."

Winter looks at Hudson. He checks his watch, hails a cab, and they head south to the office.

38

At first glance it appears like any other suburban house in a quiet residential cul-de-sac in Mill Hill. That's until you realise each house has its own gated entrance and more cameras than GCHQ. I never expected to get an early lunch invite but how could I refuse from a man who has come to see himself as my boss. Poor deluded fool. The gates open as my bike purrs up to the camera. There's no need for me to raise my visor. If I were Razor, I would have made me take off the lid to make certain my visitor was the one expected.

One assassination is unfortunate; two means there's a war. I park the bike up in a garage whose doors open at the same time I ride in. An intentional invite, I call it. I doubt my host is updating his social media status. I've come to know him as a man of few words. I too am not my status update. The bike's engine noise dissolves into the garage walls and I'm left with the sound of my leathers creaking.

"Take the lift to your left, Sky. First floor." A familiar voice comes through an intercom system. I notice the lift and step in. It has three levels: basement, ground and first. I do as requested and press the first. The lift glides up quickly and I arrive at my destination. The doors open and I exit. "Thanks for coming, take a seat." Razor points at a leather chair and footstool. "I could do with getting out of these leathers."

"Take them off and dump them over by the bar. Faye will

get them when she comes through with the drinks."

I take off my leathers. A woman who I assume is Faye enters the room carrying a tray and two glasses of what appears to be whisky. She takes my leathers, smiles and leaves. There's no introduction from Razor. "Your wife?"

"No, domestic help. The wife's out with my mum at a hospital appointment. The lift's for her. She lives on the ground floor and we care for her here. She's ninety but at this rate, she'll out live us all." I take my seat and drink and look out through the open plan panoramic windows at a garden that's in better health than me.

"I've given you enough time to make your decision. I know you've come to the right one or you wouldn't be here in my home drinking my scotch and taking in my family photos." He takes a drink and I nurse mine.

"You're right, I have made up my mind. I'm in. I've come to recognise you as a man who knows what he wants and gets what he wants, as am I. I know you've got this laid on and you just need it executed quickly and efficiently. Thing is, I can't afford to mess about waiting. The wipe out of his son is still fresh and that's a good time to seek peace. It's also a good time to send the message to others if he doesn't come on board."

"Good. Suits me. I need it done today. There's no money upfront. I need to know the job's done before you'll see the cash, but you'll see it. If you don't, well you know where I live." He raises his glass and I reciprocate. The job's on.

"Time is everything. If I stay longer I'll get pissed and be good for nothing. I thought you might insist on a quick turnaround. All I need is a photo of the target."

"I had a feeling you'd only be hungry for one thing. On this paper is a number for Polish. He has something for you. It's clean and he's told me it's better than the pile of shit he gave Trigger. Kat has an envelope with the photo in it. I've told her to shadow you. Snowy put himself forward and I told him where to go. She's a trusted of mine. She'll be strapping should you need to come out fighting. This firm are brutal. I wouldn't put it past the head of the family to have ordered the execution of their own flesh and blood. The Turk's at a different address this afternoon. Here it is." Razor hands me an address on a small piece of paper. It's the same as the one Mike told me he'd been moved to.

Razor's phone rings and he presses a button on it. A CCTV image appears on the TV screen. My shadow has arrived.

39

Main Operational Control Room – National Crime Agency

"Control from Alpha eleven."

"Alpha eleven, go ahead."

"Subject Batford is still in premises along with an unidentified subject. Possibly subject Mills but no facial confirmation as wearing a crash helmet."

"Received by Operational Control. Alpha eleven remain in situ. Alpha twelve leave current location and cover Alpha eleven at target premises, over."

"Operational Control from Alpha twelve, team leader, all received. Making way to vicinity as directed."

"All teams from Operational Control are advised subjects may be carrying firearms. You're not to engage unless authorised or life is threatened. Control out."

Winter straightens up from her leant position behind the controller's chair and pats him on the back. "Keep tight on these two. I don't want them lost at any stage of this operation. This will be fluid from here on in until all teams are stood down on my command only. Other intelligence is being operated on as we speak in relation to Razor and Detective Superintendent Hall. DI Hudson is coordinating that phase. It's being run by the Metropolitan Police. At times there will be a joint link with our control room and theirs. I have staff monitoring radio traffic form next door. That's all, thank you."

As Winter leaves the control room, for the first time since the operation commenced, she turns back and smiles at her staff.

40

No real conversation took place at Razor's between Kat and I. I couldn't be arsed and certainly not within the confines of his garage where she was told to wait. I need to be alone but see that option isn't in my favour just yet. I prefer alone and not to be tied to his piece of ass whilst I take out a prominent Turkish heroin importer. I have my failings like any other member of the human race. I draw the line at killing a man I've never met before who has done me no harm.

Yes, he's flooded the UK with grade A heroin and undoubtedly caused death and upset amongst families and businessmen in the same line of work, but this job isn't the great earner Mike had led me to believe. Outside the garage, I pull up my visor and Kat rolls up alongside me on her bike. We keep the engines running in case Razor can pick up outside speech at the flick of a switch.

"I make it one pm. I need to make a call, then we'll sit down and plan our next move. Wait for me in the next street. She nods and moves off. I follow a short distance then turn into a street opposite and pull over.

Mike answers on the third ring.

"It's me. I need to speak."

"Go on, I'm listening."

"Razor wants me to take out the Turk today. He's linked me up with a gun from Polish but I haven't got it yet. What do you want me to do? I've not got long; he's put a shadow on me." Mike goes quiet.

"I take it this is the Turk's father from the earlier hit?"

"Yes."

"He's not at the home address. He's been moved to a safe house. I authorised the witness protection today. He's a grass and he knows too much, Sam. He's got to go. You're the only one I can trust to do the job properly. He knows about Razor and me. He's kept it under wraps until his son was taken out. Now he's changed his mind and is ready to tell all. I can't meet you until it's over."

"Have you lost your fucking mind? Is this what this fucking job was all about, cleaning up your fucking mess?"

Mike's not listening. "I need a car. Have you still got yours at that lock up? I need to lay low until this blows over. A couple of weeks leave then I'll be back. Winter will be no problem. I've said I'll be here until the twenty-four hours is up then I'll be on leave and you can handle the debrief."

"You think it's that fucking simple. You're asking me to kill a man for fuck's sake! Have you lost the plot? The Command isn't going to let you fuck off on leave in the middle of this job!"

"Let me make things crystal. If you don't do as I say, then I'll make sure that threat to life becomes a firm hit. Razor will know you're undercover Old Bill. Between him and Big H, you won't be able to step outside whatever front door you've laid your hat at without thinking someone's got a bullet with your warrant number on. You've escaped three attempts and if you do this, there will be no more. You have my word on that. So get with the programme and we can all carry on playing happy families."

I stop pacing and lean against the seat of the bike. Mike. Mike, the man I've trusted and respected has been instrumental in trying to get me killed. He wants those who know about him gone. Eradicated. I have two options: call Winter and tell her everything or do this job my way. It's a no brainer. I'm reminded of the three Ps I was taught to be wary of early in my career: prisoners, property and prostitutes. All can land you in deep shit. I have added a fourth: pricks. Of which, Mike is one.

"You're bluffing, but you leave me no choice. Once this is done, we're history. The car's unlocked where it always is. Keys under the front, offside, wheel arch. Enjoy your holiday, sir. Now where's he been moved to?" As the information is relayed, a person appears at the end of the street. It wouldn't be unusual but this person has stopped and looked my way. He moves on and I'm left like a stalker victim's prey with no sign of resolution.

I call Kat. "Meet me at Stanmore Station car park. We may have company and after the last shock, I'm taking no risks. It's too bait to travel as a unit."

"No deal. Don't get any ideas of fucking off. You try and outrun me or lose me this time and you're a dead man walking. Razor's told me there's a bounty on your head and I'm up for collecting the cash at any cost." She makes the sign of a gun with her fingers. I drop my visor, rev up and go. She's anticipated the move and is following with seconds to spare. As we get to the end of the cul-de-sac, the person's disappeared. I U turn and Kat goes right, stops and looks, deciding what her next move will be. Whatever I do now will work in my favour and that includes anti-surveillance.

I don't expect her to know I won't be outrunning her. She could prove to be a useful bargaining tool if it comes to a life for a life. I wait two minutes. No vehicle has come in or anyone on foot. It means nothing more. If I'm being tailed by Winter, she's keeping the team loose and on the outskirts of the surrounding streets.

Mike hasn't arranged another attempt on me. He wants this job done first, then I know I'm next, despite his reassurances. This time I want Winter's lot with me. For the first time in a while, I need the security of the family I have grown to reject. I just hope she's gone against anything I've said and deployed a team to shadow me.

41

"Where are the subjects now?" Winter monitors the radio communication via a radio at her desk.

"Control, from Alpha two. I have both subjects north towards Stanmore. They're riding in single formation at distance. From the formation they can see each other. Keep all vehicles back whilst I maintain follow. Over."

"All Alpha teams from Winter, proceed as advised by Alpha two. No *mobile units to be in vicinity with the exception of Alpha two. Winter out."*

Winter comes back into the main control room and surveys the camera feed from the crash helmet of Alpha two as she addresses the controller.

"I want all other mobile units making their way towards the M1 and the nearest tube or train station. Junction 2 of the M1 I want covered too; they could hit the motorway. Where's the nearest station?"

"Stanmore."

"Get that covered. He could dump the bike and take public transport. Any mobile units are to get there taking a parallel route to the two subjects." Winter pauses and runs her hands through her hair. A two-day layoff from shampoo is beginning to take effect. She rolls off a hair tie from her wrist and ties her hair back.

"The surveillance teams know what they're doing, ma'am. They're experienced. We have to let them move with what they see and where they're being taken."

The ops room controller looks up at the screen as lights on a large map move and the other mobile teams flank Batford and Kat. Winter says nothing and turns to leave for her room.

"Just make sure they stay back and give them room to run. If I hear a shout that a team's been compromised as a result of not relaying my instructions, I'll have your arse." The controller says nothing and sips a lukewarm tea.

"From Alpha two, both subjects are turning left, left, left, from the A406 towards Stanmore, over."

"Received by Controller. Alpha eleven and twelve loose containment of Stanmore Station. Put one footy out in case they disband bikes and get train."

All units confirm. Winter hears the transmission, picks up the phone and dials and external number. Hudson answers.

"They're on the move towards your location. Are all armed tactical teams in place?"

"Yes. All in place awaiting further instructions."

"Good. Control of your plot will move to the firearms team leader. Once she's taken over control be prepared to move with the second team when I call. I've a good feeling about this one, a very good feeling."

Hudson confirms the message. She sits back, rests her head on the chair and swivels the seat round in a circuit of circles, working the chair clockwise and anti-clockwise. As she does a knock on the door causes her to stop. The door opens and DI Cooper enters.

"Car's downstairs. We're ready to go." Winter grabs her coat, puts the earpiece in her ear and puts the radio in her bag. She leaves the office, closing the door behind her. She ducks her head as she enters into the rear seat of the nondescript, blacked-out Mercedes. The two tones are activated and a set of blue lights leak out of the front grill as the driver heads north out of the capital.

42

All roads lead to a final destination. The destination is either by choice or circumstance. Today, both apply. I keep Kat in view as we leave the pastures of North London's outermost suburbs and head towards the county line. The sun is out, and the tinted visor does its job well shielding me from view and maintaining my anonymity from outside eyes. I know other eyes will be on me. They will be from a distance, either human or automated via camera.

The chances of evasion become more remote as technology advances and the needs for national security increase. I'm a strong believer in intelligence-led policing unless it interferes with my aims. Traffic cameras, mobile cameras, ANPR cameras, dashboard cameras, mobile phone cameras, cash point cameras, the list is endless. Everywhere we go we're under observation whether we wish it or not.

The only photo I agreed to have taken was for my warrant card and even then it was obsolete the moment I stepped out of New Scotland Yard. I'd decided against the man bun look and had a number one all over. It was unnecessary but I'm at a stage in service where I will do anything to buck the system and stay one step ahead even when it's as absurd as altering your warrant card's appearance. I've never carried it since unless visiting New Scotland Yard. Most of the security guards know us at NSY, which helps. My mind feels lighter as I enter junction 2 of the M1. A warrant card identifies who the bearer should be. How and when we use it is key.

I glance behind me and nod at Kat. She nods back and with that we both open the throttle and enter the M1 straight to the third lane. She's dispensed with leather trousers today and wears a pair of skinny jeans with calf-length boots. The other motorcycle I'd clocked doesn't respond. I'm left with the doubt of a follow or not. My thoughts are left at the slip road as the needle hits the ton and any cars in front move into lane two. I have no time to see the drivers' reactions as the needle increases and the ton becomes 120 as I seek junction 6 and the exit slip road towards my digs and respite before the main event.

It isn't an issue for me taking Kat. I won't be there for long and the place has nothing that would indicate any history about me. I see the junction's countdown markers and using a lorry in lane 1 as a block. I move across the three lanes and off onto the slip road. Kat has seen the move and does the same. We meet at the roundabout and stay in the nearside slip lane. She doesn't acknowledge me and I do the same.

The route into Watford is without incident. With one final sweep around the block, I pull over in a private road that leads to a lock up. I'm prepared to give this up now that Mike has requested my car. It's served its purpose and there are plenty more. I cut the engine and Kat does the same. The garage door is shut but unlocked. I'm glad my car is gone. It needed to move. It was becoming a burden. I turn the handle and the mechanism creaks. The door opens on an empty garage. Mike's been and gone. We move the bikes in and leave the helmets.

The flat is a short walk away but for today we'll use the rear fire escape to get in. "Glad you kept up. We'll get a drink at mine and talk. I've lost the front door key so we'll use the back." Kat is looking at her bike and checks herself in the mirror. "Whatever you say." I put on the kettle and watch Kat as she inspects the sparse living room. The curtains are drawn. She doesn't attempt to look out over the street.

I liked Stoner for her simplicity, ease of conversation and company. Kat is like a bee sting, irritating and difficult to remove. I bring the cups into the living room and offer her the only seat as I grab a dining room chair. My days of sitting on the floor are done due to how long it would take me to get up. The one thing I'm conscious of in a fight is the need to stay on my feet.

I learnt the hard way in my probation. By the hard way I mean intervening in a public altercation between two brothers. One brother took exception and demonstrated this by throwing me over the roof of a stationary car. At that time my legs were in good fighting order, but the ground arrived at speed along with the boots from either side of my body as they took their angst out on me.

In the end my shout for urgent assistance was answered and it took seven cops to extract the pair. It's a lesson you have time to reflect on especially when you're under observation for two days in hospital. Since that day I trained in Wing Chun and now I know where to place my feet and move around an assailant with the minimum of fuss.

"You haven't lived here long, have you?" Kat asks, as she sits down and scans the room. It has that appearance and for me is easier to explain away than have to lie through many fake photos of fake family, pets and nonexistent holidays. "I prefer a minimalist look." She doesn't buy it.

"There's minimalist and nonexistent. You're at the extreme end. Must cost a bit in rent." I know the drill. Ask the personal questions and you get to know whom you're dealing with or at least think you're dealing with. I know our time is running out and this excursion will be nothing more than brief respite. Suits me fine as my time for company is on a meter and I'm out of cash.

"It's home to me and that's what counts. Let's cut the small talk and move on to the job in hand."

Kat puts down her tea and crosses her legs. Her hands are both forward in an open gesture that suggests, *I'm easy, get on with it then.* "I don't do joint work so you'll do as the last one and wait in the vicinity whilst I talk to the guy. I need eyes on the outside so I can get out if the heat's turned up unexpectedly."

She smiles. "By unexpectedly you mean a shot squad turns up and pebble dashes the masonry with nine-millimetre shells? Yeah, I can be in the *vicinity* as you put it. When do we see Polish? We're way out of London."

"We don't. The less people know, the better. I'll bring my own weapon to the party." She doesn't like this and stands up.

"Razor was fucking clear in his instructions to me! He expects them to be followed, as do I."

"Well, life's full of little disappointments so try feeding that back to lover boy." She responds with a laugh that's infectious in its tone.

"You think the only reason he keeps me close is because I'm fucking him? Christ you're shallower than a desert puddle. I'm there because he has faith in my ability to look after him and protect him from tossers like you. Just remember how far you got across that dance floor with your unwilling charades partner. I had you and could have done more damage than a hurricane but he told me when he saw you on camera up top to make it look natural and get you into the VIP booth calmly. So shut the fuck up with the big I am. Let me know when we're off and how you see it all going down. I'm back on tonight and need to change." She brings her speech to a close with a slug of tea.

Her hostile demeanour is growing on me. I go back into the kitchen and I can sense her eyes following me. This is confirmed as she follows me out. "Don't panic. I'm not getting a gun." I open the under sink cupboard and take out a small lockable combination box. "Here's a phone. This is the one we use from here until the job's done. You don't call anyone else but me on this phone. Once the job's complete, I will call Razor. You put your phone in here and collect it once we're back home and dry." I keep the box open and wait for her phone. She seems distracted by this move. I can tell there's a part of her unwilling to cooperate. As quick as the thought arises, she takes out her phone and puts it in the box.

"All of them." She reaches into her boot and withdraws another. Her mouth parts in a sarcastic smile and she removes another and throws it in. "I'll need the combination, you know, in case you get blown away and I need to get my property."

"Sure. It's zero, zero, zero. Should be easy enough for you to remember." With that I shut the lid. My phone vibrates with a WhatsApp message. It's Mike.

Thanx for the motor. I've checked the oil and it's good for the journey.

I now know the target's in the address and going nowhere today.

"That's the confirmation I needed. Razor knows where the Turk's laid up and he's expecting a visit. The Turk believes an offer is being sent over to address his debt. Should make it easier to get in. We're good to go."

Kat shrugs and picks up the burner phone. "I best take a piss then. Where's your toilet?"

I indicate along the corridor and she leaves. Whilst she's gone I message Mike.

Good. Look after it and I'll be in touch.

He'll decipher the reply to mean I'll let him know when the job's done. He'll know in a way befitting the situation he's put me in. All's fair in work and war.

I hear the toilet flush and Kat comes back out. There's no hand towel and she emphasises this by drying her hands on her leathers. "Phone." She hands it over and I check the call and message lists. They're empty. "Good. Let's go." She takes the phone back and places it in her pocket. I check the back gardens before we exit via the fire escape. I can't see any human surveillance from my side or Razor's. I'm just hoping if my lot have people out, they have only covered the front thinking the back wasn't easily accessed. My view was it was easily accessed as long as your neighbours worked during the day and wouldn't see two people in motorcycle leathers worthy of police attention as they climbed garden fences.

We descend the stairs and traverse gardens until we're back at the garages. Everything's as we left it. A short space of time is all a team needs to lump a bike with a tracker. I reach into the roof eaves and bring out a scanner. Its appearance causes Kat's eyebrows to rise. "We need to be sure we're alone. I'll run this over the bikes to be certain." I start the process.

"I know what a scanner is. We're the only ones who know what's going on aside from Razor so why the wand? You're making me nervous as to why someone like you would know this stuff and feel the need to have it about you." She's taken a step towards her bike. I carry on with my sweep of the garage. I need to know Mike hasn't arranged any surprises and that Little Chris hasn't been told to conduct a covert modification without my knowledge. Late thought, I know.

"You forget I have a bounty on my head by a leading man in an Italian mob. I was also close to being carved in half by an automatic weapon so forgive me if you find this all a bit unnecessary but I don't give a shit as long as I get this job done, get paid and leave in one piece."

She says nothing and plays with the helmet's chin strap. "What will you do once this is over? Razor has you on the firm's payroll so freelance work seems to be out for you."

Kat's eyes catch a ray of sun through a hole in the brick. She squints and turns to face me. Her pupils calm and adjust. I struggle to maintain eye contact as I think of a reply. She has eyes that resonate compassion but change in response to a threat. Right now they're concerned with dispelling excess light.

"One thing at a time. Let's get this done then I can think about the next opportunity,"

"Most blokes don't see death as an opportunity for growth. You're weird like that, but I like it."

"Most women don't see protecting a self-opinionated, arrogant prick as a reasonable living. You're weird like that and I've no opinion on it either way." I put the wand under my seat. Whilst I'm doing this I check what else I'm carrying, and I'm satisfied I'm good to go. I shut the seat and ensure it's locked on to the frame. It's all clear. From here on in I have no idea how it will turn out.

She gets on her bike and wheels it back until she's outside the garage door. I take one last look around, as I know I won't need this place again. Before we start up the bikes, I have one last word. "I'm going straight to the target. When I arrive it will be straight up to the front door for me and in. You better be ready to follow me in and get out. If that's what Razor wants, he can have it his way."

She shrugs. "Let's go then, shall we?" She puts down her visor and we engage the engines.

43

Demo outside GCHQ – London

"Operational Control to Winter."

"Go ahead."

"The Tactical Firearms Commander wants to know your eta to the rendezvous point, over."

"Tell her I don't know. We're detouring due to a demonstration outside GCHQ. She must not, I repeat, must not, engage until I have confirmation of all subjects' movements. This is to be a joint take down of targets."

"All received by control. I will contact her. At present all armed units are at a green alert state. Just so you know it's a demonstration against broader use of surveillance.'

"Great. What's happening with Hudson's plot? My phone has no signal and I can't contact him."

"I just got off the phone to him. The area is covertly sterile and awaiting Batford. He asked me to tell you he's tried getting in contact with Alex Kennedy and the agreed answer phone message has been heard. He said you'd understand what that meant, over."

"Very well. In that case tell all units to remain vigilant and await further radio instruction. I have my laptop on and it's secure. I want the helicopter feed sent to me now."

"Received, control out."

Winter sits back as the computer screen goes from a blinking cursor to an outside image. She looks closer. She sees a residential street and a top-down view of a terraced house. The street is devoid of foot traffic but vehicles pass by. Workmen lean against scaffolding and eat. The helicopter is a mile away yet the image is as if it's above the street and the target address. She sits back, waits for the next radio contact and gathers her thoughts as the unmarked Mercedes clears the protest and heads towards her destiny.

44

Mike wipes the sweat from his forehead and sits back in the passenger seat. He pulls the internal sun visor down despite the day being overcast and maintains wearing his aviator shades. He checks his watch and rubs his hands together. Five minutes to go before his contact arrives and his journey will continue. He throws the open sandwich box into the foot well not caring since it's Batford's car. Mike knows Batford's fate. The last transport Batford will be in is a hearse. Mike stares out of the window and lets his mind churn over whether he's done the right thing in planning the final countdown of Batford's life.

As he looks at the different tones of grey cloud that his shades create he breathes rhythmically, trying to pacify himself that Batford's death will be put down to another bad job by an overstretched police force. He knows he will come under scrutiny for sending an undercover officer into a potentially dangerous situation but he will deny all knowledge of where Batford was as he had never been informed.

There will be no phone records, as he will show the phone Batford gave him and there will be no data. Mike will claim he told him to use the phone they had always been using. The phone Mike was using will show contact between them both and he can only assume Batford was acting as a rogue agent and was clearly corrupt. Razor was a mastermind in sending his enforcer along with Batford to finish off the job

Batford couldn't see through. Her instructions are clear: take out Batford and the Turk.

A glance in the nearside mirror shows a motorcycle headlight. It grows in strength casting a harsh vignette across the glass before it disappears as the roar of the engine cuts out. A figure clothed in black leathers approaches carrying a shoulder bag, the flap being brushed by the rider's hand. Mike feels his back tense and he pushes back into the seat. The rear door opens and the bag gets thrown in. The helmet comes off and Razor stares across. "Bet you thought I'd never turn up."

He smiles then belly laughs, strips away the leathers and throws them on the ground. His jeans and T-shirt are wet with sweat but he minds not. "Where's the petrol?"

"In the boot." Razor pops the boot and takes out the green fuel can. He picks up his clothes and kicks them on the floor near the bike. He dashes the bike with petrol and once the can is empty, sets it by the bike. He gets in the driver's seat and adjusts the seat's position. "Nice touch, you blagging that fucker's motor. You cops are all the same – no taste when it comes to cars."

Mike smiles. "You've got the tickets?" Razor leans over and opens the bag. He hands Mike the tickets and a roll of notes.

"All here, mum. Once we're in Greece we'll have a couple of days at the rental then the meet's set up. Four days' time we'll be rolling in filthy lucre thanks to a dead Turk and taking over his line of business. This firm wanted a change anyway and I offer a better rate. Kat will call me once it's done. She'll make it look like a hit and Big H will get the first visit from your mob and it'll be plain sailing. Good shout of yours to make that threat look real. Your dippy lot bought it good and proper. Shame my hired hands didn't get Batford. Hey ho, we got the Turk's son. Who'd have thought Batford wouldn't take the bike to the job? Shame about the old dear, though. Belt up. We've a plane to catch."

Razor pulls on his belt and Mike does the same. Mike feels

an emotion he hasn't acknowledged since his mum died and does his best to kick it into touch. He coughs, spits out the open window, bends down and throws the sandwich carton out for good measure. As they slowly pass the bike, Razor lights a cigarette, takes a draw, then throws it out the window towards the engine. The embers spark and the fuel ignites. There are no plates and the engine number's been ground off.

45

My visor steams up as we weave through Watford's traffic and head towards Pinner. Pinner is my penultimate destination before this work is retired and I can take a break. I lift the visor a centimetre and the view clears as I relax. It's ground me down. I need to recharge as much as my leg. As I work the mirrors, keeping Kat in view and scanning for my lot and hostiles, I think of how I can spend some of the money. My accountant has been in touch and I've given instructions where to move my funds. He has access to my temporary banks and a good team to manage movement of money. After all, he supplied the units the cash sits in. I have everything in place and know I can make the time to get away. I know this because, as is tradition, I will disappear after this phase of the operation. Winter, Mike and the Metropolitan Police can take a hike. I'm done and ready to cash in my investments.

The beauty of my work is that I travel light. I can ditch what I don't need and replace it so easily. I manage on little. I've never been one to consume material goods other than clothing. Even that's on an 'as required' basis. As the bike tyres connect with the uneven road surface, the scent of a petrol spill fills my nostrils. I move the bike to the right to avoid it. I look back and Kat has smelt it too and taken my route. I can't say I'll miss the city aroma other than the food.

We're all one moment away from the certainty of decay and as we near the target address, I cannot help but feel that scent emanating from me. So much has changed in my life that I no longer recognise the person I was when I first joined the job. My identity has changed in more ways than I care for. My career, for what it was worth, is multifaceted. I open up the throttle. I feel like this is my final ride of freedom.

Winter has been absent. Her relentless pursuit of my whereabouts has ceased. Mike has taken the strain in that area but she could have bypassed him and come straight to me. Her tactics have changed, too. Her team have become skilled at not making their presence known to me. The times of me compromising them have been nonexistent on this job. I don't for one minute assume it's because I'm being given a loose lead to gain the intelligence she wants to convict Razor. It can't be, as I have none to give. The only real threat is towards me, from an unrelated target.

46

Winter's vehicle's parked up in an industrial site half a mile away from the main target premise. Cooper, Winter and their driver are the only occupants. Winter's aware she is now ground assigned and acting as Gold Control for this arrest phase. The atmosphere in the car is tense. Both occupants remain alert. Winter tries her best to avoid looking at the radio nestled between her thighs. A watched radio never speaks.

"Operational Control form DI Hudson. We have subjects Batford and Mills in target area. They've ridden slowly by address and left area, over."

"Operational Control received. Gold Control, did you get that last message?"

Winter flinches as the radio comes alive.

"Yes, confirmed that both subjects are in target area and have done a ride by on target premises. All Alpha units, we have eyes on subjects. The job's on. Maintain current positions. Gold Control, over."

Winter pauses. The radio is below the car windows. She takes a breath from speaking and releases the radio button at the side of the handset then presses it again and speaks.

"Tactical Firearms Commander, from Gold Controller. This phase is

now handed over to you."

Winter releases the radio button and breathes in deeply as she awaits the response from the Tactical Firearms Commander. Her need to hand this phase over uppermost in her mind.

"All received from Tactical Firearms Commander. All Trojan units, I am now in control of this phase of the operation. Do we still have sight of the subjects?"

"From Trojan five zero. Update from Alpha eleven is that subjects are parked up three roads down from target premises. Subject Batford is off bike and on foot towards target premises. Over."

"From Tactical Firearms Commander. We are now at alert state amber. I repeat, amber. Act on my command only until told otherwise. Ready weapons. Radio silence unless active."

47

I can see the door to the target premises from the opposite footway. It's a typical semi-detached house in a Pinner street. I know from Google maps it has an alleyway running at the back that provides access to a small courtyard garden and back door. There are no obvious plain-clothes police about and no vehicles that look as though witness protection is in. They won't be. Funds aren't in place to babysit these people anymore. As far as the police are concerned, once you're safely housed, with a brief cover story, then it's up to you to keep your lips sealed and get on with life until a permanent arrangement can be made. Hotels were too costly in terms of risk management.

Kat is farther back from me on the house side of the street. She's confident in her stride. We have left the crash helmets and now wear caps and shades. As she approaches the front of the house, she turns right into the alley to cover the rear. I hadn't anticipated this move. I also hadn't anticipated the dark saloon that's appeared, racing towards me from the opposite end of the street. My instinct is to freeze. Headlights are on full beam and blind me. I know that option is certain death.

"All Trojan units from Tactical Firearms Commander, alert state red, repeat red. We have another vehicle entering the plot at speed, headlights on main beam, occupants wearing masks. Vehicle heading towards the target premises. This vehicle must be stopped."

I have no time to waste. I have to set aside my initial

feeling and do the job. I move towards the door and up the steps to the bell. I pause, have one last look left and right, and repeatedly ring the bell.

"All units: Strike. Strike. Strike."

I hear a loud bang. I duck down on the steps. It's the sound of tyres exploding. A police stinger has caught the saloon. All four tyres ineffective. The vehicle swerves and hits a lamppost ten feet from the steps to the house. Sweat forms under the nylon of my cap. I have no idea who's who or what's happening. All I feel is my instinct telling me it isn't good.

The quiet calm of the street erupts further in shouts. Sounds of car engines and tyres coming to a stop. This isn't what I expected. Fear grips me. I have nowhere to run. Fight or fright kicks in and fright takes over. I freeze on the spot. My heart races. I can feel the rapidity of my breath on my top lip. The front door of the target premises is flung open and a Heckler & Koch MP5 submachine gun aims at me. My eyes move from the MP5 to a plastic Lego-looking brick shaped like a handgun. As quickly as I focus, I'm aware of repeated shouts of *armed police*. Two metal hooks attached to cable suddenly impale me. My body convulses as fifty thousand volts of electricity runs through me. I dodged the Taser training. Now I'm the victim of it. Karma for the tube station. I collapse on the steps. I freeze and do as instructed by the armed police officer.

"Put your hands out to your side, palms up. When I tell you, slowly place them on your head. Do not make any sudden movements or you will be shot."

The instructions are clear. Judging by the array of weapons that are now trained on me from various directions, I do as I'm told. My upper torso is covered in a plethora of small red dots. There are other armed sniper units I cannot see. My breathing quickens. I just pray I don't piss myself. It's evident there's a grass. I believe I know who that grass is. If

I've got it wrong, then I'll put it down to human error and hope for the best lawyer I can buy.

I hear shouts from the back of the property as Kat gets the same treatment. At the same time shots ring out over my head. More shouts of *armed police* can be heard. As I look up from the ground, two occupants from the dark saloon are slumped against the vehicle. The Uzi pistols have been discarded on the floor adjacent to where the car's occupants lie. The black balaclava masks hide their identity. The blood patterns on the vehicle's windows and paintwork indicate they've been eradicated. I now know they weren't police. As quick as I've been taken down, the armed officers pick me up and drag me to the open rear door of a covert van. I'm hoisted up between two cops; my head is forced down. I'm pushed into the back. An armed plain-clothes officer sits next to me. The door shuts. I hear a bang on the roof.

"Let's go."

The driver nods. My last vision as the doors slam is a sea of blue lights.

48

Twenty minutes previously on the M25 towards Heathrow Airport

"It's like a fucking car park this road. How long have we got until the flight?" Mike bangs the dashboard in frustration.

"Will you stop panicking? We'll make it on time. Just sit back and let me do the driving, will ya? You're worse than the missus for bitching about the mundane. Focus on your drink in first class, the clunk of ice and the glorious feeling in your throat as one of many drifts into your gut."

Mike smiles and relaxes. "Sorry. I've had so much on my mind. By now Sky and the Turk will be dead and Kat back at the club. When is she flying out?"

"She'll be on the last flight out tonight. Now shut the fuck up and put some tunes on. How about '2-4-6-8 Motorway'?"

Razor's jaw opens to reveal a gold back tooth as he laughs at his own joke. A phone alert sounds from inside the glove box of the car.

A nondescript grey Audi estate sits back in lane two as Mike and Razor continue in lane one observing the required speed limit of a slow crawl. The Audi's four occupants check and ready firearms. Whilst they do the occupants of two other vehicles do the same. The three vehicles shadow Razor and Mike. Razor and Mike are unaware. The radio operator in the Audi breaks the flow.

"Operational Control from Trojan eight seven, we are currently two cars behind Bravo vehicle. I have other units in position to effect a hard stop. Traffic is slow and we have space presenting itself."

"Trojan eight seven, from Tactical Firearms Commander, you are now shown alert state amber, over."

"Received by Trojan eight seven."

Razor and Mike continue concentrating on their journey. Their only focus the airport and a phone ringing in their vehicle.

"We said no fucking phones." Razor slams his fist into the steering wheel causing the car to shake.

"I haven't brought a fucking phone! I thought you had. It must be one of Sky's. I'll turn it off. Mike releases the seat belt and leans forward to open the glove box. He pauses, slowly sits back, lifting a Nokia mobile phone with a half battery life taped to a 9mm handgun.

"What in the fuck is this?" Mike looks at the phone screen and the only app present shows one new message. He reads the message from an unknown number: *Do the decent thing.*

Mike shows the gun to Razor. "Do the decent thing? Is this your idea of a fucking joke?"

Razor turns his eyes from the road and looks at the gun that Mike has held up towards him.

"What in the FUCK? Put that down, you stupid cunt. Someone could see it."

From the interior of the Audi, the observer reacts.

"All Trojan units from Operational Firearms Commander, firearm seen. Held by passenger and pointed at driver: alert state red. Strike. Strike. Strike!"

The mundanity of the road changes.

"Trojan eight seven, doors, doors, doors. Officers deployed, stand by."

"What in the fuck's that Audi doing? Oh shit, it's the filth; they're fucking all over us. You grassed me up, you cunt! You fucking set me up with your lot." Razor slams on the brakes as the lead armed vehicle swoops in front at an angle, forcing Razor towards the hard shoulder. Officers in blue caps with chequered bands are deployed and Heckler & Koch MP5 submachine guns are levelled at the vehicle's windscreen. Another car is along the offside and another close to the rear. The last police vehicle remains at the rear blocking traffic. The situation is dire. They're boxed in with an arsenal of weaponry aimed at them. Razor looks in the rearview mirror at a sea of chequered police hats and gun barrels.

Mike is the first to explode. "No! NO! NO! Don't move! They'll fucking shoot. It's not me! It's not me!! I've said nothing. By now they'll all be dead. Why would I risk us when the Turk and Batford will be history? I'm not doing time. Goodbye, Razor."

Mike raises the gun under his chin and as he squeezes the trigger, the windscreen shatters and his body jerks twice as two rounds pierce his torso. The gun he was holding slides from his hand into the foot well. His lower jaw hangs loose along with his tongue.

Razor remains motionless. His face a thousand-yard stare. He's unaware of the cacophony of shouts demanding him to raise his hands. His senses have gone. He's aware of his barrelled chest rising and falling. He begins to release his grip on the steering wheel as he's hauled out of the vehicle at gunpoint and forced face down on the road.

The M25 is now at a standstill. The hard shoulder occupied by police firearms officers. Sirens can be heard coming down the hard shoulder as marked traffic cars arrive, get out and start setting up a filter lane.

"Control, from Tactical Firearms Commander. Bravo vehicle stopped.

Passenger has discharged firearm. Shots returned by police. Driver out of car and arrested. No other occupants. Firearm recovered in passenger foot well of vehicle. We're going to need the ambulance up here and the road shut down for forensics, over."

"Operational Control received. Independent Office for Police Conduct will be informed. Units requested are moving in, now area is safe. Control out."

Winter shuts down her laptop as the aerial live feed continues. She takes off her glasses and rubs the bridge of her nose as she stares out of the blacked out window of the Mercedes. The body camera of the officer who fired the fatal shots clearly showed a clean shoot. The personal data from the officer's body monitor will no doubt show a controlled shot negating a lengthy investigation.

"Get me to Charing Cross." The driver indicates, activates the two tones and heads towards Central London.

49

When your mind is a prison, being alone in a cell is comforting. It's the most looked after I've felt in a long time. I wake to the slam of the metal wicket falling against the reinforced door and a shout from the gaoler. My breakfast is served following a rest period before interview. The rest period was deemed longer by the Force Medical Examiner in light of my lead up to arrest and the apparent trauma that may have ensued from being Tasered on the steps of what clearly wasn't a safe house but a lure to pull me in. I took the bait but couldn't spit out the hook in time.

I was informed I'd been arrested for conspiracy to murder and supply controlled drugs. Both charges I vehemently deny. I was acting commensurate with my role and authority. I haven't told Winter that. I've said fuck all as is customary in these circumstances.

I indicate to the youthful gaoler I'm not prepared to hop to the wicket to get my microwave breakfast and that he will have to come into the cell to deliver. He huffs and mutters 'for fuck's sake' as he opens the cell door and hands me the polystyrene container and plastic knife and fork. He shouts at the next cell to quieten down as he leaves to push the food trolley to the next wicket. I've rehearsed this situation hundreds of times since I crossed to the dark side. I know how it will play out.

I just need confirmation of one issue before I decide to speak. That will come in about twenty minutes when Winter comes to interview me. It will be Winter, as she must have her show of power. I realise now this isn't all for show and for role. This is for real and I don't intend being remanded in custody if I can help it.

I hear movement outside the cell door and recognise the sound of Winter's voice. The keys go in the lock. The door opens and there she is holding my leg. "Time for interview. Put this on and let's go. Your solicitor is here and disclosure has been done."

"I take tea and two sugars, please. You can leave me now whilst I get ready. Shut the door on your way out." She indicates to the gaoler to stand by the door and leave it open.

The interview room feels close. A single strip light flickers. I'd had time with my solicitor prior to interview. I'm hemmed in against the wall with my solicitor on my right. Opposite me sits Winter and an officer I don't know. My brief has told me what I need to know and that was Mike's dead. Kat he doesn't know about. I sit back and wait for the introductions to begin.

DCI Winter: 'This interview is being recorded and may be used in evidence if this case is brought to trial. I am DCI Winter attached to the National Crime Agency. The other officer present is?"

"DI Cooper attached to the Professional Standards Pro-active unit."

I snigger. A juvenile and unprofessional response.

DCI Winter: "We're in the interview room at Charing Cross Police Station. Please state your name and rank for the tape."

"Detective Sergeant Sam Batford. The other person present is my solicitor."

"Simon Jones, Jones and Co solicitors. I have advised my client based on the disclosure given and he is prepared to answer questions in relation to the allegations made. I will ask for a break should I feel it necessary and interrupt should your questions fall outside of the disclosure given."

Winter nods. "Very well. Before I put any questions to

you, DS Batford, I must remind you that you don't have to say anything. But it may harm your defence if you do not mention when questioned something, which you later rely on in court. Anything you do say may be given in evidence if this case is brought to trial. Do you understand the caution, DS Batford?"

"Yes."

DCI Winter: "You have recently been working on Operation Kestrel, the investigation concerning a man named Razor and his criminal enterprise, namely importing drugs and firearms, is that correct?"

"Well, I now know what it was I was meant to be investigating. My brief, provided by you to my Superintendent, was to infiltrate and ascertain what criminality may have been in preparation or may have been committed. I understood that this was a need-to-know enquiry and that I didn't need to know so early on."

DCI Winter: "You knew full well what we were looking at."

"No. As I've stated, I kept asking my Superintendent what the main job was and he stated he didn't know. I carried on with my original objective and fed back to him my findings. He was to pass these back to you, as I was instructed to do by him. He told me I was to have no direct contact with you concerning intelligence in light of the previous operation, which you oversaw."

DCI Winter shifts in her seat. I can already see from the scant writing in her notes that she's tentatively prepared for this first bite at the cherry – the cherry being me.

DCI Winter: "You must have made records of meetings and conversations. Where are these now?"

"You will have to ask Detective Superintendent Hall. They were all handed to him. Hall told me this was a paper record investigation and nothing was to be placed on any computer system. But you can't ask him, can you, because he's dead."

DCI Winter looks across at Cooper. Both look at each other perplexed at how I would know this.

DI Cooper: "I can confirm that Detective Superintendent Hall is deceased. An investigation is underway. I cannot comment on the circumstances while this takes place. I would like to know where you were yesterday between noon and four pm?"

"You know where I was. You had me under surveillance."

DI Cooper: "And how would you know that?"

"Surely you're not denying it?"

I look at Winter and back at Cooper. They both sit and stare straight at me.

"I told my Superintendent what my deployments were and he sent me to the location where I was arrested. Prior to that I was at the safe house in Watford with an associate of Razor's called Kat. Superintendent Hall knew of this and had assured me that DCI Winter and her team were covering all my deployments. Are you saying, sir, that an operation was being conducted using an undercover officer, into a man purported to have access to guns, with no outside armed support?"

I turn to my solicitor and he raises a hand to stop me in order for the DI or DCI Winter to respond. Both remain silent.

DCI Winter: "You and I both know you operate outside the boundaries of what is considered normal operating procedure, DS Batford. Look at the fiasco you caused in the last operation, you disregarded orders, gave teams the slip..."

Solicitor: "Can we please stick to the matters of disclosure, I am advising my client to say nothing in response to your last accusation."

DI Cooper: "We have grounds to believe you and Detective Superintendent Hall were involved in a criminal conspiracy with Razor to have Hassan Ahmet murdered in order to take over his drugs empire for your own gain. That's why you were at the address yesterday because you believed Hassan Ahmet would be there as Detective Superintendent Hall had told you. You were to murder him at this address and then take cash owed to Razor.

Fortunately, we were ahead of the game."

DI Cooper sits back like he's wrapped the case up and put a pretty bow on it.

I lean across the table. "Very fanciful, and if I may say so sir, delusional story. I was sent to the address by Detective Superintendent Hall. He had said that DCI Winter had told him she wished to set up a sting, in the belief that the actual assassin would accompany me there. As far as I was concerned, I would go in and armed police would take out the person sent to the rear of the premises, as that person would be armed. I would be 'mock' arrested and taken away to make it look realistic to Razor. Instead I arrive, as does another firm, fully loaded, intent on taking me out. Now, I have a prepared statement that I will have my solicitor read as it has come to that time."

DI Cooper: "Before you do, let me ask you one more question. Did you send an encrypted WhatsApp message to this number, 07896 555678?"

"No. That number's not on my phone-a-friend list."

Solicitor: "I have been instructed to read this prepared statement made in my presence by Detective Sergeant, Sam Batford, undercover officer with the Metropolitan Police:

"I, Detective Sergeant Sam Batford, wish to state that whilst working for the Metropolitan Police Service, Covert Intelligence Command, I have been acting under the command and authority of Detective Superintendent Hall. During operation Kestrel I became aware that the Detective Superintendent was not acting in accordance with the law and on confronting the Detective Superintendent, was threatened with being exposed as an undercover officer to both Big H and Razor.

"Detective Superintendent Hall stated he would implicate me in the importation of heroin and planned execution of a leader of a Turkish organised crime group. I was already in fear for my life due to a current threat being managed by DCI Winter of the National Crime Agency.

"Detective Superintendent Hall had also used the threat to my life as a cover to have me killed. It's my belief he felt I was too close to discovering his corruption."

DCI Winter: "All sounds very convenient so far."
My solicitor continues.

"When I became suspicious of criminal activity by my Detective Superintendent I was aware I had a duty to expose what I saw as large-scale corruption. It is my belief that both Razor and Detective Superintendent Hall were known to each other prior to the commencement of this operation. Detective Superintendent Hall Had been running Razor as an unregistered informant for some years and had crossed the line into criminality with him."

DCI Winter: "Unless you have evidence of this, then it's supposition. Do you have evidence of this?"
My solicitor ignores her and carries on.

"I was being used as a scapegoat in their plans. Detective Superintendent Hall refused to meet me at any venue I suggested. He insisted I meet him at his London flat. This flat I would regard as prime_London real estate and beyond the salary of a man of his rank. I was not aware that he had inherited money to purchase the premises or won the lottery. His mother and only relative had died five years previously, penniless.

"I asked him for official flash money, to use on deployment. He said he hadn't gotten any authorised but produced two thousand pounds cash from a cereal box. I have kept this money for police. I could also see signs of white powder on a table that I believe to be class A drugs. I couldn't say anything at the time due to the hold he had over my life. I am willing to point the address out to the investigative team."

DI Cooper: "So now we get the crux of your defence. Duress! You'll have to do better than that to convince the Crown Prosecution Service!"

Solicitor: "If I get a further interruption whilst reading this prepared statement, this interview will cease and my client will answer nothing further. If you have enough to charge my client then say so now and we can get this done."

The solicitor looks up at each interviewer. "No? Well there's a surprise."

Cooper and Winter acquiesce. The solicitor continues.

"I felt he wanted to know my every move and this included getting me a safe house where he could know where I was. I had a genuine fear he had the means and contacts to have me killed if I didn't cooperate. He gave me an access card to his flat and this is where he insisted I changed clothing prior to any deployment. I am of the opinion this was to know my description should he need to pass it on to have me assassinated.

"In order to try and gather evidence I left a camera pen at the property, which I later retrieved. It was left in a steel penholder in his living room. This shows footage of Detective Superintendent Hall speaking with Razor in person at the flat two days ago. They discuss leaving the UK and the female, who I know as Kat, would follow on after assassinating the Turkish male and myself. I understand it may not be used in evidence but needed something to corroborate the duress I was under."

DCI Winter starts taking notes.

"To the investigative team it would appear Big H's men executed the threat to life against me and the Turkish male got in the way. Both Razor and Detective Superintendent Hall would take over the drugs line ran by the deceased Turkish male. Detective Superintendent Hall authorised the witness protection for Hassan Ahmet and informed me of the address I attended today.

"I had no intention of committing the crimes alleged. I was not armed and was intent on warning Ahmet to leave the property with me. I would have called DCI Winter once I had Ahmet and requested backup.

"I gave Detective Superintendent Hall another phone to contact me on, as I was wary of the other number being compromised. I will supply this number to police as it contains numerous calls I tried to make to him but were ignored. As I was directed to have no other contact with the operational team, I accepted this.

"The money and camera pen are under the bathroom floor in the

Watford safe house. I am prepared to give evidence if required. At no time did I act beyond the law and all notes and conversations whilst deployed were handed to Detective Superintendent Hall.

"To find myself arrested and accused of these offences is shocking and a slight on an unblemished career. I wish to assist the investigating team in any way possible in the pursuit of justice."

DCI Winter: "That's all very well but we now have the situation where a police officer is dead, in your car, in possession of a firearm that was observed by an armed officer to have been removed from the glove box. Present in the car was a mobile phone with one message saying '*Do the decent thing*'. Did you plant the gun and phone in the car, knowing he was under surveillance by armed officers, with the intention he would be shot dead and unable to rebut your account as you wanted to take over the heroin line, for your own gain, with Razor?"

Solicitor: "My client has made a prepared statement and I advise him to say nothing further in relation to the last question. Either you have evidence my client was involved in criminality or not. At this stage I am advising he answer no further questions unless you wish to seek clarity in the statement he has made. Once again, for the record, my client denies both offences he is alleged to have been involved in."

DCI Winter: "Let's take a break shall we? Interview stopped at oh nine thirty hours.

I'm placed back in my cell and allowed to keep my leg this time. A tea is brought and a sandwich that's seen better days. I've done all I can now. Only time will tell. Unless Winter has other evidence against me then all I can do is sit it out and wait. She won't release me tonight. My solicitor has confirmed what I already knew. I'm here for due process to take place. Winter will check out the camera pen, phone logs, cash and Mike's flat. My car is the only concern. I can't be convicted for owning a car that was insecure with a gun in it. I haven't seen or handled the gun or the phone. The evidence would be weak.

50

Restaurant, Central London
Persons present:
DCI Winter
DI Hudson
Alex Kennedy

Winter enters restaurant and catches eye of DI Hudson who is sat with Alex Kennedy. Winter approaches the table and sets her laptop case down and picks up a menu.

Winter: "Sorry I'm late. The first interview over-ran. We've tried another but he's sticking to a prepared statement. Have you ordered?"

Both indicate they haven't. Hudson speaks up.

"We've just got back from the debrief ourselves. All's done and an initial meeting with the Crown Prosecution Service has been set up for this afternoon."

"Good work." Winter scans the menu but her brain is polluted with the interview and she struggles to decide. She goes back to the safe option and chooses.

A waiter arrives and takes their orders. Alex Kennedy waits for the waiter to leave before speaking.

"So when were you going to tell me that Sky was in fact a Detective Sergeant? I would have thought I'd have been told that from the start not at the end. It was a high-risk move that put me on offer. I was trusted amongst that lot and was held in high regard. I could've died today had the occupants of the other car got inside the house."

Hudson chips in, "Look I've been through all this..."

"I want a straight answer from the lead person. That's not too much to ask in the circumstances."

Winter shifts in her seat before replying. "I'd remind you we're in a public place and that you are still working for us. You've clearly spent long enough in the company of this group and you need to watch your tongue. A decision was taken at the outset that you shouldn't know who you were targeting as there were too many variables at play." Winter pauses. A look around then continues.

"It could have tainted the way you viewed your role and how you dealt with us when we met. I needed fresh eyes on the job and you were already a key part of the setup before we met you. You were pivotal in gaining information from the inside about the whole network in addition to the antics of the Detective Sergeant. I know how well thought of you are and we appreciate the lengths you've gone to."

"So what happens from here? Do I go back to the club or do I leave?"

Winter pauses as the waiter arrives with the food and places down the respective plates.

"You're out as of now. Drop your number. DI Hudson will take you to Empress State building for a meeting with the Met's Chief Medical Officer. The Met will offer after care with psychological support. You conducted yourself in an exemplary manner DC Burns. There aren't many officers who could sustain an infiltration at this level. You did your undercover role superbly. I know it had been a long deployment before we arrived but it was necessary to establish links with possible corruption."

Winter takes a drink. "I will speak with your line management from Manchester and ensure you're placed on leave for two weeks. For the record you're no longer acting in the role of CHIS as Kat Mills and your authority is cancelled. Your use of the pseudonym for both Alex Kennedy with us and Kat Mills for your undercover deployment are terminated. You deserve a rest period, Holly. I will update you after our meeting with the Crown Prosecution Service as to where this job will go. We know we have enough evidence to charge Razor, thanks to you, and his associates will follow." Winter smiles and places her hand on Holly's.

Holly allows Winter's show of warmth. "I'm sorry. It's been an intense deployment. I'm glad to be shot of dealing with a bunch of testosterone-fuelled arseholes. I'm not hungry. If you don't mind, I'd rather get back to my hotel and freshen up before going to see the shrink. I'm fine so don't worry on that score. I'll be fit for court. I'll see you at Empress State Building, DI Hudson."

With that DC Holly Burns parts with her seat and reaches for her cigarettes as she departs the restaurant and heads for the tube and her hotel.

"So what did Batford have to say for himself? I bet he couldn't believe his number's up." Hudson sits back.

"It's far from up. I'm not hungry either. Get this bill and let's get to the CPS earlier than arranged. You can brief me on what Holly has evidentially against any of them. I hope it's good news or we're looking at a lot of paperwork for no result, again."

51

Sometimes in life, roses smell good despite not having a garden in which to grow them. The ones I've selected for Mike's funeral are a vibrant blood red. They were arranged in the standard funeral wreath with some greenery but in all respects selected from the value range of floristry. I told the florist to await a call when the funeral is arranged as to where to send them. They'll be sent anonymously. I have little time for words in cards or sentiments of any type. Even more so for a callused, underhand bastard like Mike.

In the end the worst criminals get greedy and that greed devours them. I did the same for Klara Winter except hers are a vibrant white to go with her habitual blouse. All's fair in love and war, after all. I enjoyed my three-day lie down at the behest of the Metropolitan Police and National Crime Agency and saw this as benefitting my cover and exit strategy.

The Crown Prosecution Service had taken the right view on any proposed charges and deemed any evidence against me weak and unsubstantiated: They took into account how I attempted to assist the prosecution by trying to obtain evidence through the camera pen. They couldn't disprove that I hadn't passed evidence to Mike and he'd destroyed it. Mike's flat was ripped apart and a small amount of drugs found along with twenty thousand pounds in cash. Further documents indicated a safety deposit box that contained a further two hundred and forty thousand. All now subject to forfeiture by police. They also recognised I was lucky to be alive. A tidy result, I'd say.

I gave authority for Winter to look at my bank accounts. There's nothing revelatory there other than a Detective Sergeant trying to do his best on poor pay.

Razor, on the other hand, was not so lucky. A raid on his club found the firearm from Trigger and a substantial amount of Class A drugs. His prints were on the gun. His house and cars were seized as part of a financial investigation.

His mother has been moved into a residential home and his wife still loves him. My threat to life remains, as they can't prove the validity was false. Big H was paid a visit by police and he naturally denied all knowledge. I'm certain Mike played his part in it but how I will never know.

Where Kat is? I don't know either. What I do know is that she did her role well. She had me over until she rode the bike. Textbook advanced riding gave her away to me. That and her warrant card. I never saw her actual card. She'd never be that stupid. You see, the first rule of undercover policing is never carry your warrant card in the back pocket of tight jeans.

Even when you remove it the outline is obvious to the best criminals. I don't blame her. She's one of the good ones. She'll have to get out of bed earlier to catch me though. I take a cab from the florist in Tring High Street to the canal footpath and get dropped off. I haven't been allowed back to the Watford safe house. My meagre belongings have been packed and deposited at New Scotland Yard.

A warm breeze embraces my face like a lover's palms. I walk towards the bankside and a canal boat with a freshly painted red door. The name Legacy is also new, burnt into carved wood and screwed onto the boat. I walk past the boat first and check about but no one is to be seen. I get onto the walkway from bank to boat. The door is partially open. I knock. I smell the scent of cooked pork coming from inside and I'm met by a boy who can be no older than nine. He turns and shouts. A male voice says "Come in." I follow the kid in and shut the door.

"Mr Sky, come, come, sit down, we eat, yes?"

Adok beckons me to sit and shows me a place at the small dining table that has been pulled down from the side of the boat. Adok looks well as does his family. All seem relaxed and at peace despite having their family home raided two days previously, but nothing untoward was found in terms of guns or ammo.

"So Adok, how do you like the place? Does it suit your needs?" He beams a wide-eyed smile and places his hands out at the boat's fine interior. "Mr Sky, it is all I ever wanted for my family. To live a good life. It is a wonderful thing you have done for me. To give me this opportunity to be the man I once was. I have job now, looking after other people boats and doing work on them. Here is phone you gave me. I left gun and other phone in right car? I look at tracker dot on phone you leave me in car. I send message if it goes within mile of any airport like you told me. I send message at right time?"

"The message was delivered perfectly."

His wife squeezes past with a large plateful of meat and sets it down. "Please, help yourself."

"I can't. I'm sorry. I need to go. I wanted to see you settled in your new home. All is paid for. The boat and mooring fees until your son finishes school. No one is looking for you, not police, anyway. Razor will think someone has talked so you must be vigilant. If you think you're at risk, you can move along the canal well away from the area. I may call on your help again, Adok. Metal is a rare commodity and you never know when it will be of use. I'm afraid the last one you gave me got lost in my car along with the phone. Not to worry though as I have heard it can't be used again."

I get up and see myself out. I start back along the canal towpath. My phone goes and it's the Commander's PA. "DS Batford, you're to report to the Chief Medical Officer for psychological assessment on authority of the new Authorising Officer for your department. The appointment is set for tomorrow at ten hundred hours."

"New AO? The old one isn't even in the ground yet! Who is it then? Do I know them?"

"Oh yes, you've worked very closely before. The Commander has offered Klara Winter the role and she's accepted. One of her first tasks was to ensure you were properly cared for after your last deployment. I hope you get passed as match fit or else it's back to a main CID office for you."

In war you're part of an army, but on the field of battle, you're isolated by the system.

Laters.

The End

Epilogue

Decision Log - Closing entry - Operation Kestrel

Fuck. Fuck, fuck, fuckety fuck, fuck it.

Not a decision but I had to express my utter dismay at the result somewhere. It felt appropriate to record it in this sensitive log as no one else is likely to see it other than the Independent Office for Police Conduct in closed conference.

Even they will appreciate my disappointment that this investigation has ended this way.

DI Cooper, from the MPS Professional Standards, is noncommittal but by his smug attitude considers this a result with Detective Superintendent Hall dead, Razor behind bars and two guns for hire deceased.

I have spoken with the undercover section for Manchester Police. DC Holly Burns (Kat Mills / Alex Kennedy) provides evidence that will secure a decent stretch for Razor, Snowy and Trigger. This will be in relation to firearm possession and drug supply. I'm hopeful we will have other evidence that will negate her use in court. I wish to keep all covert tactics out of the judiciary. This includes undercover officers.

The Crown Prosecution Service have taken no action in relation to DC Burns being present when Detective Superintendent Hall supplied Razor with the four kilos of cocaine.

The CPS sees this as a commensurate part of her cover and role for a crime that was already laid on. No agent provocateur element present.

Police located Razor's bike and leathers after surveillance called it in.

Forensics also places Batford at Detective Superintendent Hall's flat as Batford had stated.

Kat Mills's phone, aka DC Holly Burns, was found at Batford's flat. Batford claimed he had given Mills another phone so that police could interrogate her old one after the operation was complete. I'm of the opinion he knew she was a police officer and this is why he did it.

Batford has managed to convince the CPS that he was under duress and acting for the good of the crown. He has shown this through his actions to obtain evidence against Detective Superintendent Hall and the attempt on his life at his arrest.

The covert camera pen recording shows Hall and Razor engaged in a conspiracy to murder Batford and Hassan Ahmet. There is no evidence to suggest Hall had disclosed Batford as a police officer.

Detective Superintendent Hall had accepted the witness protection request as true. The last conversation he had with Razor sealed his fate. Without this we would have struggled to know when and where he would attempt the murder of Batford and Ahmet.

Intrusive surveillance isn't always a bad thing. When used lawfully, it can protect life.

Hassan Ahmet was never in the house when Batford arrived. He was away from London in an undisclosed location under armed police guard.

DC Burns had sent a separate text from Batford's safe house and wiped her phone clean. Along with our other intelligence from the phone tap of Hall's mobile, I was able to respond quickly and accurately using armed officers.

Clothes for Batford were found at Detective Superintendent Hall's flat as Batford had claimed. No notes made by Batford have been recovered from the premises.

I believe these were never made.

The firearm in the car couldn't be attributed to Batford. The garage where the car was kept was not able to be secured and Batford insists he left the vehicle open as he didn't believe anyone would want to steal such a 'piece of shit'. How the gun got there I will never know.

Razor has been charged with possession of the weapon. It's a long shot but nothing ventured, nothing gained. CPS have authorised charging. He has made a no comment interview to all allegations made against him. This suits me.

In summary, I am still of the opinion Batford is corrupt, planted the gun in his own car and initiated the call to Hall. How? I cannot prove.

Cell site analysis shows the phone couldn't have been in Batford's possession at the time the message was sent. Batford was under surveillance. He was not seen calling anyone.

If the gun was never there, I would have left the car. Let Razor and Mike go to the airport to prove intent to leave the country. Sometimes we have to react to circumstances when they present themselves.

The phone attributable to the call was not in his possession on arrest and has not been recovered.

I have now accepted a promotion and transfer to the Metropolitan Police, Intelligence Policing Command. I will be responsible for DS Batford.

I am of the opinion you keep your friends close and your enemies closer.

I will enjoy the opportunity to oversee DS Sam Batford's career development.

I truly hope this will be via an open university study programme from Pentonville Prison.

Log Completed

Klara Winter - Detective Superintendent
Metropolitan Police
Authorising Officer - SCO35
Covert Policing

Author's Note

For the sake of clarity I have left the National Crime Agency ranks as traditional police ranks. Although the staff work under the auspices of the civil service, with a different grading system, the role to detect crime is the same. Both the Metropolitan Police and the National Crime Agency work tirelessly under extreme financial constraint to keep us safe. It isn't an easy task when your own government does not support you.

Places change, command names change, ranks come and go. Don't sweat it just enjoy the journey.

This is a work of fiction and should be enjoyed as such. Names, places, characters and scenarios are all from my overactive imagination.

You can Tweet me @IPatrick_Author should you feel compelled to.

Acknowledgements

Any writers' journey is never a purely solitary pursuit. I had some fantastic support along the way. I would like to thank the following: My wife, Emma, for having the belief in me. Being my first line of defence as a reader and keeping me sane during the whole process.

Samantha Lorriman for her advice for *Rubicon.* I look forward to seeing her words in print one day.

Jane Isaac for her continued support, belief and friendship.

Uncle Mike for encouraging me to read at an early age.

Simon Craig for all the help and advice when my policing memory fails me.

Phil and Laura for letting me use the pub to write in. Bullshit corner, an appropriate writing nook.

Annie and Sally B. For the coffee and distraction while trying to write. (Phil/Laura – I did pay!)

Miriam, Chrissie and Amy for letting me use the back room at the village hall in the warmer months while you entertained my youngest daughter at playgroup.

Sarah Ade for supporting my writing through the local paper.

Steve, Sally and Tom. I still pinch myself that you had the faith in my work.

Paul at Rubicon Tattoo for the ink and back story that inspired this series.

My publisher and team at Fahrenheit Press for having continued faith in my writing.

The book bloggers and those on Twitter who have supported my writing. I'm honoured.

Most of all, you, the reader. You make all this worthwhile. I'm truly grateful for your support.

More books from Fahrenheit Press

Rubicon by Ian Patrick

Needle Song by Russell Day

Know Me From Smoke by Matt Phillips

Burning Secrets by Ruth Sutton

Vinyl Junkie by Richard Cox

29536420R00146

Printed in Poland
by Amazon Fulfillment
Poland Sp. z o.o., Wrocław